WATER PROOF

AARON BUSHKOWSKY

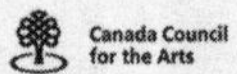
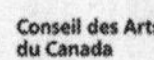
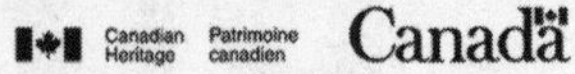
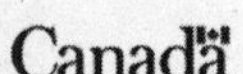

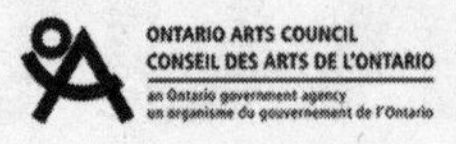
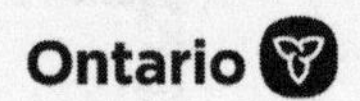

We acknowledge financial support for our publishing activities: the Government of Canada, through the Canada Book Fund and The Canada Council for the Arts; the Government of Ontario, through the Ontario Arts Council, Ontario Creates, and the Ontario Book Publishing Tax Credit. We acknowledge additional funding provided by the Government of Ontario and the Ontario Arts Council to address the adverse effects of the novel coronavirus pandemic.

LIBRARY AND ARCHIVES CANADA CATALOGUING IN PUBLICATION
Title: Water proof / a novel by Aaron Bushkowsky.
Names: Bushkowsky, Aaron, 1957– author.
Identifiers: Canadiana (print) 20210211954 | Canadiana (ebook) 20210211970 | ISBN 9781770866362 (softcover) | ISBN 9781770866379 (HTML)
Classification: LCC PS8553.U69656 W38 2021 | DDC C813/.54—dc23

United States Library of Congress Control Number: 2021938488

Cover: Angel Guerra / Archetype
Interior text design: Tannice Goddard, tannicegdesigns.ca

Printed and bound in Canada.
Manufactured by Friesens in Altona, Manitoba in August, 2021.

CORMORANT BOOKS INC.
260 SPADINA AVENUE, SUITE 502, TORONTO, ON M5T 2E4
www.cormorantbooks.com

For Jane, who knows,
and in memory of Diana, who knew.

ONE

LET ME FIRST BE CLEAR about kayaking: I don't like it. You're at the mercy of the sea and when the sea is angry, you're just a bug to it. One misstep and you're in the drink. And once you're in the drink in late September, you have minutes to live. People die all the time doing this. But I'm doing this to save our marriage.

Desolation Sound.

East of Vancouver Island and quite far north of Vancouver, British Columbia.

It's called Desolation for a reason, especially in late September. There's nothing up there except kayak tours and whale watchers. Occasionally a nice sailboat splashes by helmed by aging stock-brokers who name their vessels *Lucky*, *Serenity*, or *Providential*. The view is to die for: endless blue waters; mountains as pristine as bachelors wearing brand new tuxedos, stiff and formal in the biting, cold, cold wind. Our paddles cut the flat waters as precisely as surgeons' scalpels. Ten kayaks, mostly orange and red, moving silently across the open, still water. Gulls follow us suspiciously as we make our way to our bivouac on the east side of Cortes Island, on the north end of the Gulf of Georgia. We've seen killer whales and seals and, in the distance, the telltale plumes of whale spouts. Humpbacks. But it's cold. And the fog starts to gather us into her skirt, the shore turning soft focus, movie-like and foreboding.

If there were a soundtrack to go with this, it would be a cello, naturally. A build to it.

You'd need a big lens to get all this, maybe a Nikon 14-24mm or something like that. Something professional to get all the blues and greens and browns and white — yeah, there's white. The tops of mountains everywhere around us: white, white, white.

I'm actually tired of breathing all this in.

My lungs hurt.

The wonder in my eyes is draining.

I'm overthinking scenery, experiencing too much, too long.

Even my ears ache. I'm tired of listening to silence all day.

And watching the forever horizon for the water's dark blue edge.

Nothing happens except for views to die for.

And it's a slow death.

My shoulders are killing me. My hands shake. And my cracked lips feel like Mister Salty pretzels. The ones before they eased up on the coarse salt. We've just paddled for two hours across open water. The first hour we kept our bows turned into the three-foot swells, up and down, fighting the waves and wind, and eventually nausea. Watch the kayak in front of you. Watch it disappear six feet away. Watch the kayak ahead of you. Disappear. Don't panic. Never panic. Paddle. Throw your fist out, jab the air with your hand on the paddle. Jab the other fist. Establish a rhythm. Steady. Steady. Back and forth as the sea writhes in slow motion.

You can do this! You can! Dig! Dig! Dig!

This is the coxswain in my head and he's a bastard.

The shore doesn't appear until the second hour when the water flattens out into an ominous, green, belly swell. I see dark shapes low under my bow. I can only imagine what they are: killer whales, sharks, giant otters, the kraken.

It's quiet. As they say in the movies, too quiet.

It's *Waterworld* out here except with more islands and fewer smokers and minus Dennis Hopper, who was brilliant in the movie. Brilliant.

Out here is a lot of flat wallow. The ocean senses us. And we're ruining the planet. Well, not all of us.

It's empty beyond empty, and for all we know, we could be on an alien planet searching for land.

Distance. Lots of distance between us.

Anna has ear buds in, you can barely tell because she has shoulder-length hair and a Tilley hat on. Loves Lady Gaga on the water.

In her own world in this world.

My wife is.

Strange.

We met online years ago when meeting online became the thing to do. She showed up late for the date wearing a jaunty nautical hat and white gloves with the fingertips cut off. Her short, mousy-brown hair was tied back by elastic bands. Her big cheekbones only exaggerated the runny mascara because she had been crying a lot worrying about first impressions.

And. Things change. Mostly when you're not watching. You grow apart. You drift. You forget what kept you in sight. What was it she said that first date that made you laugh? What was it that made you stop and look around? What did she smell like? Where did she go when you dropped her off in the Safeway parking lot? Swinging her purse like a lasso. Stumbling a bit in her black high heels and dark yoga pants. Looking back at me in my car looking back at her, tossing her short, Princess Diana hair. Both of us smiling and thinking here it comes. Here comes my future; the asphalt shimmering between us.

But where am I now?

What am I doing?

Then a majestic oil tanker appears and crawls toward us; its massive, rusty hull sweating water. It seems to take forever, but then it slides by an island and disappears like a gator on the prowl.

I hear a ship's horn.

Across the water, of course.

Then.

I feel the water bulge under me. I imagine it, I guess. It goes by fast.

The others look around as if trying to figure out what just happened.

Holy crap.

A warning?

A bad sign?

An accident?

We don't say much because we're worried about dying. You don't want to ditch in this shit. Not a chance. You'd never last.

My opinion, of course. And I'm an extremist. Also I'm terrible in water and on water. I was never much of a swimmer, and I get nauseated fast because of vertigo. There's also a rhythm to the ocean and I can't dance.

It's swell to have swell, but as my mother used to say: enough is enough, go to your room if you think you've got moves.

Wow, is it quiet out here, I say to nobody in particular.

Not a single murmur in agreement.

What's with these people?

The ocean gurgles. It's a deep one, far beneath our skinny hulls and fat asses.

A silence. As vast as it is out here. All-consuming. The edge of dusk swallowing us slowly. We mean nothing. Nothing. The great expanse has not been expanding our minds, that's for sure.

A real quiet ride, wave after wave.

Solitude with each stroke, building.

Later Anna will say nobody talked because nobody talked. It was because of the natural beauty. The sky. The mountains. The water. Etcetera.

The inescapable fact is, we feel totally insignificant in the emptiness out here.

You do. And you start to regret many things that are out of your control.

Like global warming. Or my marriage.

I shiver like hell. Can barely swallow. Or talk.

Also. It's Friday, the 13th. It really is.

Most of us beach without a problem. We scrape the shore with the bottoms of our boats, snap off the Oh Shit handles on the spray skirts, and creep out ankle-deep in the cold, cold water. My feet feel like they just went to the dentist, completely numb. I stumble getting to the shore and look amateurish because I drop my sunglasses a couple of times. I want to throw up. I might be seasick. My fingers are white raisins. Our fearless leader, Emma — a bright, curvy dark-haired Environmental Sciences major from the

University of Victoria — wades out in her bright yellow gum boots, scanning the soft cloth of fog starting to muffle our very existence on the rocky shore.

Andy, Anna, Allan, Faith, Colin, Kayla, Robert, Chris … and Sarah?

Emma reads from her list.

Sarah?

Sarah?

She says the last Sarah as if knowing what the answer is.

We all stand like sentinels, each on our own rock, to study the fog. We're knights and our watch is the endless, dirty, green water. Our bright waterproof jackets lose their glow as the fog settles even though we're blinking a lot.

Am I tearing over?

Through the veil, and I don't use that word lightly, an empty, bright red kayak drifts toward us. And somebody behind me screams.

It's Anna. Her scream.

Sarah is her best friend in the world.

Was.

TWO

THE SEARCH FOR SARAH BEGINS immediately. We break into groups of three and two of the groups head down the shoreline. Three others tie off the kayaks and drift back into the fog, calling her name. Anna, Allan, and I grab our hiking poles and flashlights and start heading north, hopping from rock to rock looking for the telltale yellow of her jacket. We're dreading finding her washed up and blue in the face with seaweed in her hair. I speak for everyone. Yes, this is a nightmare. It's a very bad horror flick, and we're all stuck in it looking for the happy ending. Not the genre for that. And I know it. This is the kind of moment that stretches out; even a cough becomes memorable. Sarah's name gets repeated over and over again. And Anna and I both know this is defining us, the two of us, with each toxic passing second, each breath.

Our marriage is finished.

We'll realize it later.

Right?

Right.

Why does it always take a tragic event?

My parents broke up after my father lost his job. He was in the business of saving lost souls, but lost himself in the church. Some preachers are like that.

It moves toward dusk now. I notice how the sky has become the shore, dipping down to embrace the grey of the rocks. Anna shivers. I watch her struggle, trying to keep her balance along the sharp rocks because she's crying. Allan, who still wears his Oakleys under his Toronto Blue Jays baseball cap, isn't talking. He's in his head, man. His beard gathers moisture from the ever-present fog and starts dripping rain on his chest, not that he cares. Allan is a Philosophy grad from UBC who teaches high school part-time, and this trip was supposed to be his sole reason to return to the classroom. I live for the stupendous, he always says. Pedantic, right? He's thirty-six and wears explorer shorts, the kind that have seventy-two pockets and are mosquito proof. They're off-red. Russet, he says, of course. I like them. It's easy to follow Allan from rock to rock even as the fog fogs and we begin to get vague.

Look, we're disappearing. Look.

Allan says that from a rock over there. He holds out his arms all Moses like and looks out across the already-still water.

Can you still see me from over there? Can you? It's phenomenal. Astonishing. Formidable.

We ignore him.

Then he steps down and disappears along the shore, quiet as a cougar.

I shiver.

It's a half-hearted, but heavy-hearted search.

The dreadful time we will always, always dread. The Fall of our lives. At the end of the world. Desolation Sound. Cortes Island.

This is something I wanted to avoid, particularly in my fifties. Who needs soul-crushing dread just before retirement?

After an hour or so, we head back to camp, depressed and scared and covered in bug bites. I have one on my chin. Anna's off-brown eyes are bloodshot from crying. And she's somehow broken her hiking pole, probably in anger. She tosses it at the tent. It bounces into the weeds instead.

The RCMP speedboat shows up in the dark an hour later, red lights barely visible through the dark haze. Tiger eyes, I suppose.

There's nothing we can do, the cops say. Until tomorrow. It's the fog. Their voices muffled by the heavy mist. And the dark.

The fog.

Slowly making things worse.

I have a chill that won't go away.

And a chin itch that goes crazy right to my ears, and now *they* bug me so much I pull on them until they stretch out and bounce back into shape, which is still big ears. They are getting bigger as I age. Soon, they will make up the majority of my head.

In the smelly, blue, impermeable tent later that night — the one we bought from Canadian Tire — Anna sobs. We're not sleeping, she says. Not a chance. Just lie there and look at the mesh. Anna asks why, why is this happening? This isn't like her. Sarah. Oh, Sarah. Why? She's a good kayaker and she doesn't make mistakes. She's careful. And she's a great swimmer. She can swim ten lengths. And she was wearing a life preserver. It was the best life preserver you can buy and the water was way too calm.

Anna wears red long underwear from top to bottom. It makes

her look like a skinny Santa Claus. No beard, of course, but make-up running down those enormous cheekbones again. Tears, lots of tears from those also enormous, sad, almond-coloured eyes. Her hair nearly stands on end. But her hair always looks like that unless she gets extensions, which happened on our wedding. I barely recognized her then … long, beautiful, dirty-blond hair spilling down her back. But now it's pulled back with a hair band, one that she found while hiking the Powerline Trail in North Vancouver.

How can she do this to us? It was our first vacation together. This isn't fair. It isn't.

I nod and nod.

You're right about everything, I say.

But mainly I'm studying the tent mess, our clothes scattered to the side, feeling my heart creep up my throat. My phone lights up the tent. I'm getting a message, but I ignore it.

Here's the thing: I have a part in this. I know I do.

It's not a good part. Not in the least.

I imagine Sarah walking over and ripping open the front flap. Hey guys. She's bleached out and bug-eyed. Hair still dripping wet. I'm fine, she laughs. Just a little waterlogged, that's all. You can all come out now. Let's open some Chianti. It's nothing. Nothing. Does somebody have some cave-aged gouda?

It's very dark now. Our little tents are lit up like giant wine gums. Red, green, orange. Probably because we're all using our phones. Yeah. We are perfectly placed across the rocky shore every twenty feet. Six tents.

Somehow, we eventually drop off. Surrender to exhaustion and bad dreams. The night air in the middle of nowhere is a sleeping pill. No matter what, no matter who you are. But the sleep comes with a slight taint of death. This is not an exaggeration. It's the great outdoors, and it can kill you in a gasp.

In the morning we're all up at the crack of light, stumbling out of the tiny tents, although we wear very expensive outerwear and boots ordered online from Italy. Of course, we rub our eyes. It's bright out. No fog now. Blue on blue, sky and water ablaze with the rising sun. Blinding. There's a fresh smell to everything like it's a new car outside. I say this to the sky hoping for an audience reaction. Anna just says please stop with that, it's not that funny anymore.

I rub my chin hoping for a more interesting description.

My face feels vibrant, although I haven't shaved for days. I can honestly say my heart has slowed, and I can taste the air; it's thick with misty salt.

My armpits smell like sea breeze.

I feel so alive, I say to Anna.

Don't, she says. Enough. Please.

Settle down.

We collect our bearings. The dread of the day sets in like a toothache.

Anna's bloodshot eyes have bags under them. The kind you can pack a lot of anxiety into for a trip to Crazy Town, although to be fair, she rarely goes there except to visit friends.

On our second date we visited her cousin in Abbotsford, a tiny man with an old-fashioned film camera around his neck. A museum piece. His name was Tom, all sinew and bones and bloodshot eyes, wearing a white T-shirt with fast food stains on it, probably Arby's.

You're a brave man to take her on, he said with a grin, one bony finger on the shutter. She's the crazy one in this family, you'll see.

Anna said, Back in your trailer, Crazy Tom. The cats miss you.

She pulled out her wrap-around sunglasses and used them to point to the broken-down Airstream gleaming in front of us; a convex mirror of a trailer reflecting sun in our eyes.

Love the facilities, she laughed, shielding her face. Love the facilities. We can see ourselves in this. Warped or what?

Then she did a little dance, finishing with a big spin.

This is my world, she gushed. This is it. It's so weird. I love it!

Aren't you going to dance a little? Anna said. Let yourself go, Andy. Let it all go.

We look like akimbo clowns, our legs stretching into stilts, our heads oblong in the reflection of the trailer. A little pathetic over here.

I think that part I said aloud.

Well, I don't care, Anna said. Watch me. Watch and learn!

In this moment, she was genuinely happy. I could see the joy in her face.

Tom snapped the shot mid-twirl.

Got it, he said. Got it good!

But now we're far from the pastures of Abbotsford, British Columbia. Far from any Arby's or McDonald's. Or Wendy's.

The only air stream we have is off the water.

The ocean is quiet. Cold. Distant.

There are three red Kodiak boats out there with big numbers on them. They're dragging the bottom of the sea with chains or hooks of some kind. Police boats, I'm told. From the shore, they're just bugs on the water, crisscrossing in regular patterns, back and forth, forth and back. No waves. The sea is as flat as a bowling lane. Maybe even as shiny. Like I said, it's bright out. The sun scatters light across the water in shivers. It's probably a scene that will remain etched in our minds for decades.

A cop, Constable Deborah Shiner from the Powell River RCMP, stands on shore with our fearless leader, Emma, checking stuff on a beat-up old iPad. Deborah frowns and keeps scratching her butt nervously. Her pants are too baggy for a cop. Unflattering, even. Emma nods and nods. This is the worst day of her short, uneventful life, and on top of everything, this tour was supposed to have two guides, not one. Shortcuts cause accidents and Deborah knows it; she's seen it before many times.

There. That's where we were, Emma says. And that's how we came to the beach.

Where?

She points out across the water at some islands in the distance. Remote. Bird sanctuaries. Mainly. Worlds ruled by eagles who perch on the tallest trees and scream at passing paddlers, the occasional seal, or dreaded orcas.

Deborah says the islands aren't ruled out.

The ones the orcas patrol dot the horizon with emerald trees and invisible crows.

One of the red boats is over there now, searching the shore, the low murmur of its motor a purr across the flat water.

Deborah is patient. She has a hand on Emma's shoulder and talks very quietly. It's okay. Everything's going to be okay. Breathe. She explains the process. First, we're going to make sure we follow procedure; second, we're going to be professional; third, we need to remain calm. Breathe. It's very important to remain calm. Emma cries and tries her best. She's on her phone a lot. We have connection here. Solid bars. But this is a situation that isn't getting better even though communication is. She's talking to her boss at the tour company between huffs and puffs and tears, barely making sense.

It's crazy, she says. She disappeared. Just like that. We were maybe a hundred metres from shore. Not even that. And the whole group was ready to beach. Crazy. I turned my head and the next second, gone. It's not my fault. Believe me, I was doing my job. Honestly. Not my fault, Dennis.

Breathe, Emma reminds herself. Breathe.

I watch this from a distance, shivering a little.

Cops have come from everywhere to help with the search, even though it's the weekend. Search and Rescue is part of it. Everyone is doing their best, Deborah says. It won't be long. She was wearing yellow, she says. Easy to spot. High viz. And the water's calm. We have a plane. We have a helicopter. It won't be long. Not in these conditions. Just let us do our jobs.

A plane appears on the horizon. Perfect timing. It passes by a distant island. I can barely hear it. It's lower than I thought. The search is very coordinated for so early on, I decide. This must happen a lot.

Another oil tanker drifts by, so distant the mirage makes it look like it floats just above the horizon.

Light plays tricks with the water and the curvature of earth.

As usual.

I notice a bunch of gulls sitting on rocks behind us up the slope. Above them, crows who sit on higher rocks, studying them. Above them in the tall pines, eagles as large as bobcats, studying everything.

Other paddlers emerge from their tents, rubbing sleep out of their eyes, collecting their bearings. Colin, a voice actor, strikes a pose beside his green tent, holding a big stick.

Look at that water, he says, pointing with the stick. Look at it today.

I nod. Yeah, I say. Yeah. Look.

He watches me out-damn-spot my Maui Jims over and over again. I obsess over clean sunglasses.

He doubles over and crawls back into his little green tent. I decide my sunglasses are scratched, but I slip them on anyway; this is not the day for naked eyes. I look around for sound. Lots of thin voices crackle through little speakers.

Deborah is double-fisting: cellphone in one hand, walkie-talkie in the other. Police crackle. No, cackle.

To the right, she's saying. To the right.

As she talks, she's looking out at some of those distant eagle-only islands. She's pissed now.

She alternates between the phone and walkie-talkie in double-time.

Can you hold? she says. Can you hold, please? This is important. Don't talk to me, Charlie. Not now. Please. I'm in the middle of something. What's wrong with you guys? Get it right. I'm telling you it's right, right.

The police boats hum by. They look like the kind of boats the Navy SEALS use, big motors in the back and bulbous in the front. Obviously, they are filled with air. A man in uniform waves from boat two. The one closer to the shore. I notice a police car pull up, an SUV of some kind. Another RCMP officer gets out carrying a box of bagels and wanders over to Deborah, who just ignores him.

Anna tells me she's worried about our team leader. She's been standing beside me breathing quietly and not saying anything for a long time.

She's scarred for life, Anna says. Poor girl. She's shaking. Look at her.

And she is.

Clearly this is her first kayaking incident, I say.

I hope she survives it, Anna says, holding out a coffee, and it's then I realize she's had enough time to collect herself and the wherewithal to make me a decaf with soy. I need my coffee in the morning. Although mine comes without the buzz.

I take a sip from the tin cup she purchased for eighteen bucks at Mountain Equipment Co-op and watch Emma squirm. Her face looks terribly pinched, and she's probably wishing like crazy that she was staying at a downtown Holiday Inn sipping a Starbucks double-sweet latte far away from kayaks and open water.

Emma has written down her questions on her iPad.

Number one.

She wants answers. Company policy. Because this has never happened before. Not for Northwest Kayak, the company owned by her two brothers, Dennis and Brandon, now living in Seattle, counting the money, and changing their name on the website to something else.

Number two.

Why me? Why me? Why?

This is Emma's plea.

Emma and Constable Deborah look like mother and daughter. Touch heads. It's sad. Terribly, terribly sad. In whispers.

They talk about currents and timelines.

The unseen.

What happens next.

Relatives.

When to speak of the dead.

THREE

IT'S JULY. THREE MONTHS BEFORE the accident. We meet at a hipster bar in Gastown. The Alibi Room. Sarah wears a shiny red top and tight blue jeans. High heels. Red ones with gold buckles. She looks like a tall, robust, sexy elf. She has too much makeup on, but I don't mind; she's smiling a lot. Her reddish blond hair bounces in all the right places, and she smells like an ocean breeze. Deep breath through my nose. We're just having drinks. No big deal. Right?

I tug at the ends of my stupid shirt, my faux cowboy one with the blue and green stripes. I bought it in Calgary one year when I had a gig near the tower and lots of shops were in trouble because of poor oil prices. I felt sorry for the owner because his cowboy apparel shop was shutting down after thirty years in the business.

I love your shirt, Sarah says as we sidle up to the bar where the bearded hipster bartender named Joel takes our martini orders.

He's probably forty, but he's working the youth angle. He's auditioned for me before. His beard is Greek-like. It's brown and frosted on the edges, and it might be the best damned trimmed beard I've ever seen. Joel hopes it distracts women from the fact that he has no hair, I think. His head has been waxed. It looks like an apple.

How are you two doing tonight? Joel asks. Yes, he's wiping glasses as he asks this.

Fine, I say.

Leave the kids at home tonight? he asks us.

No, I say. I'm childless and my wife here is barren.

Cool, he says.

I try a smirk.

Plus, we prefer dogs.

Right.

Joel nods and immediately retreats to mix drinks.

I know he knows I'm not funny to anybody who's hip and happening and under thirty.

I settle in and take off my jacket.

I love this place, sighs Sarah. Love it!

It's happy hour and we're just having fun after work, I think to myself. That's what people do on Wednesdays. Have fun.

The place is made out of oily wood, although flowers dry over the bar, purple ones. I feel like I'm in a fancy garage where motors were once hoisted and drained of all their black blood and wish I had worn plaid. Joel wears plaid. Naturally.

Plaid is the camouflage of the disillusioned, I say.

Funny, Sarah giggles. You say the funniest things, don't you?

I'm not sure, I say. What's funny?

Sarah laughs at that, and this confuses me because it was a real question.

But what does that mean about us? Sarah asks. I mean, look at your shirt and look at mine. We've gone with the obvious, right?

Right.

This is a stupid conversation to be having before you're drunk, I think.

We order apple crantinis. I have apple on the brain, I guess. And a homemade pretzel. With bright yellow homemade mustard. I always order pretzels and pickles because I'm German. Joel places our order in front of us like it's an idol. It's on a wooden plank, of course. He backs away saying, At your service, m'lady … your Holiness. Enjoy.

He doesn't ever turn his back on us, I notice.

Hey, listen to that, Sarah gushes. Love it!

They're playing Prince on the speakers, and it's Prince when he was bad. The song is "Movie Star," and it's just weird and not funky and some people in the back sitting by the washrooms ask Joel to change the music. They don't care that Prince is now dead. No respect. None.

What is that shit? I hear one woman say.

I love this, Sarah says. It's so me. Me, when I was somebody else. Ancient times, right?

Right.

Who were you yesterday? Sarah asks. Or should I guess?

I'm not sure I've ever been anybody but me, I say. Except maybe when I go to Toronto. Then I'm just depressed.

I try a dry laugh. I'm less and less funny, I decide.

A Toronto joke is low hanging fruit, I quip. I think I add a wink too. For compensation.

Oh, you know what I mean. Stop joking around. Everybody

was someone else for a while, and we all look back at that person and smile, right?

Right.

Alter egos are fun, mister, she says. Maybe you're being that person now, and how would I know, right?

Right.

Sarah has the kind of restless nervous energy almost every guy loves. She touches my arm a lot as if checking to see if I'm heating up, makes terrible jokes about my hair, and drinks too fast.

That song is nuts, she says. Who would play that today? Love it.

Alcohol makes her hilarious.

Crazy.

I think we order more drinks before finishing our current ones. Keep the flow going.

Are we crazy? she gushes. Look at how young these people are. They are hip and we're not. Especially your hair. Did you even comb it today, Andy Man?

You're hip to me, I say.

She smiles. I'm just hippy.

Right. Now to be clear, I wouldn't normally laugh at a joke like that. It's too corny. But it doesn't matter. I'm hooked.

You're funny too, I say, laughing out loud.

Really? she asks. I mean, really? I'm humorous?

Absolutely. I drink. Almost slug it back like a rugby player on a Thai vacation.

Most people think I'm weird, she whispers in my ear. What do you think?

So, this is how an affair begins. And, this is how the guilt builds. It gets worse from here. I'm thinking this part, by the way.

Who is Sarah, really?

Sarah asks me this, while pulling my drink hand away from the bar. She pulls it toward her chest. I know, I know, this isn't normal. It parks between her cleavage, wedged between Boob Number One and Boob Number Two. Yes, I've already named them.

Sarah continues her monologue. It's a PowerPoint presentation without the PowerPoint, but completely third person. I wonder if this is part of a larger plan, but here we go.

Sarah. Yes. Sarah. Well, let me think. Okay, Sarah says out loud.

She sells air-time for a local radio station. She loves dogs. She comes from a broken family. She hates Christmas. She loves Hawaii. At Christmas. She's good with numbers. She's willing to try anything once.

That's it? I ask.

Sarah looks me over.

No, that's not it! Sarah says. I'm being superficial for a reason here. I don't think we're ready for an in-depth conversation about my life, do you?

I might be, I say. Come on. Tell me more.

Sarah takes a look around the room, fondling her drink elegantly.

I'm the kind of person who's been passionately in and out of love for all the wrong reasons, Sarah says. Men run to me, then run away. Maybe because I'm so intense. Maybe because I get obsessed. Or maybe because I'm on meds.

I stop her.

Wait, I say. What?

Who isn't? Sarah smiles, then adds, Oh, and I forgot, Sarah loves drinks after work with tall, handsome men.

Why am I doing this? I say. You're nothing but trouble, young lady.

Sarah snorts back a laugh, then holds out her hand like she's stopping traffic.

Okay. Listen. This is about connection and destiny. And I just happen to be a woman, all right? Sarah says this while trying to bite back a grin. Stop giving me that look, okay?

What look?

Sarah smiles. Pats my hand.

Listen, I appreciate the attention, but not the stares, she says sternly. Boob one is especially shy.

Ha. I think. Is she reading my mind?

I fumble with my drink.

I don't want to be known as somebody who objectifies women, I say. So, I wasn't eyeballing anything, okay?

We lean closer to each other, angle our stools in so that we can touch our knees.

Sarah drinks slowly, and I see her one eye through her glass as it's raised and it's magnified, obviously. And green. Although I'm not sure that's her eye colour; it might be the crantini. She's going goblin on me, I think. Goblin!

All very freaky here. Very freaky.

I'm suddenly as quiet as a fuse.

Sarah notices and leans in, her face mere inches from mine, so close I can feel her aura. It's a tiny current of electricity that enters my body through my eyebrows. I'm instantly connected to her, I wrongly think.

Your wife thinks you have a problem with women, Sarah says. You're on a path that clearly isn't healthy.

I pull away to drink, but there's nothing left really. Where is the next round? I wave at Joel, but he ignores me because he's making a drink with dry ice or something, and there's a little patch of fog sitting on the bar now. Joel channels Gandalf. It's magic hour.

Look, I say. I shoot commercials. They're successful. They may not objectify women directly, but they promote stereotypes. And that sells. It's just formula. That's what I sell. Formula and clichés.

What are you promoting right now? Sarah asks.

I'm promoting friendship, I say. How about that?

Really? Sarah says, putting her glass down carefully.

I've always been committed to relationships, I say.

The voice in my head says being committed to relationships might not exactly fit my reputation around town. But word gets around and sometimes you can't control that word. To be clear: I've been called "that asshole." And sometimes, I think: I'm going to change. You watch. And then I don't. Because I'm that kind of asshole.

I fondle my drink. Try to look normal.

Don't you believe in destiny? Sarah says.

I find it a bit unpredictable, I say.

Sarah says, It's my life. My life. And I sometimes hate it. Really, really hate it. Fuck destiny.

I worry she might throw her martini glass against the back of the bar.

But she doesn't. Instead, her eyes water and brim over the edge.

A tear tears down her cheek.

She wipes at it and flicks it away from her like it's ash.

Clears her throat and actually holds her right hand down to the bar as if steadying herself on a very tipsy boat.

Shit, she says. Shit.

She grabs my hand.

She does something to my fingers with her fingers.

What follows is an unpleasant silence. I think this happens when you start thinking of which piece of clothing you'd like to remove first — I mean, if things work out. When you get over fifty, you usually start with shoes because it's a long way down and your glasses will fall off and you might get dizzy. But. I do think about my wife, currently visiting her ailing parents in Toronto. Both of her parents have issues. And let's face it, we're all at that age when parents give out. Sarah wanted to talk to Anna about her lousy life, but it turned out I was the only one available. So, that's why we're here.

I blame this all on the fact we still have a land line. Call me old-fashioned. I'm getting rid of it soon.

I should have let the phone ring, but I've had some car problems. I thought it was the dealership.

We just exchanged a bunch of how are you doing and are you bored like me and I need a drink.

I didn't think you liked me, Sarah says now. When I called at first, I thought you were just being polite.

I was being polite, I say.

You made me laugh when you told that joke about working with a priest.

I did work with a priest, I say. I was shooting a commercial for the archdiocese. And it wasn't supposed to be funny. He loved turtlenecks and men with goatees and lead crosses. And he told dirty jokes on set.

Are you religious? Sarah lets go of my hand and tugs at a small cross on her necklace, feigning hope.

No, I say. I'm a total atheist.

That worries me, Sarah says. You're my first one.

First one for what?

Oh, you know, Sarah says. Maybe I should pray for you.

She stifles a giggle, then adds, Or at least lay hands on you.

I try to imagine where she's going with this, but now she begins to chew on the end of her hair and rubs her eyes as if trying to focus on me and failing.

We finish our drinks. Our first and second ones very quickly.

Excuse me, Sarah says. I need to use the washroom.

She pushes my knees apart and moves away, across the crowded floor to the back.

I watch her and see there's a line-up at the front door, mostly disenchanted millennials with super-large iPhones texting their millennial friends in other bars standing in other lines looking just as disenchanted. There are a lot of beards and Blundstones and bitterness crowding the entrance waiting to find their place at the equally crowded bar. Some wear masks over their mouths. Others wait with craft beers in hand, hoping for one more meaningless conversation about finding a reasonable place to rent in a city gone mad for real estate. We're all lost. Why not converge? And then drink to excess?

Joel wanders in.

You two finished?

I don't know, I say.

Take your time, he says, moving away to answer his phone.

For some reason, the music dies and I suddenly am aware of small talk everywhere. It washes over me.

And then Sarah appears again, looking out of breath, and I notice a faint wisp of white around her nostrils.

She pushes my knees apart again. Plops down. Thinks.

Change? We can't change.

Sarah says this.

We are who we are, right? Who, Andy?

Sarah touches my arm the way children test bath water.

We should go somewhere, she now whispers. Shouldn't we? I have an apartment nearby, but I'm never there. Weird, right?

Right, I say back. Right.

We must vamoose, she declares to the room. Everyone ignores her.

And so, we do the vamoose. And the fandango. We flee as fifty-year-olds should, gracefully, politely, and without a negative thought in our heads. We've got money and they don't, and our future came with high-paying jobs and retirement packages. Fuck, millennials, you got unlucky, you sorry bastards. Enjoy your plaid and your craft beer and your special bars. And your neat beards. We leave you with global warming. Unaffordable real estate. Debt. And Kanye West. Enjoy.

We head out into the darkness, lit by the cellphones of others like us, wandering the streets holding hands and dreaming of no-guilt sex. We've each done this before. I love you. I mean it. No, really. You complete me. Totally. I know everyone says this shit, but it's true, beer goggles turn us into hopeful vampires and bad poets.

We push past pedestrians. They mostly move to stay under awnings even though it's not raining.

Look at how everybody ignores everybody, Sarah says as we head down the street. I hope we don't turn into people like that.

She punches me a little in the arm.

We're not going to ignore each other, promise me that, she says.

I promise, I say.

We grab a cab because I don't believe in Uber. I've heard it's owned by a giant corporation and they believe in world domination. Google that shit.

To be serious, Uber is like the zombie apocalypse for cab companies, and there's nothing they can do about it. The virus spreads as we move, one block at a time, city after city. It won't take long. The end is near. And soon, these cars will be driverless. We will be assimilated. Resistance is futile. But seriously, I don't want to drive when I'm eighty-five anyway, right?

This is what I'm explaining to Sarah in the cab, and I have no idea how I decided on this topic.

I should think about what's really going on, but instead I love her perfume.

I think I might have said this out loud. Did I? Why would I be that stupid?

Yeah, I know. That makes no sense at all. Just shut up.

We go maybe three kilometres, and mostly we go in silence.

Get out at an empty intersection and I notice how wet the streets are even though the sky is clear. Maybe they're sweating; I know I am. It's July and it's very humid even for the West Coast.

No traffic on the shiny pavement except a street sweeper. Or is it a garbage truck? Its tail lights fade.

It's after eleven. And it's Wednesday. The city snuggles up to the mountains. Tomorrow is another workday.

Sarah grabs my arm when she slips slightly on the sidewalk, and then she doesn't let it go.

I really should have not worn new shoes, she whispers. I didn't test them or anything, so I guess I'm lucky I have something to hold on to, right?

Right, I say, slowing down slightly to accommodate her slowing walk.

You're a nice guy, aren't you? she says into my ear. A nice guy.

I hope so, I say. But it depends on who you ask.

Everything depends on your point of view, Sarah says. Some people think I'm too needy, but you can tell I'm not, right?

Right.

Maybe we've drank too much, I think. Was it only one drink, though? Or two? I can't remember.

An Audi honks at us, zipping by on the left.

Why are people so angry? Sarah mumbles. What did we do? What? Answer me that, world!

Nothing, I say. We just are.

And we are.

At this moment.

Almost innocent.

FOUR

THE DOCTOR'S OFFICE. THE SPECIALIST. The cancer expert. The one who you get to see three days after visiting Emergency with abdominal pains. The one with the wild, red hair and black-rimmed glasses. The pretty one with the plain name, Dr. Jane.

Her picture is on the wall behind us.

Her grad picture from medical school.

Stiffly holding roses.

Hair everywhere. Like it belongs in a Harry Potter movie.

We are planted firmly outside her office in an adjoining room at the cancer clinic in hard, green, metal chairs. These are the kind you find in backyards or gardens. They hurt your ass. Anna sniffles quietly. Sits beside me beside herself. Looks at her phone a lot. A friend. A friend from Toronto should have texted her minutes ago. Arlene. That's her name. Arlene who works in PR.

Something is wrong.

The room is off-white.

We wear black.

There's an old analogue clock facing us on the other wall. It looks like a prop for a scene in a hospital. So does the bookshelf. It has books about CANCER! On every shelf. Thick. Numerous. Voluminous. Ominous. Tedious. Spaced to fill things out. Lots of blood-red book spines. Extra care taken to make it look like there is order in the universe over here.

Two posters fill the opposite wall. They show insides of people.

Their guts spilling out with arrows pointing. They are cancer maps and no one is safe. No one.

But let's not label things too much.

Fuck.

We haven't slept in two days.

After the visit to Emergency … they said the cause was unknown. What you have. Who knows? We don't. And we see a lot. We can't say for sure. But there you have it. See the specialist. See the specialist, please.

Several nurses and two doctors said this.

So, we sit.

Drift into the Unknown. Stare at our iPhones. The glow working over our faces.

Someone must be out there. Someone. Talk to us. We need you. Text us. You worthless friends. You worthless, shitty, healthy friends.

In the meantime.

Listen to music from the speaker above. What is that?

Electric Light Orchestra, Anna says.

Why would they play that?

Why not? Anna says. It's uplifting and it's from the eighties when we were full of hope.

Seventies, I say.

Seventies? Are you sure?

I'm sure, I say. Yup.

Then she sobs.

Fuck me. What's happening? What? What? I thought we had more time!

A quiet series of shoulder pops while she holds her face. The shudder is a series of train cars coming to a stop in front of a granary. Goes right down to her legs. Then feet. Until she stomps them hard to stop the wracking. Nothing cooperates. Nothing works. Not even prayer when you are in the waiting room of a cancer specialist.

Our chairs feel like chains.

Arms too.

Legs.

I'm cold, Anna whispers. Why am I so cold?

She dabs her eyes with a tissue pulled from a box on the table behind us. The one with the vase of old candy canes and Get Well cards with cats on them.

I can't stop even if I tried, Anna says.

She muffles a good sniffle. Then several more down the line. I try to move in my seat because my butt is numb. The chairs in any waiting room are not made for sitting properly. Everybody knows that.

We're here to hear good news, I say. Remember. Nobody in the hospital knows for sure. That's what they told us. They don't know. It might just be a blockage. Or something normal.

Nothing's normal about this, okay?!

Anna stomps her foot again.

We watch the clock. The sweep of seconds. Time moves around us like we're not even here.

I'm having an out-of-body experience, Anna says. Her face floats in front of me, tears dropping on my lap.

Right, I say. Right as she swims in faraway thoughts.

There's smell to the room. Root Beer. A hospital cleaning agent possibly? Who knows.

Fuck. What's happening to us?

Anna grabs my fist.

Don't make a fist and try to hold my hand like you care, she says.

I DO care.

You need to care more, she says.

It's the unknown that makes it hard, I say.

Fuck the unknown, Anna says. Let's try to be empathetic. Can you do that? Can you?

I am empathetic, I say. Then try to free my hand with my other hand.

Who are you texting?

Will, I say. I'm trying to figure a shooting schedule.

You can't figure schedules out, Anna says. Not while we don't know what's going on with our lives.

Life goes on, I say.

No! No, Anna says. Life does NOT go on. That's why we're in this fucking room.

Anna, I notice, has clenched fists. They are mini white-knuckle balloons. She stares me down.

Lick my lips a bit. Think hard.

I'm just saying we need to face this head on, I say. With decorum.

Oh Jesus, Anna says. Who are you? Who? Just shut up. Please shut up.

A lot of shutting up overall.

We sit there.

For a long time … nothing.

Not even a single text.

Then.

Will you take me kayaking again? Anna says.

Really?

We can't let things stop us from enjoying the great outdoors, she says, twisting my fingers in her hand.

And …

And that's where I find myself, Anna sighs.

Despite everything?

I ask this as quietly as I can because this room is incredibly bright and quiet; the fluorescent lights above us buzz slightly … but very softly.

Despite everything, Anna says. No matter what Dr. Jane says.

Right, I say.

PROMISE ME!

Anna faces me with her face pinched up now, tears flowing. Around her eyes it's red and white along the wrinkle edges, her crow's feet. Her slight Roman nose flares. She has both hands around my right hand in a vise. Very tight.

Why are you so impervious? Anna says. Why? Can't you see what's happening? Can't you feel it? What's wrong with you?

My chair actually moves.

I think because of the power of her words.

Or because inside I'm actually trying to get away.

Either way, this is when time really stops.

In a relationship.

Full.

Stop.

It seems then Anna moves closer to study my eyes.

I know I have lying eyes. I was born with them. What can I do?

I always try to make things funny. It's a thing I do. I've been doing it regularly since my father stopped hitting me at thirteen.

I will NOT be my father.

He didn't find anything funny. And that's exactly why he married my mother. She saved her laughs for when he wasn't around. When he died, she found her sense of humour hiding with her grandchildren.

Games, right? You scatter on command.

One potato, two potato, three potato ...

ANSWER ME!

Yes, I say. We will go kayaking again.

What?

If that's what you want, we'll go kayaking, I say, thinking this is a very good answer.

Anna thinks about what I just avoided, then sighs.

Someplace near the end of the world, Anna says quietly.

Someplace where we can sense the beginning or the end. Someplace where things run together. Someplace where time can hold us. Where we can find ourselves. Someplace where we can take a look at the world, and where we can breathe the air deep into our lungs and feel hope. Can you do that for me? Can you? Because I really need to be with you, okay? I'm talking about a peaceful, easy feeling. And don't say anything funny right now, don't you dare. Don't even think about it.

Of course, sweetie, I say, licking my lips. Anything you want.

Don't say anything you want either. It's not something I want to hear in the waiting room of a cancer specialist. Okay?

Right, I say.

Anything else?

Would you pray?

No, I say. I'm an atheist.

Could you for once in your goddamned life not be so cynical? Anna says.

Jesus, I say. Je-sus.

Thank you, she says. Then she tries to recite the Lord's Prayer.

Our Father, who art in heaven. Hallowed be thy name. Thy kingdom come. Thy will be done on earth. Give us …

Fuck.

Fuck.

Fuck.

I can't even remember that.

She nearly collapses into a pile of herself. Her off-green-and-white sweater swallows her. And she sobs. Not the kind of sound you want to hear from any human, particularly your wife.

Come on, I say. Come on.

I try to pull her chin up like my uncle used to do. He knew how to be strong. He was an engineer for the Department of Highways in Saskatchewan. And he was a schizophrenic. But he was kind and crazy, but mostly kind.

I try to be understanding, right? I have that capability, right? I know what it takes, right?

So it goes. Come on. Please.

Rocks in our heads replace holy prayers. Cementing our thoughts. Our wait gains weight. A finality to everything. Not good. Not good at all. Then nothing. Just a big empty space.

We sit there. Planted, you could say. Fixed in time and place. Phones held in mid-air like torches. A pause to end all pauses. Our fate behind that door over there. The white door with the sign. “There is no medicine like hope.”

Yes, that’s what it says.

In the cancer clinic. Just over there. I’m not sure if I’m breathing or sighing. Or mixing them up.

Tell myself. This too will pass. It seems Biblical for an atheist. Say it over and over. This too will pass.

Anticipate Dr. Jane. Anticipate.

Hope she will sweep into the room smelling like roses and spouting somewhat good news, which is exactly what she does in three, two, one …

I can’t believe my timing.

FIVE

THE SMART CAR COMMERCIAL. A car so smart it drives itself. The car of the future. Relax and let the car drive you. Buy one today. You'll never regret it.

It's almost a year before the kayak trip with Sarah and Anna. My big job of the season. Something I had been looking forward to creatively and financially. Get to work with my buds. My drinking pals and gals and those who just adore me. We're going to have some fun and spend copious amounts of money that doesn't belong to us.

It's going to be a killer shoot.

We film across the street from the football stadium. It's raining. The kind of rain Vancouver always gets: a constant drizzle like you're walking through a despondent cloud after a breakup. Most of the crew complains. What is this shit? Everything sweats. There's a glisten to every cord and cable, every forehead and fist. The cameraman constantly wipes the lens and bitches about the troubles with focus. The actors stay in their trailer like they've been herded in there by a border collie and play with their smart phones until called out by the assistant director who carries a big black Nike umbrella. Jess. She's just graduated from college and made the mistake of wearing a short, tight dress on set. Everyone hopes things will clear up. But the rain stays committed for most of the day. The sound guy hates the interference from the pitter patter, but the lighting pro doesn't care; the grey is perfect, let's get at 'er.

His name is Dave and he's a total ass-hat. But he's MY ass-hat and the best lighting guy in the city bar none.

He's a squirrel monkey, quick with his jumps to set up stands and his nervous little hands fiddle with lights like they're candy. But he's a genius. And everything looks amazing. The kind of light you dream of.

Also, he talks shit all day on set. It keeps things loose.

I could have sex in this shit, he says while the camera is running, and I have to tell him to shut the fuck up.

Shut up, Dave.

Dave rubs his red Expos hat like it's on fire.

Okay, okay … just chill, Andy Man. I didn't know we were shooting, and it's really nice light right now so that's all I was commenting on really —

Shut up, Dave.

I love the grey. I love it, he says to the clouds. Keep it up, sky guy.

We're doing close-ups of the car door closing over and over and over again.

Rolling.

Cut.

Rolling.

Cut.

That was a good take, I say.

Were we running tape? Dave asks. Did that get picked up? Was I talking again? Shit.

Yes, obviously, Dave. It did. Just … shut up.

Shit, he says. What an amateur move. My deepest apologies. My kid is failing math and I can't seem to focus.

Then I see another problem in the playback.

The car window has glare and you can see us in the reflection. Just in the corner. Shit.

Dave snuggles over and looks at the monitor.

Oh yeah, I see it. Oops.

How do we get glare when there's no sun? I ask. How?

It's the light I put up.

But I don't want a light, I say. No extra lights, please.

Sorry, Andy Man, Dave says. I fix.

Reset, I say. Reset. First positions.

Dave pulls the light, but I notice he sets another one further away and somewhat brighter, and this fussing enrages me. Why do they fuss so much? Can we just finish on time for once? Please. I want to shoot the final sequence. I want to go home eventually and have a double Scotch.

Dave, get away from the light! Now!

He backs away from the light like it's an idol.

All good, man. Sorry, dude. It's gonna look amazing. Trust me.

Dave looks apologetic. He's now down the street a little, trying to focus the light where the Smart Car will be, not where it is. He clambers down from the double apple box he's set up beside the light and wipes his dirty hands on his jeans.

Reset.

The car absolutely glistens. It's parked beside another Smart Car, a white one, to make it look like the city is packed with them.

Dave scampers up trailing a cord like it's his tail and throws it out of his way.

I gotta say, this shoot is great, Dave says. We have some very nice close-ups of the door, and I love the shot of the feet as she gets into the car. Love the feet. The actress has great ankles for a Smart Car. But why isn't she wearing a Swatch watch, all things considered?

What are you talking about, Dave? I ask.

Well, everybody knows that Swatch started the Smart Car, and Mercedes jumped on board after, Dave says. Google that shit. You'll see. She should wear a Swatch, dude. Get on the irony train.

The actress slash model slash driver wanders over from the car.

What's happening? Why aren't we shooting?

Please go back to the car, I say. We're about to go again.

The car is supplied from a local dealer. It's black and very shiny. The actress we've hired — Gili — loves to sit in the driver's seat as the car drives up and down the block over and over again, smiling and laughing and showing teeth and swinging her dark hair back and forth like a pony on meth. The sponsors are deliriously happy with her.

The girl next door. That's her. Perfect.

And here's the thing about the Smart Car: it's self-driving. It's the car of the future and we're shooting the future. The tag line is "This Smart Car is Brilliant. It cannot make a mistake because it's the smartest car ever made. The smartest of the smart. Cars."

Something like that. I didn't write that shit, trust me.

Gili sits behind the wheel because that's what the law says. But mainly the car drives itself, and we have a computer specialist on set to make sure it does.

I'm ready when you are, Gili says to us through the open window over and over again.

She tosses her hair.

Dave stares at her.

Wow, she has this hair thing going great, he says. It's awesome like pony mane awesome.

Can you please not talk, Dave? I say. I'm trying to concentrate on the shot.

You should probably get a GoPro on the dash and pick up some of that great hair action, Dave says. It's gonna make a difference, trust me. And the Swatch. You need the Swatch.

We're not using a GoPro, Dave, I say. Stop with the GoPro all the time.

I used a GoPro on *Mushroom Men* plus a drone and my footage was awesome, Dave says. I have one in my car — it'll take me fifteen minutes max to set it up, dude. Quick, trust me. Very quick.

Gili waves at me from the car.

Are we a go?

Yes, I say. We're going.

Love that girl, says Johanna, who was sent by Mercedes Canada from head office in Toronto. Johanna is in her fifties too and always has her kid in tow; a strapping teenager, Malcolm, who wants to be an actor himself. He wears a black leather jacket and secretly vapes bubblegum-flavoured liquid smoke when his mother isn't looking. He hangs out with the grip at the crappy black tent we've set up. The grip is from Nigeria and he's tired of this shoot. And he's cold. His leather gloves are always folded over his belt like spent bat wings.

I will fix anything, the Nigerian says. You ask. I make it happen. You will see.

Best grip ever.

Wears flip-flops.

Yeah, I know.

Malcolm. There's a sadness to the kid like the world is weighing him down, pushing him into a sagging slouch under the canopy of the playback tent watching take after take. Yeah, he acts like his life was over six minutes ago. And this is an everyday thing, for sure. But, really, he should cheer up because he's on my set, and everything is going perfectly great on one of the best shoots ever.

The TV ad is my twentieth in two years. It's what I'm paid to do. This time: a one-minute spot showing the WONDERFUL INTELLIGENCE of the SELF-DRIVING SMART CAR in an URBAN SETTING. It's what they spelled out on my contract. With caps, of course.

They are paying me over thirty grand for this shoot. It just needs to look good, not be good.

That's why I hired Gili. She's thirty-something, but looks twenty. She's got the *it* factor, plus a great smile and hair to die for. She's got *wonderful intelligence* written all over her. All guys are attracted to her because she makes them attracted to her. Kind of tells them that, first, they are all full of shit, and second, she's not interested. Then she punches them in the arm and tosses her beautiful mane. Mostly that does it for every guy and mostly they're hooked. I'm one of them.

How smart are you? With a Smart Car, all you have to do is drive it home. Or better yet, let it do the driving for you.

That's some of the narration, and, to be clear, I did not write that shit.

Gili talks through the open window before taking off down the street, and I guess the concept is: who was she just talking to? You, her boyfriend, a random handsome man?

She mainly says hi. And does a little wave.

Before we started, we talked about objectives over double-sweet lattes Jess bought at the local bean place next door called JJ's.

Jess said she'd call us when the extras were ready.

Gili wanted to sit, but I wanted to watch for a change in weather by the door.

I want this to be honest, Gili said.

Oh yeah, I said. It will be. Honest.

No, don't just agree, Gili said, putting down her coffee on the counter. I want this to have the feeling of authenticity. I want people to not just like me, but to feel I'm somebody they can relate to. That's why I decided to wear a blue outfit instead of black.

I thought the costume person said we were going with black, I said.

Well, I told that costume person he was full of shit, she said.

It's what the Mercedes people wanted, I said.

Well, Gili said. They will get it when they get it, right? I'm wearing blue and the car is black, right?

It is black, I said.

So I'm blue in the black. What does that tell you — and be honest, Gili said, pulling on my sleeve.

I stood there and tried not to get mad.

Eventually I said, Maybe we can try it with you wearing black and then also shoot it with the blue, just to have a choice.

She dumped her drink in the trash and winked at me.

Yeah, she said. Maybe we can.

Back to work.

I look at her now wearing the blue top and suddenly it all makes sense. She looks more sophisticated and trustworthy.

In the car.

Smiles.

Do you like this look? she asks, sitting there trying to be authentic.

Yes, I say. Wow is she cute.

Here's the shot-list: a bright, happy, intelligent woman wearing a blue top jumps into the car carrying books from the library because she's smart and she drives a Smart Car, get it? She spots two handsome men — probably lawyers with colourful socks and short beards and nice suits, dark blue and grey — stepping across the street. She drives past them, waves because she knows they are in love with her smarts, pulls over, and says hi through the open window. She drives off smartly (very important) and then spots a mother walking with her nine-year-old child in front of her at the intersection; the car recognizes the pedestrians and stops all by itself, and the mother points out the Smart Car to her daughter. Look how smart that car is, right? Then more voice-over as they cross the pedestrian crosswalk in super slow motion. Big smiles from everyone.

Easy, right?

This is the kind of shoot most directors could do in their sleep.

Mindless. Stupid.

Money.

Say that over and over and over again on the way to your bank while driving your Audi convertible along the beach.

And it is ridiculous money. Obscene even. Did I mention the thirty grand?

Money. God, I love money!

I thought this ad would make me forget about the empty life I had chosen to live. I always do that. This one will be different. It will be art. It will show people I'm not full of shit. I'm creative. I'm better than all those hacks out there. I am. Also, I thought it would make me interesting and funny at backyard barbeques and openings of plays and at bars where actors hang out taking selfies with their new phones and posting shit on Facebook saying Look Who I'm With. Look. A Director. He's Famous. He makes Obscene Amounts of Money. He drives an Audi. He makes beautiful pictures. He creates moments of wow. And he cares about his craft. He cares about us.

No one expected what would happen next.

No one thought the worst-case scenario would happen.

No one thought the rain would change anything.

But it did.

It made everything sweat. Everything.

Take 15.

Quiet EVERYONE!

QUIET PLEASE!

Jess waves her black umbrella like it's a machine gun spraying out evil thoughts: you people suck; you have no talent; this is a waste of time; no one will get famous; life is meaningless; and the coffee is shitty.

I look at my phone: it's 6:37.

Near the end of the day. A long day. We have less rain, more light, no wind. Great. I'm pretty sure I'll make my dinner reservation with Anna.

ROLLING!

Gili complains about Dave's light suddenly appearing in her rear-view mirror as a blinding spot. He's put it on a long stand twenty feet in the air near the streetlight behind the intersection. I don't think much of it at the time. But it makes a difference, obviously. As the car slides to a stop in front of the passing mother and child, it hydroplanes and with a soft thud like a hockey stick hitting a bag of feathers, hits the child, not very hard, but hard enough for her to fall over and smack her head on the pavement, also with a soft thud, like a seagull hitting a telephone pole. I know, I know, two similes when one would do just fine. It is contact, but contact so tender and so innocent, the cameraman actually giggles, *giggles*, and says, That's what I call a love tap.

Crap.

The self-driving car mostly stops in time because the computer recognizes the pedestrians crossing in front, but the wet road changes everything.

A barely-there bump.

At the time, really, nobody thinks much of the incident. The girl is fine afterward and even laughs about it. So do most of the crew.

Oops, says the makeup person. Oops. And ouch.

Gili jumps out of the car immediately.

You okay?

That was embarrassing, the kid says, getting to her feet and doing the proverbial wipe-off.

Her mother laughs, Well, that was close, wasn't it? You okay, sweetie?

Stupid me, the kid says to the crew. Sorry. Sorry. Sorry.

She salutes us like a Girl Scout, three fingers in the air straight up.

That's the part that I clearly remember. The salute to the crew.

And her giggle. That kid could giggle for a living, I said at one point, looking at the playback. Jess asked, Go again? Less giggle?

The kid was gold. Absolute gold. A trooper. There, I said it. A real trooper.

The so-called love tap didn't faze her a bit even though her mother wasn't sure what exactly had happened.

She insisted we finish the shoot. We did ten more takes. The self-driving Smart Car stopped perfectly on each one, and then we did some close-ups. Nothing unusual. In fact, the rain stopped, the sun peeked out between the clouds, and we had a nice clean final take and Gili nailing her smart grin, the Smart Car lurching to a smart, tidy stop. Done. The nine-year-old smiled on cue and pointed to the car like she was jealous teenager.

I love that car, she said to her mother.

Her name was …

I can't remember her name.

Or maybe I can and I'm just blocking it out.

Gili said we called her Kiddo throughout the shoot. I don't remember that. I just remember thinking … she was a trooper and a real pro for finishing take after take perfectly happy and smiling like she was told: with conviction.

Be real, I said to Kiddo.

But be yourself.

Have fun out there.

It's a game.

And your friends will laugh and smile.

Because they will see you on TV.

And you have something they will never have.

You have spunk.

I can't take my eyes off you for a reason. You're beautiful. You're perfect. You're the daughter I never had.

Kiddo smiles, wiping her bangs away at the same time.

I notice she's missing a tooth.

Uh-oh, I think. Uh-oh.

You're so nice to me, Kiddo says quietly.

It's super nice.

I look around.

I feel very fatherly for the first time in my life, and suddenly I am filled with regret being childless and barren, but I decide not to say anything more.

Places please.

Some of the crew giggle a little behind my back, and I wave them to shut up.

We get a bit of sun suddenly.

Beautiful, I think. Beautiful.

One last take. One more and that's it.

Let's do this, people. Let's make history.

Kiddo has got one more in her, for sure.

Right?

Kiddo beams. And rubs her head.

Johanna, the official representative from head office, said it was the best direction she's ever seen.

Official cause of injury: epidural hematoma.

Hours later.

Kiddo goes into a coma.

SIX

THE INQUIRY.

The WorkSafe people, plus all our lawyers, plus the families, plus the doctor, plus the other government and civic people, plus the Smart Car people, plus the self-driving computer experts, plus our whole cast and crew, all of us, are required to participate in the investigation of what the hell happened on set. After a week at the courthouse, each day for around six hours, I find myself outside in the hot sun with Gili.

We're on the courthouse steps. The cement is very hot. No clouds. A day of just sun. And it's a dinner plate of heat boring through my forehead and forcing my thoughts into sweaters of doubt.

It's June, almost ten months since the accident and we're melting. I can't remember the last time it was this hot this early.

My limbs feel like they've been weighted down by big, heavy, hot things.

Barbeques. A brick of tin. A pallet of Bibles. Scarborough in the summer near a mall. A large pillowcase stuffed with dead kittens. A death in the family, usually a favourite cousin with a drug problem overseas, probably Berlin or Copenhagen. Golfers who complain about their wives after smoking copious amounts of dope. Debt. Affairs. Guilt. Sin.

I'm doing this to distract myself.

Shit.

What am I doing? What?

I wear a white shirt with a green tie. Anna purchased the tie for our tenth anniversary. It has a scene of the Austrian alps on it. I've never been to Austria. And, I wish like hell I was there right now. Sort of. I would be much cooler, no doubt.

Gili says, I think I'm doomed.

I say, Don't say that. If anything, I'm doomed.

Right, says Gili. Double doomed.

We sit and dream of better days, watch the hipsters walk by pulling on their beards and taking selfies. The concrete under our bums is a Coleman and we're slabs of pork. The sun melts the tops of our heads, our matching black hair turns into radiators. My brain is fried.

God, it's hot, one of us complains.

God.

We're here because we're waiting for the judge or the head of the inquiry to come to a decision. Who's at fault? Who's responsible? Why did this happen?

Gili says, it's going to be me. They're going to find me guilty. Me.

I say, don't say that.

I hit the brakes, but they didn't stop the car fast enough, Gili says. It's my fault she ended up in a coma.

Don't say that, come on, I say. Plus, she came out of the coma eventually, right?

I want to take her hand while I talk, but I don't.

Look. The car was new. It was supposed to be self-driving and you were watching very carefully, I say. Plus, it was wet out. You have nothing to worry about. It's a black mark on the future of self-driving motorized vehicles, that's all. It might set the industry back a year or two — especially since the artificial intelligence nearly killed a child. But that's about it. And we'll be okay. Especially you. Because the court saw you in there and you have a wonderful way with people. You're very nice. You're funny. You've got that great smoky voice. And this is important: You're genuine. You're the real thing. Don't ever stop being yourself.

I'm not falling for that, Gili says. It's BS. Don't BS a BS'er.

We sit on the concrete and bake a little more.

Gili leans over with her lips.

I think it's for a kiss. I'm hoping, but it's an old man's hope so it's tainted with a little desperation and sadness.

What about you?

Gili asks this while hovering a few inches away from my face.

I blink it all in and avert my eyes.

I look out at the skyline.

Oh. Don't worry about me. My production company has insurance. *If* this whole thing goes to a lawsuit down the road, which it might. But I'm covered. I'm sure I'll be okay. Positive.

Of course, very little of this is true. We're covered to a certain degree, but if things go against us, it's the end of a very profitable run. The end of our company. The end of my partnership with my fellow producer, Will. My pal of pals for the last fifteen years. Nobody will hire us again. Why would they?

Maybe I'll do a feature film after this, I say. Maybe I'll just quit shooting stupid commercials and finish my movie.

You have a script? Gili says.

In this town, everybody does, I say. I mean, you walk up to random people in Safeway and ask how is your feature film script going and almost all of them will say, how did you know? How? That's the way it goes in Vancouver. We're a movie town. We're creative because of all the mountains and rain.

I don't have a script, Gili says. Who has the time? I need to work on my nails.

Mine is still a work in progress, I say. Like me.

I'm impressed. You should send it to me, Gili says. I like works in progress. Usually I end up dating them.

I don't laugh.

I'm not sure it was meant as a joke.

We sit for a moment longer, just soaking in the heat.

Fuck, it's hot out here, I say. Then I play with the laces of my brown shoes. Then I stop doing that and rub my eyes and try to pull out my loose eyebrow hairs, the long, thick curly ones that start growing in when you turn fifty.

You look worried, Gili says. You're pulling your eyebrows out.

Oh, yeah, I do that sometimes, I say. I hate my eyebrows. I think they're wrong for my face.

You have an honest face, says Gili.

The hell I do. I'm in my fifties, so apparently I'm now middle-aged, and I'm white. Nobody should trust me. Plus, I make obscene amounts of money doing a job that a sixteen-year-old with a MacBook Pro could do in his sleep. I overcharge for everything and book the second-most expensive hotel in every city and charge the clients. I order room service and leave most of the food untouched on my tray in the hotel hallway, especially fries. My champagne bottles, though, are all upside down in the ice bucket. And they're Cristal.

Which hotel?

Gili looks at me.

I'm at the Sheraton and Mercedes is paying for it.

Holy shit, Gili says. You've got balls. We're on trial here.

Oh, they know, I say. They know. Everybody knows. This is a big deal. This could mean millions. They want me to be happy. I want me to be happy. We're fine. Absolutely fine.

Why aren't you staying at home with Anna?

Convenience, I say. Just convenience.

I'm lying very poorly, I decide.

We both watch pedestrians walk by. A steady stream of them with heads down, oblivious to the snarl of traffic around them, the buses parked at the curbs barfing out more people just like them. Everyone texting everyone. Where are you? What are you doing? What's real?

My cell vibrates. It's Anna.

Gili looks at my phone.

Answer it, she says. It's your goddamn wife.

I answer it.

Yeah?

Look, Anna says. I've been thinking … If things go wrong with the court, we have to hide our money somehow. We can't let them know about our huge bank accounts.

I've thought of that, I say.

What?

I said, I've thought of that. And I have a plan.

Well, I really hope your plan isn't spending our money on making your stupid movie.

I gotta go, I lie. It's time.

There are ways to legally hide small fortunes, Anna says quickly. Have you heard of Bitcoin? Have you heard of property in the Cayman Islands? Or Belize? My cousin took me to Belize twenty years ago; the banks have tiny guys with big machine guns in there.

I cut her off in mid complaint. Put my phone in my breast pocket. And then I feel it vibrate again and again. I ignore it. It eventually stops like a dying hummingbird.

I sit there feeling guilty for a bit.

Shit, I say. Anna isn't happy.

Gili says, I'm way worse.

What?

I can't sleep anymore. I don't have the energy for it. And, I had to quit my day job.

When did this all happen?

It's been happening a lot, Gili says. I'm seeing a shrink. She thinks I need a therapy dog or something. Maybe a dumb dog like a bulldog, but that's usually what my dyke friends have and I'm more of a cat woman.

You don't sound depressed, I say somewhat hopefully.

It's beyond that, Gili says. I'm trying to walk it off. You know, in pristine forests full of chirping fucking songbirds out by the university, but it may not be working.

It's all going to be okay, I say. I promise.

I'm going to get sued, Gili says. You're going to get sued. I can't afford to get sued. I'm still living like a fucking student. My bookshelves are made of bricks I stole from a construction site. I take transit all the time and I can't eat out. I'm barely making my rent. Or my Botox injections.

I barely pay attention to Gili.

I take out my phone and start running numbers with my calculator app. I know how much my company has in the bank.

Can't they garnish my wages or something? Gili asks.

She looks at me hoping for a rebuttal, but I keep my mouth shut. And I don't want to look at her; she's too beautiful, and plus she looks wildly desperate like she belongs in a spaghetti western. Her hair is in her eyes now, maybe it's intentional, but I can't stop staring at them because they kind of dart now, nervously watching strangers go about their business around us who have no idea. No idea at all. I think most of them are bankers or insurance brokers.

The wind catches us by surprise and I taste dirt in my mouth. I wipe at my lips with my forefinger.

More wind. It stings my eyes.

Holy shit, she says again. This is brutal.

Gili wears black because her lawyer told her to. But later confesses it's a tennis outfit and the skirt is far too short for legal purposes.

How's your tennis game? I say, trying to change the subject.

I need to work on my backhand, Gili says. It's my big weakness.

Yeah, me too, I say.

Then we sit there.

I play with my phone now, waiting for the message from my lawyer. He has told me to stay within walking distance of the court. When he texts me, I'm supposed to return fast.

You have nothing to worry about, he has told me. This was an accident. The judge would be crazy to find fault with you.

Gili wears flat black dress shoes with yellow flowers on the toe. Her lawyer — Nathan, a six-foot-nine former basketball player — has told her no heels. You need to look vulnerable, he said when we met months ago over poutine and beers at a local joint specializing in pizzas and doughnuts. It was raining then too. And Gili cried through most of the meeting. I wanted to hug her, but decided to remain cool and aloof because I thought I was being professional. Plus I'm old.

Her lawyer told me he wanted to date her, but couldn't because he was her lawyer and that would have been wrong.

Nathan had integrity. Has.

He was recommended by Dave, who met him during a shoot in Jamaica.

I twist my eyebrows with my fingers and pull at them.

Gili grabs my hand from my forehead.

Don't, she says. Soon you will have no eyebrows and that will look stupid. You'll look like Mr. Clean's older, straight brother.

Andy Clean, I say.

Andrew, she says. Andrew.

I feel dirty, I say. Hardly clean. Not after this.

The city bakes at our feet. Twenty stairs down, pedestrians carry on, doing what pedestrians do in big cities: wait for the light to change before rushing across the street to nearly full bars to drown out their daily sorrows with full mugs of foamy local beer. We're all doomed. Gili and I just happen to be really doomed. There's a lot riding on the inquiry. Lawsuits could happen, people would have to pay, and careers would end. All because a little girl fell over and hit her head during a Smart Car commercial shoot.

Poof. The world changed.

Gili holds my hand and squeezes it. She's a good squeezer.

And I love how cool her hand feels in this heat, her small fingers wrapped around mine.

I throw her a glance. The wind, the hot wind, catches her black hair again and sends it to stand on end briefly. It's an unexpected gust, and Gili drops my hand to pat it all down. Fuck my hair, she says. Fuck it.

You look good. No worries, I say to her. Everybody likes you. That judge-person always smiles when she looks over at you.

Gili sighs. You're making shit up. Stop making shit up. Just stop it.

Come on, I say. Come on.

I'm pretty much a complete disappointment so far, Gili says. Oh yeah. Ask around. You'll see. I don't even have an agent. I haven't got any film or TV offers. I haven't played Ophelia. I've never been to Broadway. And I'm still single in my thirties and I happen to be Jewish. My mother is going to kill me. I should have two babies by now. Fuck me.

Her mother doesn't know about the trial. And Gili never really got along with her because sometimes that's what happens with mothers and daughters.

Mostly it's just harmless anger, the kind that makes her slam on car brakes when somebody follows too close. She'll laugh about everything later. Much later. Except this accident. It is the kind of thing that takes a long time to get over. Which is what she tells me later, at her small bachelor apartment at the edge of where rich people live. She has an apartment in a Tudor-style house on the top of a small hill. The inside is decorated like a funeral home, lots of black and fake flowers and pictures of loved ones, particularly older people, most of them Jewish, who refused to smile because of the war.

And Gili does yoga, but it might not be helping.

I'm not the vision of joy you cast in that commercial, am I? she says on the steps with me. I'm basically fucked up, and that's not a good thing for an actress to be.

I want to disagree with her, but shut the fuck up.

She sighs.

You want to know my theory of self-driving cars?

Yes, I say.

They will be our worst nightmare in a short time because after they start causing accidents, we won't know who to sue or who's responsible. Are we going to start taking computers to court? Are we going to imprison the people who wrote their code? Are we going to lock up the cars? I mean, can we put a Tesla behind bars?

I laugh. Funny.

Don't, Gili says. I'm being serious. I mean, I was just sitting in the car trying to mind my own business and smile for the fucking camera, and then it hits a little girl, and there was nothing I could have done about it except maybe slam on the brakes earlier, but the car had already done that for me. There was nothing I could have done. Nothing. That stupid car wasn't that smart, if you ask me. It acted like a moron, and now we're stuck here awaiting our stupid fate.

Shit.

Gili sighs again.

The world will be fucked over very soon by self-driving cars, she says. And to think it all started with Roombas. Trust me. The age of robots. It's coming. It is.

So, this is kind of when it all starts between us. Us sitting here on the steps at the courthouse above the fray. Waiting to be judged. The world exists below our feet, and it's a little like we're sitting at the edge of a large, crowded pool waiting for fat people to get out so we can drop in and be romantic. Maybe drift around each other, noses touching — and you can imagine the rest, particularly below the surface where our legs mingle. You'd need a waterproof camera to capture all this, and it would need to be super slo-mo because there's something primal about naked legs intertwined underwater.

The world waits for us, too. People pass below like loaded freight cars. Two million people in this city and most of them have bigger problems than us. Most. And most of them are thinking, I suppose, of how to solve their issues before the weekend comes. Or before the in-laws land and the judgment begins. Or the next phone bill.

The inquiry will turn into a lawsuit and eventually lead to money changing hands and jobs being lost and maybe a car becoming demonized along with a brand.

Don't buy a stupid Mercedes. Think for yourselves, people. And don't use Google Maps, have fun exploring, just drive and drive and drive. Find the edges yourself, please. Find your horizon, people. Explore the great unknown.

Guilty as charged, says Gili, grabbing my hand again. She pulls it in to her body briefly, and I watch where it goes.

She leans in close and says, This is the worst day of my life. What about you? You okay in there? You're making a fist, it's probably not intentional, right?

Right.

Her phone beeps, and she pulls it out like it's a dagger and swipes at the edge, almost asking for a cut.

Oh shit, oh shit, oh shit.

She puts a hand over her mouth.

I hold on to her like she's a kite, but she pulls away with the hot wind, wandering back into the coolness of the air-conditioned courthouse.

I can't take it anymore, she says to the sky. Sorry. I just can't take it.

The glass door closes behind her with a click. A movie click.

She drifts toward the checkpoint where the security people wait for her like vampires, hiding behind metal detectors and big desks. They never smile.

I follow, my shirt now dripping wet. My pants soaked through. My thoughts filled with lead balloons of various sizes, making my head wobble and my neck ache. I'm going to be sick. I know it.

But I'm convinced I'm in love.

And I will sleep with her.

Because I'm weak and stupid and completely untrustworthy, and maybe even slightly psycho.

But why stop there?

SEVEN

THE TOWNSFOLK HAVE ARRIVED CARRYING homemade walking sticks, stainless steel water bottles, and Snickers bars. They tell us not to worry, things like this happen all the time, all the time. It's the middle of nowhere, and this is where a lot of things die without being noticed much. Here, have some chocolate. Stay calm. Do you have enough water? A stick?

Anna and I walk with Holly, a retired botanist with a Tilley hat who lives on the island. Holly. Gangly. Giraffe-like. But eternally gracious. To a fault. A frozen smile that's smiled at too many horrible things, I'm sure. Twice divorced. Her latest husband has slowly become a Mormon.

He's his own person, Holly says without a giggle. And he's changed, obviously, into a man who thinks Jesus came to America and lived with the Indians.

Holly has a thin face. It's a bit witchy. And she has enormous feet like they belong on a basketball player.

We talk a little while we walk.

Fuck. Back up.

Holly. Let me describe her here: she's important to this story. She's maybe fifty, but looks thirty-five. The kind of hair that looks off-white. But not really grey. Stringy. Thin. In her face. Wet, mostly. Pale. In fact, as a whole, Holly's so white she's practically blue along the edges.

The oddest thing about Holly: she wears a long, grey dress that looks vaguely Amish with big boots underneath, like workman boots — man shoes, I guess. Maybe they're her former husband's, I don't know, but she stomps from rock to rock like a really pissed Alanis Morissette at a stadium concert after a breakup. In retrospect, I think I actually tell her that too — but Holly doesn't crack a smile. She's not one of those women who think I'm funny. This bugs me. I try too hard around her and become irritating.

We've been walking the shore for three and a half hours now in groups of four and five. The RCMP have organized the whole thing like it's a school hike, and each of the six groups are assigned a cop, a local, and two or three kayakers. Anna and I are the kayakers. Our cop is Ashley. He's Asian and very fit. He's shorter than all of us.

You can call me Ash, people, he announces. Ash is perfectly acceptable. Let's go.

Holly is our local. She's the second tallest after me. I don't know why that's important, but it is. A lot of short people live on islands. Don't ask me why.

We're maybe two kilometres down the shore from the camp. We're hopping from rock to rock again, then along the shore where there's sand. Nothing has worked out right today. One RCMP boat broke down and needed to be towed back to Powell River on the Sunshine Coast. The search helicopter also broke down and headed back to Campbell River on Vancouver Island. The locals, mostly from Squirrel Cove on Cortes Island, are a nasty bunch of adamant environmentalists, retired people, and yoga instructors wearing Gore-Tex hand-me-downs and man buns. Each group has a couple of walkie-talkies and an armed cop. We're being safe and communicating and very professional. Mostly our job is about keeping our eyes peeled for clothing or body parts clinging to rocks or bobbing in the surf. The usual.

But for us, it's tedious work.

Nothing.

Nothing is very painful after three or four hours.

Your eyes tend to hurt with all that looking. Look at that. No, look at that. Is that … no. Keep looking. It's nothing. There's a lot of that.

No answers hurt.

It's tense. I'm tense. Everyone is tense. That's what you get for looking into the abyss.

My feet also hurt. My shoes aren't really made for rocks; the soles are too thin. They're New Balance, but they don't give me much balance, new or old — mostly I feel like a tottering, semi-drunk librarian. I'm out of my element with these shoes, trust me. They're made for light hiking, not rock climbing. And they're soaked. My feet are ice cold and they itch, too.

Holly points out another incredible view, too many to count by now. Soon we give in to the sheer splendor of the wilderness and wonder of it all, the blue sky around us, the deep green of crashing waves beside us, and the smell of forests everywhere. It's the best vacation ever, except I'm searching for a dead woman I slept with and my wife is right beside me grinding her teeth and crying into the wind because that was her best, best friend. Yeah, I know ... not good, not good at all. In fact, this is a shitty set-up, let's be honest here.

I'm not a likeable character, I'm sure. I guess my father was right about me. When you get to be my age, he said once, you're going to be a big disappointment unless you start going to church regularly and commit to a God-fearing life.

I feared my father until I turned seventeen, and that's approximately the first time I had sex. You make the connection. And don't jump to conclusions.

The horizon, I decide, looks horribly empty today. Devoid of even little boats. But when I look away, I notice an oil tanker creep from behind the tree line of a nearby island, as if on the prowl.

Holly is near my elbow on the left.

They sneak up on you, she says. Every day I notice more and more.

What is going on? I ask. Up here?

The terminal is up north, Holly says. They fill up and come back down through the islands and then to the coast of California.

Should they be doing that?

Holly pulls a long wisp of hair from her eyes.

No, she says. No. They will be the end of us. And soon.

We space out, ten to fifteen metres apart, along the wide part of the beach. Anna is in front of me, using a long stick to poke around in the rocks. Ash is in front of her. He uses a broken hockey stick he found earlier to probe the rocks. Holly is in front of him, kicking at seaweed and moss with her big boots. We're getting close, I think. To something.

I kick at clumps of sea shit and gravel. It's all a big mess of flotsam and seaweed and plastic. Yeah, lots of plastic, even in the middle of nowhere. Coke bottles, lids from yoghurt containers, coffee cups. That shit is everywhere. I find a strap from a wristwatch, also plastic. It might be from an Apple watch.

What is it with people? Why can't we be more responsible? Where is our fucking humanity? Is everything disposable?

I actually find an unopened package of Gillette razors, the ones with four blades. I pocket it because that's my brand.

How long have we been at it?

I start to sweat a little and feel my cheeks burn. My face cheeks. The wind doesn't help. It spits sea water at me. I probe between big rocks and small, keep my eyes peeled for anything remotely Sarah-like, but steel myself for the worst-case scenario. I worry about finding a head lolling in the surf caught between two big boulders, a grin on Sarah's face, her sunglasses intact.

Yo, dude, what's happening? she'll say. What's with the long face?

We cross over a small outcropping of rocks where the surf is subdued and there's lots of seafoam.

That's where I find it.

Sarah's blue waterproof Nikon camera, still bound by a float strap, bobbing softly against a small rock like a heartbeat.

I look around. Everyone else is heads-down, I think, as they stickhandle through the debris the surf has thrown up over the last million years or so. They search with intensity; Ash has motivated them. He's a good cop. And he's kind of stately, too. He talks like a deposed general, his orders apologetic and terse. Sorry, let's not clump together people. Sorry, but you need to get off your phone. Sorry about this situation, people. Sorry. Keep looking, keep looking.

The camera. Yeah, I found it.

I bend over, pick it up, flip open the back, and quickly remove the memory chip. I slip it into my back pocket.

Camera! I yell to the sky. Camera!

Ash turns and runs back. I'm astonished how much ground he can cover in a matter of seconds, hopping rocks like a possessed frog.

Don't pick it up, he yells. Leave it in the water. Leave it!

I quickly put it back in the water and pretend to point at it. Well, actually, I do point at it.

There it is, I say. Look. Camera.

Ash is beside me now, breathing like a dragon. He has a plastic bag in hand, and somehow, he's managed to slap on a latex glove too.

He scoops up the camera and a little bit of water too in the plastic bag. He holds it up to the sky.

Holly now joins us. The bottom of her dress is wet and her eyes are kind of misty.

I found it against the rock there, I say very loudly. Right there.

She just looks at me. Doesn't nod. It's then I notice how blue her eyes are. Dark, dark blue. Like they belong on a beluga.

Anna, huffing and puffing, grabs my arm.

That's her camera, all right. That's the one she bought at Best Buy when I went shopping with her at Christmas. It's a Nikon. And it's blue. That's the one, for sure. It's hers. She wanted to buy something cheaper, but I talked her out of it. And later she said it was the best advice I ever gave her.

We don't need all those details, I tell Anna.

It was important, Andy. SHE was important. Is, I mean.

Yes. IS, I say.

We have an uncomfortable moment. The four of us.

Ash looks around and notices a big black cloud heading our way.

He takes out a can of spray paint and marks a rock nearby with a sloppy pink check mark.

Okay, sorry everyone. Let's just finish up here and head back. It's going to get ugly out soon, he says, then ties up the end of the bag with the camera.

We tramp around for a bit, work our way down the beach another two hundred metres. There's nothing to see, nothing to find. Then it starts raining a bit, and Ash motions for us to go back to the campsite.

The tide's coming in, and some of the beach we've looked over is now under water. If we missed something, it's now below the surface of the waves.

That's it for today, Ash says. Sorry, guys. We did our best, right?

Right.

We head back, and it's then we hear the news from the walkie-talkie that another group has found a running shoe. It's a Nike. It's pink.

I'm pretty sure Sarah wore Nikes, but she's not the kind of woman to go with pink. At least from what I remember. Although her kayaking outfit was beautifully put together and all brand new.

I'm hoping we don't find her.

I'm hoping this is all some kind of huge mistake or cover-up or deception.

I'm hoping she's lost.

Finding her way across the island after bumping her head.

I walk with Holly. She moves gracefully for somebody wearing construction boots and stomping a lot. She practically glides over rocks and actually guides me, grabbing my elbow when I start to lose my balance.

There, there, she says. Watch it.

For a brief moment we have this connection, like a bolt of electricity has charged through our bodies. I look at Holly, who just smiles and nods.

We have to be careful, don't we, Andy?

What?

Careful, careful.

Yes.

She pulls a strand of hair from out of her face and stares at me for a second.

Everything okay? I ask.

Sure, she says. Watch yourself.

I'm attracted to her obviously. And I'm attracted to her at the wrong time. I'm a dick. I know I'm a dick.

I try not to look at her because our situation is awful.

The beach is cluttered with slippery rocks, a moonscape of them, the waves sweeping through them without hesitation. The pattern is the pattern and pretty soon you get used to it. Waves in. Waves out. Rocks in the middle. Waves in. Waves out.

In the distance, more ominous clouds gather like protesters at a political rally. They frame the horizon.

Holly says, It won't be long now.

For what? I ask.

Things can change here very quickly, she says. You have to be vigilant.

I look at my watch — yes, I still wear one. It says 4:45.

How long has it been? I say.

Holly says, five hours. Five hours and a bit.

Walking tenderly in and around the rocks and the pulling tide is exhausting; you need to watch your every step. I have a small backpack, and it throws me off-balance occasionally. I blame my water bottles. I have three of them. They bounce around back there constantly. God, I'm tired. My thighs ache; my ankles are swollen; my shoulders feel the effects of paddling for five, six days. There's a fire in two spots, just below each shoulder blade. My breath smells like salted fish and jujubes. I shiver and it's the kind of shiver that makes you want to pee even though there's nothing to pee out. When I lick my lips, I can taste the salt: the wind working its way off the water has painted our faces and coated our mouths.

In the distance, along the tree line facing the shore, eagles do the equivalent of pacing, flying across the treetops back and forth, watching us watch the water.

I nearly slip again.

Catch myself and slow down.

Holly and I stay behind Anna and Ash, maybe twenty metres. Anna is all about the camera; it's invigorated her.

Sarah, where are you? I love you!

Anna says this over and over again, throwing her voice against the curtain of trees facing the water as if Sarah might have somehow retreated into their branches to watch us struggle.

Sarah? Sarah? I love you, baby! Please, Sarah! Please come out!

I stall a bit as we walk because I want to talk to Holly. She senses this and also lingers behind. We pretend to find our bearings or catch our breath. I poke at some seaweed on the beach, which has flattened out a bit. I watch as Holly straightens her hair, then her dress, and touches her boot tops, wiping some sand off them slowly.

Wow, I say. Wow. What a day.

Holly gives me a long, long look. Then studies the waves in the distance is if calculating how long we have before the whitecaps hit the shore. It's clearly getting rough. The wind picking up, clouds racing in like cougars.

Your wife really loves Sarah, says Holly.

They were inseparable, I say.

How does that make you feel? she asks.

I'm not sure, I say. This whole trip was their idea. I thought it was going to be a lot different than this.

No kidding, Holly says. No kidding.

I've only kayaked once before in my life.

What did you find? Holly asks.

What?

Never mind, Holly says. Let's go.

She grabs my hand and pulls me off a rock. I nearly lose my balance, but catch myself. My feet splash through the water, and I don't like how cold I've become. Very cold. Not convinced I will ever be the same again.

As we approach the camp, I notice someone from the other search groups has started a bonfire along the shore. And with the coming dark, it's a beacon. The flames struggle as the wind picks up and the rain starts, but it guides us in.

We are living in medieval times. We just need more armour.

As we trudge over the crest and down into the camp, the fire suddenly goes out, then mysteriously comes back to life.

Deborah, the RCMP officer, pokes it with a stick. Stands practically on top of the fire, but she looks cold and wet. And miserable. It's been a long, horrible day, and the best she can do is spark the fire.

She sees us walk toward her; the four of us, also a little wet and miserable.

How are you four doing? she yells. What did you find?

Ash holds up the camera in the plastic bag like it's a rabbit at the end of a stick.

Her camera!

Wonderful, Deborah says. Wonderful. We're making progress, people!

Anna runs to Deborah and hugs her. Her muffled sobs are cleared away by a growing, persistent wind.

Sarah. Sarah.

Sarah.

Holly looks at me. I look away.

EIGHT

HOLLY'S CABIN IS A MENNONITE's dream: simple, full of stout beams, simple lines, and clean, clean, clean. The logs are red cedar. The open floor design means the kitchen, which is mainly stainless-steel counters, flows into the living room, which flows into the back rooms, where I haven't been. Copper pots and pans hang over the stove and a beautiful photograph of the same pots and pans hangs over the couch. Weird. The carpet under my feet — which is enormous and thick and red — is from Afghanistan, and the kitchen floor is pine. Everything about the place looks like high-end IKEA, although it would be a great insult to suggest that.

Lots of plants everywhere. Herbs? I don't know.

It's a jungle in here. Some of it might be pot.

Holly makes tea in the kitchen while I thumb through my phone. She has a great connection, three bars full. She needs it because she runs a bed and breakfast; this main cabin sleeping five while the mini-cabin in the back sleeps two.

Where's your wife, Holly asks from behind the counter.

Anna is still looking for Sarah with the cops. They're checking out Read Island just north of here. They took one of the police boats.

What? Why? Holly stops fussing with the tea.

The currents might have taken her that way, I say. I mean, that's the theory. If she's dead.

Or alive, right?

Holly waits for me to answer.

I don't.

Why aren't you helping?

I'm helping in my own way, I say. I'm here. The cops have a base camp near the beach. So, I guess I could go there to find out how things are going. They're just down the road.

Holly watches me watch my phone on the couch beside one of her two cats; a Siamese named Rudy, cuddled by my elbow.

I think you're full of shit, Holly says.

I keep my thoughts to myself. Again.

Because really, I'm here because I need to download a script. Yes, I know, how callous to think of my art at a time like this. But you can't stop creativity just like you can't stop progress.

I'm not sure how much of this I'm explaining aloud. Holly begins to slow her movements. Her hands rest on the counter, then on her hips. She's studying me. Or as my mother always said, sizing me up for a major correction.

We've always wanted to shoot a feature. My partner Will and I. Our first. Because we're going to make something brilliant and hopefully resurrect our flagging careers. Will owns the production company with me. We started the whole thing up over twenty years ago because we loved cars and cameras. It turned into commercials. Will. Who most call William or Bill or Billy, but never Willy. During the last shoot, the Smart Car commercial, Will was in Scotland trying to find his roots. Everyone's doing it because we need to find out what we once were in order to do things today. Without guilt. Whatever that means.

I'm righting myself, I say. It's my story. About my story.

Go on, says Holly. I'm all ears.

We'll write the script of our lives; I'll shoot it and we'll be famous. Absolutely. Then we'll travel to film festivals and do presentations and get grants and tell people it's a small picture with a big heart. Don't laugh. It's personal. It's true. It's who we are. Etc. The best kind of story. Write what you know. Everyone knows that. And it — this film — will add meaning to our miserable lives.

This is exactly what happens when you're in your fifties. You realize you've run out of time and suddenly you NEED to be creative, you NEED to say something about your existence, you NEED to try to find an audience, somebody to listen to you, to believe in your cause even if your cause is selfish and self-serving and self-indulgent. At least it's about yourself, I say. Even if yourself is beside yourself on the edge of sixty and almost completely irrelevant.

Holly watches me explain shit like she's targeting my left nut. She's staring even.

How long are you going to stay?

Holly leans over the counter and shows cleavage and I try to ignore it. Them. Boobs. Whatever. Boobs. They're perfect. Boobs. Why should I be surprised?

Boobs.

The RCMP said we can go anytime we want, I say, not looking up now.

Why don't you, then?

My wife wants to stay as long as it takes to get some answers, I say. Sarah was her best friend. Obviously.

Was?

Is.

I lick my lips. And stand up briefly.

I have high hopes, I say to the room. That Sarah is still with us. She was with us the whole way in, and we were maybe ninety metres from the shore, if not closer. I mean, it wasn't very deep, I don't think. I could see the bottom. Even if she ditched, she had a personal floatation device on and, hell, she could have walked to shore. Honestly. And she's tough. A great athlete, too.

Really?

I was just as surprised as everybody when her kayak drifted in empty, I say. I mean, the water was flat, it wasn't windy, and it wasn't cold. It's a big mystery what happened.

Were you beside her? Holly asks.

I turn to face her in the kitchen. She gathers things, expertly putting together a tea tray with little homemade cookies and wildflowers. Purple ones. I notice she has one or two in her hair, too. It's all very exotic and homey at the same time. She looks like a middle-aged fairy with only a little magic left ... mostly in her eyes, but those eyes, those eyes.

No, I was further in. I was one of the first ones to beach. I wanted to stick close to my wife and especially our guide. Emma. She's the expert. I always listen to the experts. Especially when I don't know what I'm doing. Which happens a lot.

Holly brings out the tea on a wooden board that's been turned into a serving tray.

That's a beautiful tray, I say.

It's a piece of wood from just around the corner. I found it under some deer shit, says Holly. Wiped it off. My husband cut it and finished it. Natural oils. You can put any food on it. And wash it with soap. Just not in the dishwasher. That would be a disaster.

And where is your husband?

He's in Utah getting married again, Holly says.

Ex partners. We lived together right in this very cabin, which he built — thank you very much Todd — but then he suddenly became a complete idiot and converted to Mormonism and went AWOL. I blame Google. And isolation. We had too much time to think on this island. When you start to think too much, religion sets in. Also, Todd throws axes for fun. And professionally. On the circuit apparently. The axe-throwing circuit in Salt Lake City.

Wow, I say. Did you just make that up?

Why would I do something like that? Holly says. You'd see right through me, wouldn't you?

I love how you talk, I say. It's so interesting. Like you could be in my movie.

As soon as I say this, I realize how shallow I sound. Like I'm a teenager in the mall.

I hate acting, Holly says. It's so superficial. I'd rather stick to plants. They don't argue and they're rarely full of shit.

Ha, I say. But it's a nervous ha.

I watch Holly saunter over to me, her face as solid as granite.

Holly sets the tea down like this is now a Japanese tea ceremony and long pours me some into a tiny cup that's decorated with clowns.

Todd made the cups too, if that's what you're wondering, but he was only seventeen when he did those. The style isn't very mature. Bottoms up.

I don't drink right away because I hate hot, hot tea. It'll ruin your day, trust me. You'll lose your taste in everything.

So.

Sit there. Try to think of something nice to say. Avoid the cleavage, avoid the cleavage.

I squeak with each squirm in the couch. It's dark brown and very, very comfortable.

Where did your ex-partner learn to throw axes?

He built a range for himself out back. In the trees. Twelve feet. The axe needs to rotate once. So you measure it off. Twelve feet to the target, which is a stump of wood hung on a tree.

Wow, I say. Do you throw axes?

What do you think?

Holly flexes her arms. But that's not where I'm looking.

She knows, oh she knows. I swallow loudly.

Love this place. It smells great in here, I say. Like it's a living forest.

Oh, sorry. I left the window open, says Holly. It is the living forest.

Right.

Right.

Holly looks at me.

I look at her.

How far are we from the beach campsite? I ask.

Holly takes her time thinking of an answer. I think we're maybe one-and-a-half kilometres away. Not quite. It's a nice walk, don't you think?

I love walking through the forest, I say. That was the first time

I've felt safe in a week. Not like out on that water with all the killer whales and seals and shit.

What are you, a big chicken? says Holly.

I'm just a newcomer to this kayak thing, I say. Like I said, it was my first trip. I love the scenery, but, it's not safe. Obviously. Obviously not, after what happened to Sarah.

Again, with the obviously. Shit.

There's a moment. It's a long one. We sip the tea a little. Actually, I fake it. Still too hot.

So … I heard the shoe they found wasn't hers, Holly says, running a long finger down her sort-of-white dress.

Where did you hear that?

Holly thinks.

I don't know where I heard it.

Holly sighs and drinks her tea. She swings the tiny cup up to her off-red lips and slurps in the politest way imaginable, like royalty. I study the way she studies me.

What's going on?

Holly takes my hand and places it on my tea cup.

You're insulting me. Drink. Please. Drink.

I pick up the cup, her hand acting as my guide, and I actually take a sip. It tastes like mushrooms.

It tastes like mushrooms. Shit.

It's an extract, says Holly.

From where?

I extracted it from the forest. Just out there. Under some very large trees. In the shade.

Oh. I sip again. Very mushroomy. Very.

I put some lemon in it too, Holly says. You should taste that as well.

Yes, I say. Yes. Lemon. Lemon it is. Very lemony. Mushroom shit.

Another moment. How long have I been here? I think.

The room seems larger all of a sudden. The carpet on the wall. What is that?

I stare across the room at the carpet that depicts a large wolf. It's over the fireplace, and it's the only artwork that isn't about kitchenware, anywhere.

I laugh.

What is that? I say.

That's a carpet of a wolf on the wall, if you're asking, says Holly.

I am asking, I say. I just said that. What? Aren't you listening?

Holly laughs. You're really funny, aren't you?

I don't mean to be, I say. Wow, I feel great. Wow.

The wolf is my protector. His name is Wolfgang.

Holly crosses her arms. And forces a weak smile.

Wow. I laugh. Great name. Not obvious at all.

Holly stiffens, I think. But it's now that I notice her long, off-white dress has a slit in it, and she's got runner's legs. Great knotted legs. Super. Cool. Legs. Wow. Angelina Jolie legs. Wow. And …

That carpet, I say.

I got it in Vancouver. It was made by a Dutch woman in her seventies after her grandson was killed walking backward on a railway track under the influence. He was listening to Coldplay and ignored the train because he was caught up in their very deep lyrics. Very tragic. And ironic because nobody really likes Coldplay. Right?

Coldplay is lame, I mumble.

What do you like then? Holly asks. Or should I care?

Well, I like that carpet, I say, drinking more mushroom tea. What part of Holland is it from?

Port Coquitlam, Holly says. She has a little store there. All of her carpets depict my spirit animal.

Right, right, I say blandly. That wolf is really staring me down. Love it. Love it. Love it.

I'm dizzy from repetition, I think. What am I doing? What? Fuck.

Who else do you love? Holly says, leaning over more, her breasts now mere inches from my nose. Wow. Wow.

I laugh.

This is weird, I say. This is really weird.

What?

This whole trip has been one big trip, I say. And you. Look at you here. Leaning over at me and I'm sorry I looked down your top. I didn't mean to. I was distracted, obviously. And what's with that wolf. He's pissed. And he's just carpet. Right?

Are you feeling okay?

Hell, yes. I swallow. My stomach feels funny.

That will pass, says Holly. It's a side effect of the magic mushrooms.

They're magic? What?

They are, says Holly. *Psilocybe semilanceata*, commonly known as the liberty cap, is a psychedelic mushroom that contains the psychoactive compounds psilocybin, baeocystin, and phenylethylamine.

Wow, I say. You're really … did you just google that shit?

No. I'm. A. Botanist.

A real fucking botanist, I mumble. Wow.

Yes, says Holly. I'm what you call an expert.

I love how my hands feel right now. Look at them. Monster hands.

I hold them out. Dangle them. They twitch like mad. Really squirm. Like nervous worms.

Take them, I tell her. Take them. Please make them stop doing whatever they're doing there.

She holds my hand and it's electric. Just relax, she says.

The room has this energy. It's everything right now. This place. Me. This woman named Holly. A real-life botanist. And the forest waving at me from outside. Stop that. You stupid forest.

Wow. The ferns out there are coming through the window.

I think I say that. Not sure at this point.

That carpet is amazing, and I love how everything is so real in your place. Those pots and pans and the smells in here are amazing and you're amazing and I love this leather couch. I love how soft it is. I mean, I'm literally sinking in here. Sinking. Fantastic. Really.

Holly smiles.

Have more tea, she says.

You're making me trip, I say. Aren't you?

Yes. Yes, I am.

Holly leans over and cups my chin.

Where's the memory card you took?

What?

The memory card. You took it out of the camera. I saw you do that along the beach. You took out the memory card and I want it.

Oh sure. I say to the room. Sure. I put it in my pocket. Obviously. You can never be too careful.

Holly fingers my front pockets, and I let her do this for a bit because who knows what might happen next, right? I'm an idiot. Yes. I'm an idiot.

Back pocket.

I'm confessing like a cheap junkie, I say.

Holly sighs and reaches around and digs it out of my jeans. She holds it in front of me like a broken thumb nail.

You're a little devil, aren't you?

I smile. I feel so warm and so incredibly loved right now, I say. It's amazing.

It'll pass, says Holly. Why don't you just lie down and feel happy on your own for a bit while I check things out on my MacBook?

She pulls me down onto the couch, and it feels like I'm on the kayak again. Surrounded by carpeted wolves and orcas and clouds and water. I love how the rain plays with my brain and how the roof logs line up so perfectly that it's a cedar sky worth remembering.

Cedar sky, I say. Cedar sky. Just look.

Keep talking, says Holly from over there. Keep talking. I love listening to you go on. And you do go on, don't you? Right, Andy?

Oh yeah, I say. Oh yeah. I DO go on. I love stained wood.

Holly is over there. Her face lit by the computer. And suddenly she looks just like a witch, grey and bony and with those beluga eyes. Her hair straggly and longer than I imagined. Whiter. Older.

A photo. Another photo. She goes through them. My photos. My videos. My secret sex life.

It's not real, I say. Nothing is real!

She momentarily looks at me from across the room, and I know what's going on. I know what those eyes have seen. But I'm tripping now, and my world shifts as I squirm on the couch, my stomach rolls and I want to throw up.

Instead.

You have beluga eyes, I say.

Yes, I know, Holly says. Keep talking.

And you might be a witch, I say.

Yes, I know, Holly says. Keep talking.

And you know my secrets, I say.

Yes, I know, Holly says. Keep talking.

What's going to happen next? What?

Holly's face turns redder with each passing image reflecting on the computer screen. Click. I hear the mouse. Click. Wow. Click. Click. Click. Wow.

My life passes me by in sections.

Someone else watches.

In sections.

In flashes. Actually.

Bits and pieces. Let's nail this down. Let's be honest. Real. Please.

I'm naked in some of them.

Sarah is naked too.

Sex. Like we need a record of it.

This is my most lucid thought at the moment. I want to stop this process, but I can't … I can barely move a muscle. A little finger thing maybe. A squirm of frozen. A twitch of ecstasy. I love it, but I hate it. Helpless, but what the hell.

What is this, Andy? What?

Holly's voice now, from over there. Way over there. Off the cedar sky and through the carpet and all around the couch I'm sinking on. Slowly sinking. And Rudy, that fucking cat pushes my chest down now with his front paws. Kneading the dough of my chest. Feel the claws. They're sharp. Wow. Your cat is weird. Look at this cat. Look. Pushing and pushing and making these weird little pig grunts. What is with this cat? What is going on here? I'm sinking.

Holly's voice now above me.

What did you do, Andy?

I'm confused. Sinking. I reach out to her. I can't sink.

Her face drained of all blood and with a pointy chin.

She's naked, isn't she? Or?

Am I?

What is she doing?

The world shifts on its axis.

Andy Man. What did you do? What?

I'm trying to answer. I reach out with my stupid, stupid long hands.

Her skin feels like warm rubber. Or maybe it's my skin. I want to laugh. Or cry. Or something.

She looms. She actually looms over me. Her hair cascades.

Picks up the cat and tosses it aside. Like it's nothing.

A small soft thud. Over there. It lands just over there.

Holly straddles me, and I feel my heart pound in my ears.

A rushing sound.

Then nothing. Just quiet so quiet you could pack it into cans and sell it.

I lick my lips because I'm sure she's turned me into some kind of lizard. What I was always meant to be.

Holly's face stretches across the room.

You killed her, didn't you?

Andy.

You killed her.

NINE

AFTER THE INQUIRY WE'RE FOUND liable for ten percent of the accident that put a child in a coma. But officially we will bankrupt ourselves. I will make sure of that. They won't get a dime.

Anna stands by the end of the bed wearing my blue housecoat. She's naked underneath and holds my big toe sticking out of the bedsheets because I refuse to get up without my morning cappuccino.

We will be sued. We will not pay. It's that simple.

Why don't we transfer the money to my father's account instead? Nobody will ever know.

Anna smiles and pinches my toe.

He's very good with dough. He's a former bookkeeper, and he used to do the books for Blue Rodeo when they were famous. I mean, that takes talent.

Anna waits me out.

I'm not giving your father my money, I say. He's nearly ninety, and he can't remember any of his accounts. He took me to the wrong bank the last time I visited him. The wrong bank. In the wrong part of town. Then he called me Herbert. Do I look like a Herbert to you?

He's always been there for me, Herbert, Anna snaps, finally releasing my toe and inadvertently flashing me.

And this is how you treat me?

I'm not treating you, I say. I'm ignoring your bad advice, there's a difference.

My father gave me fifty grand after I married you, Anna says. Don't forget that.

We spent it on your Honda Fit and a vacation to Slovenia because that's where your DNA came from, and it rained the whole time.

You're being a jerk!

She storms off as only Anna can storm off, leaving my housecoat on the floor, shedding it like a second skin.

I'm jumping in the shower, she says from the bathroom. I'm late for work.

The money. It will be spent on our new feature film; the one Will and I have been dreaming of making for a million years.

I can't hear you, Anna says. I've got the water going.

I've got to meet Will, I say.

I can't hear you, Anna yells. But whatever you're planning, don't be stupid.

Plus, I've been working on this script for twenty-three years now. It's taking shape. Draft three or four by now. Lots of changes. Lots of new reveals. The dialogue is tight, tight, tight …

By the way …

Gili is found to be not responsible. We should have replaced her with a trained stunt driver. We didn't. She did what we asked her to do. She tried her best. Poor thing has nearly been to the Funny Farm and back, but she's surviving. Working a nice bar on Granville Street where the pours are barely legal and the servers, also barely legal, wear mini-skirts and stilettoes and say how can I make you happy? It's the kind of bar where chefs go to do shooters after their long, horrible shifts frying halibut to perfection with a Chardonnay reduction cream sauce and capers.

Gili. I know what she's going through. Her feet are killing her. But the tips from boozy customers buy her great insoles.

There is some good news.

The car dealer was found mostly responsible. They had not properly serviced the car before releasing it to us. The brakes were found to be slightly faulty. They should have checked. They didn't.

The computer on board the car was working properly, driving exactly as designed, with care and expertise. But the bad brakes changed everything.

Self-driving gets off the hook. Those kinds of cars aren't supposed to hurt little girls, are they? No way. Computers love kids, right?

Oh, and the other news. The child had a pre-existing condition. Apparently, she had always suffered from miserable headaches and blackouts. Doctors were actually doing tests on her long before she showed up for the commercial. The results, although inconclusive, showed a possible brain injury. It might have happened when she was a toddler because the family was in a serious car accident, also with a Mercedes. A black one.

Irony noted.

Either way, we're partially liable.

Will sits with me outside a bar at the old Olympic site. He's been pretending to listen to me for the better part of an hour. We bask in our narrow escape. We formed our company eons ago to make enough money to shoot our own movie once we retired. And now we're going to do it. Bankrupting ourselves should be fun and therapeutic. And we should always do a story that we know. We know us. And we think we're worth it, dammit.

When you write yourselves into a feature, you will right yourself, I always say.

Will says stop trying to be witty. You're too bitter for that kind of shit. Just fucking drink, asshole.

Will wears a white linen suit. He's going Old School and looks a little like Jack Nicholson in *Chinatown* or Robert Redford in *Out of Africa*, but a lot bigger. It's the kind of suit missionaries wear in Gabon under palm trees. When I tell Will this he doesn't laugh, just grunts and slugs back more wine.

Wasn't it French once? he asks.

Oui, I say. Oui. Independent now, I suppose. Free as free can be.

Cheers to that, he says. And to the Gabonese.

He throws back his drink.

Will has the face of an accountant, round and trustworthy except for the beads of sweat cresting his massive eyebrows. His cheeks are always red, drinker-red. Don't judge. He has bad skin, as well, like it's always shredding.

Will reaches into his leather man-bag slung over his chair. He pulls out a bag of ketchup chips and struggles to rip it open.

What the hell are you doing? I ask. We're at a restaurant. You can't do that.

I have a nasty urge for these things, Will explains. But you need to be a gorilla to open them.

He pulls on the seam and grunts.

You gotta find the notch, I say.

What?

The notch. You find the notch and rip it. It opens the seam.

There's no notch, Will says. It's a bag of chips.

No. They build in the notch, I say. To make it easier. So, run your finger along the top.

Will strains to pop open the bag.

Maybe it's a defective bag, he says.

It's not defective, you are, I say. Find the fucking notch. You're embarrassing me.

Fuck these chips, Will says, throwing them back into his bag. They don't go with the wine, anyway.

Yeah, but it's nice ambiance here, I say.

Yeah, Will says. It's all about the ambiance.

And the servers.

And the servers.

This is the kind of dialogue you end up with after two bottles of rosé. Some of it works. But you don't laugh because inside you're just rotten and empty, the product of a superficial life with dirty secrets and lies and too much money.

But we have the time for it. Neither one of us will work another day of our lives. Except when we work for ourselves. That's the retirement plan. Pass the rosé, please.

It's hot out. Late June. A full year after the accident with the car on the set. And eight months after Sarah went missing on the kayak trip. I want to put things in perspective. My marriage might just have survived the whole thing. I still have money. Gili sees me on the side, but we plan things very, very carefully. The accident with the Smart Car has made us all cautious.

Will says, I don't need to hear your entire history. But why do women want to sleep with you anyway? What do you have that I don't? More hair?

He always says this.

I'm just lucky, I say. But I always say that too.

You're a flawed character, Will says. But look at me. I'm a mess, right?

Right, I say.

Cheers to Anna, Will suddenly says, throwing back another drink.

Cheers, I say.

Anna still works. In a dentist's office. Although she is constantly sad. The kind of sad you only see on refugee faces, the ones that come from camps in the Middle East. I guess it makes sense, when your best friend goes missing and is presumed dead on a kayak trip that you suggested for bonding purposes.

She had a health scare, too. Still does. She could be gone tomorrow. Any of us could. That's life, pal.

Yes, it's a horrible story. But I'm in deep now.

We drink rosé.

It's cigar time without the cigars.

We survey the scenery through our wine glasses, through the pink of the wine swirling at the bottom. It's a shimmering vision. Totally false. Speaking of which … False Creek ripples in diamonds across from us. It's just after one in the afternoon, getting hotter by the second. Across the water I see giant white tents setting up for the annual Jazz Festival. Glass condos frame the water and behind all this, mountains frame the condos and behind that, majestic white clouds spread their wings. It's the kind of framing to die for. I love my film side. I see life in images.

The patio is half full. Mostly patrons who want to be seen preening in the June heat, women wearing tank tops and short shorts, the guys wearing T-shirts with funny slogans on them like Wrap Your Brain Around This Sucka and Jesus Loves Cold Pressed Juice and Beaver Town Red Hot Blues. Whatever that means.

There're maybe twenty tables on the patio. Half of them shaded by huge umbrellas with Coors Light written on them.

The servers are mostly women in their early twenties wearing too-tight miniskirts or short shorts wobbling between tables with trays laden with french fries and tall, cold beers, none of them Coors Light. There's one male server who seems to mainly wipe tables.

"Philadelphia Freedom" plays from the tinny patio speakers overhead, Elton's worst song ever.

Outside the patio are two dogs tied to trees. A poodle and, farther away, a bored boxer. They pant like crazy even in their shade. Occasionally a server comes out and pours water into their stainless-steel bowls and coos over them.

Nice girl, nice, nice girl.

We're all slightly drunk. But we're well-fed. And warm. And most of us carry no-limit credit cards. Life is good. Right?

Nobody wants to leave. It's that kind of afternoon.

We bask like seals on a rocky beach watching the orcas pass by in the distance, not giving a shit. And, for a moment, the world and all the problems that come with it don't matter a hill of beans — a saying my father said a lot, and now I'm saying it.

We toast nothing.

It's nice out.

It's Vancouver in the summer, baby.

We need to make this movie or we'll die regretting it. Will says this while sipping his wine.

I nod.

Two hundred thousand. Maybe three. That's what I figure it will cost. We've got that much easily, Will says.

And, if we spend it all, we're wonderfully broke. Try to get the money from us then, I say. Go ahead, sue us. Sue away. Perfect.

Perfect, Will agrees.

Nobody can touch us. The money is really gone, I say. And we have our feature.

And the script is really tight now, I say. It's really ready.

The two leads are still misunderstood assholes, right?

Right.

Charmers?

Of course, I say. They're the kind you'd want to sit on a patio and have wine with.

We can improv a lot once we get shooting, Will says. We'll do some Christopher Guest stuff. Blue sky it. Right? "Best in Show"?

Right, I say.

I want to make this thing beautiful, Will says. But I need to do most of the directing if that's okay with you? I have a fucking vision for the piece that is amazing.

What?

I can't verbalize it yet. It's still gaining visual shape, Will says. But lots of handheld shots ... nothing fancy. Consistency is the key. We have to be consistent. Okay? And we need to be on the same page, okay? Let's not argue on set. Let's be the kind of collaborators people want to collaborate with. But let's also be true to my ... our fucking vision. It's the dialogue that's key to this thing. Right? And make it snappy.

Right, I say. We remain true with the dialogue.

No fucking monologues, Will says. Get over your internal thoughts. It'll just slow the picture down.

Right, I say. Limited monologues.

No monologues! Zero, Will snaps. I can't stress that enough. We've got to keep it flowing.

Right, I say. Very few monologues.

Jesus, Will says. Jesus.

We're on our third bottle and we're obviously bullshitting about our script. It's an oddball rom-com with dire consequences for older people. We've got friends of friends lined up to play the parts. B-list actors, some C-list, too. Everybody wants a piece of the action because it's a story about them. We're all in our fifties. We know what's left of our miserable lives. This is one last kick at the proverbial can. It will be meaningful and funny, and all our relatives will be forced to crowd into an indie theatre to see the thing at some stupid festival and then it will be forgotten.

But we'll have credit.

And. We'll have reputation.

And in this business, reputation is everything.

Plus. We need to scout locations, Will says, looking across the water at the condos. Something hip. We need something hip. And cheap. A condo rooftop where the affairs begin. I'm thinking fig trees and rosemary. Lots of green. Then we'll frame that shit with steel and glass. The harsh world around us, the city spread beneath like a living, breathing thing. That kind of bullshit.

I nod only because the wine makes it easy.

It's then my iPhone buzzes and I get the text. The message that changes our lives forever.

I have the memory card, it reads.

Signed, Holly.

What memory card? Will asks.

The one with my sex tape, I say.

Sure, sure, Will laughs. You have a sex tape. Hilarious. How old are you, anyway?

The one on her camera. The one that washed up after the kayaking trip last year. I say this while trying to look nonchalant, which is a feat in and of itself considering how much I've now drunk.

Why would she have your sex tape?

It's stupid, I say. I was stupid. I was with her at her place. She gave me this tea and I tripped out.

Who were you having sex with on the tape?

Come on, Will. I'm not telling. That's personal.

I down the wine. Throw it back. Look out at the angel-wing clouds that have turned into huge anvil heads, undersides darkening quickly.

What does she want? Will sips his wine like an educated man. He usually does.

I stare at the phone as the words form.

Two hundred thousand.

Or she'll release the sex tape to Anna and the cops.

Will stifles a laugh.

It was Sarah, wasn't it?

I nod. Yup.

For a moment Will just sits there thinking, then says, You had sex with your wife's best friend, and then she goes missing on the kayak trip?

Yes.

What were you thinking?

I want to explain, I say. But what would be the point? It was a bad decision. I was obviously quite stupid that day. Maybe I thought that taping sex was a funny idea.

Taping sex when you're in your fifties isn't funny, Will says. Just sad. Nobody wants to watch that shit. It's pathetic. I've seen you naked.

I realize that now, I say. I saw the video and I can never unsee it.

I bet, Will says. I bet.

A moment.

What were you hoping to do with the video?

I don't know. Watch it, I guess. Be inspired. But then I did and I wanted to scream and erase it, but Sarah insisted on keeping it because I think it made her laugh. She was high at the time. So was I.

Were you hoping to improve your ground game?

Yeah. Funny. Real funny.

The sex tape has nothing to do with Sarah's disappearance, I say. Nothing at all. We had come to an understanding. About the sex. And the tape.

Will wrinkles his forehead. And now you're being blackmailed by another woman you might or might not have slept with? Why did she wait until now to try to blackmail you? Why didn't she make that kind offer earlier?

Jesus, I say. I don't know. Her name is Holly, by the way. Just to keep the women straight.

It's been a long time since you were kayaking, and it seems a little weird that this crazy woman just now has come up with the blackmail.

Maybe she googled me, I say. Maybe she found out how much I'm worth. Maybe she's got a gambling problem. I don't know. And don't ask me if I slept with her because I don't know.

Will looks at me. What makes you uncertain?

About what?

Whether you had sex with this Holly person?

I pour myself another big glass of wine without spilling a drop, which is amazing considering how much my hand shakes.

It was a weird time, I say. I wasn't myself. I think it was because I was so dehydrated.

Dehydration makes you uncertain about whether you had sex?

Yes, Will. It does. And don't forget I'd been looking for a woman's corpse all day along the beach with no breaks.

Will studies me. I finger my wine glass.

What the hell? he says. What the hell are you talking about?

Look, whatever. I'm being blackmailed. Let's focus on that, okay? Forget about the sex. Just forget I ever mentioned it. Not important. Plus, I might have been drugged. With some tea she made.

You don't know for sure?

I do know, I say. I just don't know about what happened after I drank the fucking tea.

Did you have an erect penis?

Very little was actually erect. Actually.

Fuck, Will shouts. Vague sex. I hate vague sex.

Stop yelling, I say. People can hear you.

Actually, the patio seems to be emptying out. Patrons going

back to their loser jobs — mostly in real estate. This is Vancouver, after all. We sit there and act cool.

I break the momentary silence.

Look, she's got us ... me ... over a barrel, obviously, with that memory chip thing. I do know I had sex on that. It was a very clear video.

Will leans back and goes all gangster on me.

Two can play at that game, he says. Cracks his knuckles. Makes a fist. A big one. Where does she live?

Cortes Island.

Where the hell is that?

Desolation Sound.

Where the hell is that?

In the middle of nowhere. But it's very picturesque. Stunning wildlife. And vistas too. Bald eagles everywhere and seals. And killer whales.

So, a beautiful woman you may or may not have had sex with in the middle of nowhere is blackmailing you over a sex tape you made with your wife's best friend? And this blackmail happened just after you were searching for Sarah's dead corpse? Something like that?

Well, technically ... but being dead obviously means she would be a corpse, I say. You're being redundant. And the sex with the aforementioned dead woman ... whose death, by the way, hasn't been confirmed by the authorities because no body was ever found ... that sex happened long before she went missing, so that should count for something.

I pout.

Will thinks.

Will drinks.

Yeah, I get it, he says. I get it. But that money was supposed to go into our feature. Our feature we've been planning for over twenty years. I mean, that's unacceptable.

Will slugs down a big wallop of wine.

Will shivers a bit and coughs.

Then.

Will says, what a crock of shit. We. Will. Not. Pay.

Never, I say.

We need a plan, Will says.

We shouldn't do something stupid, Will. I mean we're older now, we're supposed to be more enlightened and shit. I mean, you have two grown children, and we have to be good role models and have people look up to us.

Then we should have never gotten into film, Will says. Right?

Look, it's only money, I say. Who cares about the money? Let's just pay her off and go from there.

It's the point to it, Will says. It's wrong to blackmail just like it's wrong to cheat on your wife.

My mouth feels like it's made of chalk.

Isn't it just as wrong to spend all the company's profits on a feature film just to avoid paying a possible lawsuit? I ask.

No that's different, Will says. That's just being smart.

God, I'm hot. I'm melting.

Where's our fucking server? Will says. Where?

The sun makes my face red. I'm full of bad radiation; I wish for my life I had brought a baseball cap. It would be a lifesaver now. My favourite cap is one that reads JUMP NOW ASHOLE. I bought in India because asshole was spelled wrong and I thought why not, I'm a terrible speller anyway. My forehead feels like a toaster. Eyes are red and getting redder. I haven't slept in weeks. I play with my phone. No other messages appear. Weird. A ploy, I'm sure. I start to sweat under my knees. It feels like blood running down my legs.

We sit there and wait for our pretzel. As mentioned, I'm a pretzel guy, and we always order one at the end of the meal here. It comes with a cheese and beer dip. Our server, Katey, is a tall redhead who took an acting class from me a long, long time ago. She's nowhere to be found. I'm guessing she's baking the pretzel herself. Or grating the cheese. Whatever. We have our bottle. And the sun is still out. Whatever.

Why is it so hot out?

I put down my phone.

I make a horrible sighing sound like I've lost all the air in my body into the Martian atmosphere, if I was on Mars. Obviously.

What are we going to do? I fidget like a ferret.

How did she get that memory card again? Details please. Will sips his wine.

She roofied me with magic fucking mushroom tea. I had the card in my back pocket. I found the camera on the beach and ripped out the memory card before anyone saw. At least that's what I thought.

Will thinks. What are magic mushrooms like?

It's a nice trip, I say. But you lose your inhibitions faster than dope or booze. Like in five minutes or so. It was hell to lose control, mainly because I'm German. I prefer my inhibitions just like my invasions: organized and efficient.

Yeah, I guess that's why you made a sex tape, Will says.

That's the Russian side of me, I say. I just hate it. That's why I drink, obviously.

And that's why you can't remember whether you fucked her?

Yes, I say. Obviously.

A moment.

Fucked whom exactly?

Well, that's the whole point, isn't it? says Will to the sky. That's the whole point. Cheers, mate.

He throws back his wine like a half-blind pirate which he only does when he's really, really pissed. Which is what he is.

We order another bottle when Katey brings the pretzel. We rip pieces out like it's a twisted, stupid heart and shove them into our mouths like we're unemployed werewolves. But we take our time, one piece after another, and chew them slowly. Oh yeah. We're in no hurry, none at all.

TEN

WE WALK IN THE FOREST near the university. It's the kind of late afternoon where the wind has decided to ruffle only the very tops of very tall trees. On the ground, in the shade, we're all a bit sticky. It's hot out. We're here because we're out of the sun. And we love the rocky path into darkness, the crooks and crannies of the park that cool our bare legs, arms, and heads. The scent of pine needles is heaven-sent.

Gili climbs the knobby hill carefully avoiding the rocks on the narrow path. She thinks about each step without looking back at me. I'm huffing and puffing a bit because I'm older and I probably drink more.

My feet hurt because I'm wearing new hiking boots. This is their third time out and I'm regretting it, especially my right foot, second toe from the end.

At the top of the hill, she spots a park bench perched to the side with a dedication on it: "Diana, a park lover, 1962–2019 — her place to rest and to consider the world at large. Enjoy the peace. Enjoy the struggle."

Gili watches me pick my way up to the top to sit beside her. The hill isn't that high, but it's an uneven climb, and it's full of tire ruts from mountain bikers. Also, it's somewhat muddy. It rained a couple of days ago. Rained so much it broke a record. So, the forest smells extra good and extra rich like infused mud with rose petals.

I feel it seeping into my skin.

Gili waves at me.

You having trouble?

No, I say. All good.

I plop beside her and notice her bare knees are scratched up.

What happened to your knees? I ask.

Nothing, she says. Just the forest being the forest and me being me.

We sit and listen to the tall timbers, the sway of trees moving to the wind.

I wear cargo pants. Brown ones that are two sizes too big because I've lost weight over the past few months. I can't eat, although drinking is no problem.

One of Gili's knee scratches looks particularly red and puffy. She rubs at it with her soft, pale hand. She knows I know.

The accident, I say. You ever think about it?

Gili looks me over like I'm her new shrink.

I don't want to talk about it, she says.

I want to, I say.

Why?

Because I feel it's getting in the way of our relationship, I say.

Gili sighs.

You know what's really getting in the way of our relationship? Your marriage.

She kicks at the dirt under the bench with her pink Nikes. She has tiny feet, but beautiful thin ankles, the kind you see in fashion magazines.

Look, I say. I'm going to end it. I am.

I don't believe you, Gili says.

I've got a final kayak trip planned with her and after that I'm going to break it off, I say.

Right, Gili says. Like I haven't heard that before a million times.

We sit there.

Listen to the trees.

Breathe.

Gili grabs my hand and uncurls my fist.

Why are we doing this?

What?

Why are we doing this? I mean, look at you and look at me. What are we doing?

Her hand feels cold. I notice her arm hair is bristling too. Obviously not a good sign.

I look up. The pine trees are so tall they make me dizzy. Also, they sway and my head wants to follow them rhythmically. I need to look down and when I do, my sunglasses slide down my sweaty nose. I pull my hand back from hers.

Gili wiggles a bit on the bench.

I thought we were doing this because we have a connection, I say.

You think I care about connection? Gili says. I connect with everybody, that's just my personality. I need more than that. Is there somebody else you're seeing?

Just my wife, I say.

You're lying, Gili says. I know you're lying.

I'm not lying, I say. Why would I lie to you? You can see through me. You have that ability, and I would hesitate to test it.

If you're seeing somebody else other than your wife, you will live to regret it, Gili says. I mean, being with me when you're still with your wife is bad enough.

I'm not double cheating, I say. Honestly, that's very low.

Right, Gili says. Right.

I realize I've sat on my phone and dig it out and immediately see a message from Sarah on it. I turn it on mute and quickly place it in my front pocket, the lower one on my baggy pants.

Did you get a message? Gili asks.

Yeah, my wife wants to know where I am, I lie.

I thought she was at work, Gili says.

She is.

We sit and I fidget.

Suddenly out of nowhere, three tall teenagers walk out of the trees wearing togas and drinking from flasks. They're drunk.

Hey, one of them says to me. Dude, where's the party?

I look around.

I don't know, I say.

They told us it was in the clearing, another one says. A freckled red-head with extremely long arms.

Do you see a clearing here? Gili says quickly. Does this fucking bench look like a clearing?

The three dudes shuffle their feet and all of them wear sandals, the kind you'd wear near water if you were a professional surfer. They look expensive.

One of them coughs. I think another one giggles. They try to be good boys. For a second.

One of them, who happens to be East Asian, motions to the others to leave.

Dudes, let's move, he says. Come on.

The wind picks up and it's then I notice an awful smell, like teen desperation and menthol cigarettes.

The three guys sweat profusely and the shortest one, the one with thick greasy black hair stumbles toward us, leans in with his flask raised.

Beware of betrayal, he hisses. Then he turns on his heel and they all disappear down the path and into the dark.

They seem to float.

As the forest swallows them.

For drunk guys wearing sandals and togas, they are unusually light on their feet.

I say that.

Gili waves her hand in front of her face.

I'm overheating, Gili says. We need to get out of here.

Wait, I say.

I pull her down, back to the bench. By her hand.

Then I pat it.

Look, I say. I know you think there's somebody else. But you're it. You're the one.

Gili sits and thinks.

Really?

Really.

I rub at a smudge on my cargo pants. It gets worse.

How did we end up here? Gili asks.

Where?

I mean, we're too far apart in age. Neither one of us has friends in common. We have different ambitions and dreams, and you think we have a chance?

Why not?

Are we together because of a stupid tragic event? A little kid nearly dies and suddenly we're involved intimately and exclusively. Is that it?

Gili stands and says most of this to the forest. She doesn't look at me. In fact, she throws on her oversized sunglasses and stamps her feet.

She is wearing dark tennis shorts and an off-red tank-top. Underneath, a T-shirt that says Do It Now in huge black letters.

She waits for me to say something.

I swallow.

Grab the bench with both hands and brace myself as if waiting for a wave to roll under me.

People get together for lots of different reasons, I say. Who cares. We're together because we belong together. We talk. We have fun. We do things. We're doing something right now. Look at us. We're in the middle of nowhere and we're fine with that. We just ran into three drunk guys wearing togas and we handled them fine. I sure didn't expect that.

I think I have said something brilliant. I wallow in it. But it doesn't last.

Somehow a few drops of water hit me in the face, and I look around trying to figure out where they came from.

The trees hush innocence.

I notice far above, a single dark cloud.

Do you love me?

It's not the question I expect from her, but there it is. She crosses her arms and I notice again the hair arm, still bristling.

What kind of question is that? I ask.

It's the only question, Gili says. And you're not answering it fast enough.

Then she turns and quickly walks away.

I sit and listen for the forest to give advice.

It sounds like a sigh.

ELEVEN

WE MEET DAVE AT A bistro on the wharf on the west end of Vancouver. It sits on stilts. Black Bentleys park outside. The building looks very much like it was once used to can salmon, but it's an illusion. It's very modern, hip and popular with kids in their twenties. The kind who get allowances from rich parents overseas. Part of the bistro hangs out over the water — people come here to get a whiff of fresh ocean with their garlic fried snapper.

We are here to scheme. And this makes us very hungry.

Dave has told us he can give us some Rohypnol — roofies, little blue and white capsules sometimes known as the date-rape drug. Don't ask me how Dave gets them. Or why.

Will and I sit by the window overlooking the water. We order cranberry and sodas. And three orders of poutine. With B-52 shooters. Four of them. Flaming B-52s. And two orders of crab. And a Cobb salad. And a bottle of Prosecco. We're trying to keep it low key today. Don't want to attract attention. Will makes sure to take his blood pressure pill beforehand. He's on Mavik. Just a small amount: 2 mg. He usually takes it with food or alcohol.

The restaurant is filled with layers of lawyers and realtors, and it seems every table has a computer or tablet on it and business deals are being brokered. Lots of Asians in the place and they're all dressed impeccably. Lots of little black dresses with very high heels. Everybody looks like a Bratz doll.

There's a great smell in the air. Garlic and butter. Yum. Maybe to cover up the fish smell, because there's a lot being served. Along with flatbread, which is really just the new, more flattering way to describe pizza.

Will and I eat our flatbread with mushrooms and arugula.

Fuck, it's good, one of us says to the roof. I can eat this shit all day!

Nasty pizza. Nasty!

Our server Christine tells us that we're being a little too loud. I had no idea. But when I study the place, I realize a lot of the patrons are whispering. This is one polite bistro on the wharf. And the kids here are very shy.

Will says, Hey look.

A giant fiberglass shark thing hangs over our heads along the wall.

It's actually tuna, which I'll find out in a bit.

I'm terrible with fish.

We wait for Dave. And go over the plan.

Here's the plan. This is Will speaking and, to be clear, his face is even redder in this restaurant. It might be a reflection from the large faux-Persian carpet under our feet, but I think it might also be because of how much time we've been spending on outdoor patios drinking Riesling and eating pretzels. But it also might be because we're a little evil now, planning shit and thinking of ways to break the law on remote BC islands, taking advantage of a woman who is trying to take advantage of me. Will wipes at an invisible fly hovering near his nose.

Fuck that fly, Will says. What's it doing in here, anyway?

I drink. Fast.

Okay, he says. Okay. Here goes. Holly will think we're there to pay out the blackmail. We'll show her the money, right? But we're actually there to reverse roofie. She might feed us magic mushroom tea, but we drop a roofie in her lemonade, knock her out, and then we find the memory chip, her computer, and any other electronic device, take them, and leave.

Will has figured out how to wrap a bunch of paper inside two twenties so it looks and feels like a shit-load of dough, when actually it's more like forty bucks. He has a stack of them in the trunk of his car to make it look like the two hundred grand.

Then we will take a ferry home and destroy the evidence, dump the memory card into the Salish Sea from the deck of the boat.

Into the wake, I say. I'll flick it into our wake.

Then we make our movie.

Because we'll still have enough money.

And people in the know will say *respect the process* because in our business, process is everything.

And so is reputation.

And no sex-tape blackmail will stop our rom-com about cheating middle-aged guys who crave affairs with much younger women. That would be wrong. And we're adamant that our art will bring in a lot of awards. If not awards, an armful of nominations will do just fine. And if we don't get nominated, several trips to obscure film festivals will do very nicely. Like Sienna. Or Austin. Or even Yorkton.

Blackmail should not stop Art. Will pronounces that to the ceiling fan. It doesn't move.

Christine skates to our table and asks, You gentleman have enough to drink?

Not sure if that's an order or a request, sweetie, Will says.

Don't call me sweetie, Christine says. It makes you seem like a dirty old man.

Then she strides away, triumphant.

Wow, says Will. Did you hear that? I mean, wow. Ageism or what? I can't fucking help it if I'm white, middle-aged and male. That's just bad luck. Right?

Will drinks while winking. He also kicks me under the table. Just a little.

There's too much ageism in this world, I say blandly. Way too much.

The first time I heard the label "middle-aged man," I was lying in bed with a woman half my age, Will says. And I was in the middle of things.

I don't laugh.

Why don't you think that's funny? Will says. Because that's good dialogue.

I look Will over solemnly.

Because what the hell are you doing?

I'm single, Will says. What difference does it make? So what if she was twenty-nine?

Twenty-nine? What? I don't know whether to salute you or drop you as a friend.

Will toasts himself as if this is something you should actually toast when you're nearing sixty.

I stare at the remains of the food sitting in front of me, the shell of a crab. I'm convinced there's more meat in there but it just isn't worth the effort at this time.

Yeah, Will adds, don't forget that 60 is the new 40, right?

OK, I say. Then what does that make 29? Nine?

Touché, Will says. Nice dialogue. Finally. Put that in the script, funny guy.

I drink now.

It's weird how your realities are becoming our fantasies and now we're about to record them for others to enjoy, I say. I mean, that's the whole plot of our feature. That's it. Two assholes looking for redemption.

I say this while holding a fork, a tiny crab fork.

Or sex, Will says.

Come on, sex is the disease, I say.

Sure, sure.

Will grunts while cracking his crab and picking out the meat with his own tiny fork. He wears a bib provided by the bistro that says Yummy Crab on it. You'd think an upscale place like this would have a better vocabulary.

Think about this, though, Will says. We are creating art using us as examples of what not to do. A lot of people are going to be impressed with our transformation. And then we might even get some government funding. That's the way art works these days.

When Dave shows up, he's wearing cycling shorts and an Adidas sweatshirt and looks every bit like an unemployed lighting designer, which is sort of what he is. His hair always looks unkempt and is turning prematurely white along the edges, making him look like the son of Newt Gingrich — which is a nice way of saying he's got a punchable face. A lot of lighting pros have these kinds of faces. Industry standard, I guess.

Dudes, he announces as he slides in behind our table. What's with the tuna overhead?

Did you bring the stuff? Will asks.

What's wrong with a little small talk beforehand? Dave says. I noticed a beauty fish overhead and thought maybe you guys didn't know you were sitting under a skipjack tuna, a streamlined, fast-swimming pelagic fish common in tropical waters throughout the world.

Shut up, Dave, Will says.

Gee, I thought you guys were my pals.

Did you bring the stuff? Will snaps.

I brought the stuff. Yeah.

Let's just make the deal, Will says. How much did you bring?

I brought two, one for each of you. What's with you guys ... thinking of switching teams with each other, but you just need to get your inhibitions down?

Will frowns.

It's not for us, you moron. We're looking to roofie someone, and we need a few backups if things go horribly wrong.

Dave smiles. I thought this was for personal use.

Why would we roofie ourselves, Dave?

I don't know. You old guys never cease to surprise me.

Look, Dave. We need more than two. We need a bunch. We're on a mission.

Who you doing?

Dave looks us over. Takes our prosecco and pours some into my coffee cup and swirls it like he's a taster, then slugs it back.

Who's the lucky gal?

Shut up, Dave, Will says. You don't have clearance.

Okay. There's no clearance. You guys work in film. You're probably thinking of using the ruffles for fun, right?

What's ruffles? I ask.

Ruffles, ribs, Reynolds, wolfies. Don't be such obvious amateurs.

Shut up, Dave, Will whispers. You're a loser.

Keep up the insults, Dave says. It'll cost you more.

How much for the two pills? I say, reaching for my wallet.

Fifty bucks each, Dave says. And, that's a good deal for assholes who might employ me in the future no questions asked.

Dave brings out the pills and rolls them across the table like they're tiny footballs. I give over the cash, and Dave decides to count it even though it's just five twenties. It's then that Christine rolls up with more B-52s — we've ordered more, of course — and spots the transaction.

You really shouldn't sell drugs in my section, she says. If you're going to do that, go out on the balcony. That's Peter's section and he doesn't care.

You must be mistaken, Will says with a wink. Those are my blood pressure pills.

He picks up the two ruffles and drops them into his plastic pill vial clearly labelled Mavik. I must have dropped them, he snorts.

Dave sighs. He's enjoying this.

Look, he says to the server, can you get me a tuna fish sandwich?

We don't serve tuna, Christine says. Sorry.

Then why do you have tuna on your wall?

That's not a tuna, Christine says. It's a flying fish.

Then she waltzes off carrying her tray like a miniature Captain America.

Dave studies us.

What kind of place is this? he says. Is everyone in here stupid? That's tuna on the wall. A freakin' skipjack tuna.

Will clears his throat. Look, Dave, we're not stupid if we get hired to do commercials for Smart Cars. You think they chose us because of our looks?

Yeah, and that little adventure went well for all of us, Dave says, then picks up Will's crab claw and finds more meat in it.

You guys are sloppy, he says. And you're going to make sloppy, stupid mistakes.

Will crosses his arms. He gives Dave a laser stare, but Dave continues, this time while waving the tiny crab claw like a dagger.

I think I should warn you that those little babies affect people in different ways, Dave says.

What ways? I ask.

Well, depends on how much you weigh and how much you've had to drink, Dave says. You ever hear of chaos theory? You can't predict the way things will turn out with these pills. And, on top of that, it just might turn out completely opposite. Especially with you guys. You have no clue what you're doing. No clue at all.

Don't worry about it, Will says, then knocks back a shooter.

Dave sighs again.

Look, he says. Don't get caught. You could get in trouble. And I've got a supplier I can't expose.

Who's that, Dave? Your mother? Will asks with a big bar-room laugh.

Those I got from a guy I worked with on the mushroom documentary, Dave says.

We don't care where you got them, I say.

Just be careful, Dave says. I have a reputation to protect, okay?

Shut up, Dave, Will says. We know what we're doing. And nobody's going to know nothing. It's up on Cortes Island on the fucking Salish Sea, okay? There are no cops up there. Not even RCMP.

Don't give him the details, I say.

He doesn't know jack shit, Will says.

The Salish Sea is the intricate network of coastal waterways that includes the southwestern portion of the Canadian province of British Columbia, Dave says. I should know. I kayaked through there five years ago with my brother. I also know that's where Sarah, Andy's love-bug, went missing. And they've never found her body, have they?

Have they?

Look, Dave, I say. This has nothing to do with that.

I'm not saying you killed her, Dave says, pouring himself more Prosecco. I'm just saying whatever happens up there should never follow you back here to me, okay?

Dave, Will says, nobody wants to link you to anything, okay? You're boring.

I've already been linked to the Smart Car investigation, Dave says. I was called on, you know, to testify. And I've lost work because of it too. Thank you very much.

You'll get the work back, I say. Things are picking up in film. They are. Plus, the brakes were mainly to blame, you know that. Not us. Although your stupid light didn't help things.

Dave picks at our Cobb salad. He goes for the egg.

You guys are dicks, he says. And you shouldn't be as horny as you are unless you're popping little blue pills. And if you're making life choices on account of your dicks, you're idiots.

Shut up, Dave, Will snarls. We're finished here.
Then we order one more round of shooters.
Flaming ones.

TWELVE

WE MEET DAWN AT PRONTO Pinto, an Italian restaurant on Cambie. Dawn runs Bright Dawn Productions, a production company we want to marry to our film.

We order pizza, not noodles because we're big on class, not slurps. Also, pizza is half-price during happy hour. And that's now. We need to appear austere, but not desperate. But we still sit at a table near the door. Both of us also wear brand-new running shoes with mom jeans, the official uniform of out-of-shape white dudes over fifty.

Will wears a university prof jacket with elbow patches while I stick to leather. We sip Pinot Grigio, which apparently goes great with the smoked sardines sitting in front of us. Free appetizers. Neither of us wants to try them, though. They're nestled into a white dish that looks like it's a mini porcelain coffin. They still have their heads on and they smell funny.

Dawn drifts in wearing a black pantsuit and looks much, much shorter than her profile pic on Facebook. Older too, maybe close to sixty. She has a round, warm face and large horn-rimmed tinted glasses and lots and lots of colourful metal bangles. And she smells great, like peppermint. And smoky too. Probably because she smokes. I notice a package of Players cigarettes in her black leather purse, more like a man-bag I suppose. It's huge, large enough to house a small Canon printer. Which, I notice, it does.

She sits at the bar away from us and motions for us to join her. She does this with her nose. So, we pick up our wine and sardines and sit down on the stools beside her on the corner of the polished oak bar.

I say hi, but she waves it off. Her hand is tiny like it belongs on a seven-year-old.

What's the pitch? she says. And please don't waste my time with small talk.

Will looks at me as if I'm supposed to start. So I do.

It's a rom-com about two older guys who have affairs with younger women, and when their wives find out they leave them. It's very dark and has that *Wedding Crashers* comedy vibe to it — you know, misadventure and misdeeds lead to shenanigans, right?

It's dialogue-heavy, Will adds quickly. Like *The Trip to Italy* starring Steve Coogan.

The Hangover, I interrupt. Without the hooker, though. More about the wives.

Really? Will looks me over. Did we discuss that? Wives?

Yeah Will, wives. No hooker.

Dawn orders a bottle. Make it a Chianti, she says to our ragged-looking barkeep. We could be here for a while.

Will says, Look, Dawn, we're buying, okay? Order whatever you want. Try the sardines? Please.

Dawn waves Will off, then pushes the sardines two feet away. They smell bad even from over there.

All right, Dawn says to me, what's the complication in that story?

Well, their wives leave them, and then the husbands try to win them back.

Dawn frowns. What the hell kind of story is that?

Will says, Look, it's going to be a dark comedy.

Dawn looks bored, and I say this because she has now taken off her tinted glasses to rub her eyes.

Why would anyone want to see this movie? I mean cheating husbands are a dime a dozen. It's a little overdone, all right?

Will says, The locations are great, and it's got some great dialogue. Lots of great stuff. Funny stuff.

I think Will has just made the worst pitch ever, but decide to shut up for now.

What locations? Dawn says.

We sit there for a second trying to think of something because we really haven't talked much about this.

Look, we're going up to Cortes Island to see if we can shoot up there, Will says out of nowhere.

What? I look shocked, obviously.

Will says, Yeah we talked about that, didn't we, Andy?

He really stresses my name and I don't like it.

So. Are these guys trapped in a cabin up there or something? Dawn looks us over.

They go kayaking with their wives up there when one of them

discovers a camera full of nasty photos, Will says. Basically, it's a sex tape.

What's so funny about that? Dawn says. Come on.

This isn't in the script yet, I say. It's not in there. Officially. The sex tape.

Hilarity will ensue, Will says. I guarantee that. Once it's in. Which it will be in the next draft. It's the major complication.

And how much for that hilarity are you asking? Dawn says. Exactly?

Will thinks by scratching at his neck. Flakes appear on his shoulders.

Dawn reaches for her Chianti. It's magically appeared in front of us without anybody noticing thanks to our waiter who has also magically disappeared.

Two hundred thousand, Will says. We already have two hundred and fifty committed, maybe three hundred. And we're going to make this whether you jump in or not. But you should jump in. It's really something. We've been working on the script for years now. Dialogue is tight, tight, tight. There's this bit where one of the dudes, who's a respected academic, crashes his mountain bike.

I thought the two leads were just older white dudes in the film business, I say.

No. They're profs, Will says.

Why did that happen?

Because profs are respected, and they have a lot of contact with younger, beautiful women who may or may not be their students.

That's kind of a major change to the script, I say.

Yes, Will says. It is. But we're keeping the kayaks in. Absolutely. Imagine what could go wrong with guys in kayaks with their wives in the middle of nowhere, and, get this, their wives might know about the affairs. You bet.

Dawn stares at Will like his flesh is rotten and, in reality, it might be. He's been tanning and has patches of dead skin around his collar and because he's wearing a tie today it's clearly bothering him, the eczema, I mean. It's a fish tie, maybe a salmon. I think who the hell wears a fish tie to pitch a film idea? Will rubs at his shirt collar hoping nobody will notice the flaking skin, but we mostly notice because bits and pieces of him are falling off onto his shoulders and down onto his fish tie, scales upon scales. Gross. Very gross. I drink. Then pour more Chianti into my glass. I sip and look past Will at the rows of Italian wine bottles behind the bar.

Dawn sips her wine and cases the joint too. She may be just bored or she may be looking for a second exit.

Look, guys, Dawn says. You've been shooting commercials for over twenty years now. What makes you think you can shoot a feature?

Because of our humanity, Will says quietly.

What humanity? You work in advertising, Dawn says, looks at me and winks, hoping I'm going to get this. She doesn't laugh. Much.

Will shuffles in his seat. He rearranges his weight because I think he wants to actually throw a left hook, but instead he raises his glass.

I think you have a point, Dawn, he says. But that's why we're trying to do something different here. Right, Andy?

We're trying to find depth and meaning in fifty-something-year-old white men who have lost their purpose of existence, I say. Have you actually seen *The 40-Year-Old Virgin*? Well, this has more weight because our heroes are older, like fifty-something.

Demographics are on our side, Will says.

Dawn sniffs her wine.

It's a hard sell, guys. A very hard sell.

Well, we can throw in the hooker, Will laughs.

Crickets.

We all drink at the same time. Will finishes his glass and spins it on the bar, thinking.

Then he pulls out his phone and starts scrolling.

We've got a great DOP, Will says. Yvan. This guy from Quebec. He's a total artist. I'm sure you saw his documentary on boreal forest mushrooms. I mean, that was amazing. It was like I was picking them myself. I have some shots on here somewhere.

And we've got Dave, too, I chime in.

Who's Dave? Dawn yawns.

The lighting guy, I say. He's amazing and he's committed to the project. He did the documentary on the mushroom pickers with Yvan. The way he works with ferns is amazing.

What documentary are you talking about? Dawn asks.

Mushroom Men. It was at the Vancouver Film Festival and won a bunch of awards, and trust me, it's amazing, I say. It's about city people who have these mushroom clubs. They go into lush, exotic areas looking for pine mushrooms. And somebody almost dies from eating the wrong mushroom. It's very dark and funny. Right, Will?

Will frowns, then adds, I think you're going to love the overall look to our piece because it's promoting a part of the world few people have seen. It's remote up there. The foliage is amazing. Very lush with a rainforest. And so on.

Dawn now slugs back her Chianti and lets the bar atmosphere soak into her. They're playing Manilow over speakers hidden somewhere in the beams above.

We fidget in unison.

There's a lot of middle-aged white guys in here, she says. Have you noticed?

We look around and notice a lot of middle-aged white guys; most wear dark clothing and wire-rimmed glasses and are slightly overweight and wearing mom jeans and Nikes. Everybody seems to be eating pizza and drinking Chianti. A couple of them work on scripts on laptops in the corners.

Will answers her. No, I think there are a lot of really imaginative, creative people in here.

We don't know them, I chime in. They're not with us.

Will nods. And nods. It's a giant coincidence. That's all.

Look. I shouldn't commit money to any project that I don't essentially believe in, Dawn says.

I will email the script, I say, pointing to my iPhone.

I email it.

What's it called? Dawn says.

The Kayak Trip, I suggest.

No. *Desolation Sound*, Will says. Or *Sounds*. Yeah. *Desolation Sounds*.

I hate that title, Dawn says. I'll be honest with you. It won't sell.

I'm not sold on that title, I say. We're still thinking about it, right, Will?

The way I see it, the way I really see it, Will says gesturing broadly with his hands, is think Kafka with a little Larry David thrown in. A Canadian version of *Curb Your Enthusiasm*, but located on a remote island. That kind of thing.

You're not convincing me, Dawn says. Of anything really. Sorry, guys.

Well, we're just getting started, Will says. We could go on about the comedy.

Although I think these men are bored with their existence, I add quickly. It's too good. And it's too easy. So, there will be existential humour. Essentially.

And that's why they have affairs? Dawn asks this while stifling a yawn. Boredom? Really?

Yes, you got it now, I say. Exactly. There's a lot of irony in it. And it's going to look great. We've got a 4K camera lined up —

8K, Will says quickly.

— and we're shooting some locations with a drone. Can you imagine opening with a shot of six kayakers —

Eight kayakers, Will says. Eight. And the kayaks are all red.

— out on the open water on the Salish Sea?

I love saying the Salish Sea, says Will. Love it.

Where's that? Dawn says. Sounds made up.

It's all around us, Will says. And it's been the official name of our waters since 1988 or so.

Why don't you call the project *A Bunch of Red Kayaks on the Salish Sea*?

Dawn smirks and plays with her wine glass and studies us.

I think that's too long, I say. That's like … a sentence.

Look. It's about internal desolation, Will says. That's the theme. We won't compromise on the theme. No way. We're locked in on that. Theses dudes need to find their hearts. Or else, what's the point to their existence? Right, Andy?

Right, I say. Transformation. Usually it happens toward the end. For sure.

Dawn stares at her phone.

Okay, I'm reading your script right now, says Dawn. What's

funny about this? He says to her: "Why are you an existentialist?" She says: "I have an apartment nearby, but I'm never there. Weird, right?"

I cut that, I say. They now mostly talk about the meaning of commitment. Is commitment a condition of love?

Will says, Yes. I believe it is, Andy.

Right, I say. Absolutely, Will.

We sit there stiffly.

Oh yeah, that's way funnier, Dawn snorts. I get it now, for sure.

Dawn puts her phone down like it's a gavel. She stares at me, then Will.

Again, Dawn says. Why should I care? Why?

Well, I say. Here's the thing. You need to have your protagonists being assholes at the front end because they need to evolve into good guys at the end. I call it the Iron Man journey. I speak of the first *Iron Man* movie, obviously. The one where he's a loveable asshole making millions selling arms to unsuspecting natives, and, eventually, he learns better and announces I am Iron Man at the end. He moves from a negative to a positive. And that's what we're doing here. It's obviously a journey, right? And Iron Man accepts Gwyneth Paltrow as his equal, sorta. In the end.

She's still under-used in my humble opinion, Will says. I mean, she's an excellent actor. Very watchable. Great figure. I mean she's posing nude all the time and she's what, over fifty?

Should we look at making our female characters bigger? I ask.

Yes, yes, I sorta agree, Will says. We need to pass the fucking Bechdel Test for sure. Absolutely.

Dawn drinks her wine like it's a shooter, puts her glasses back on and straightens them carefully, as if she is about to dissect a corpse.

Call me when you have a trailer, she says.

She stretches her back, wiping down the bar with a nearby napkin.

In the meantime, I'll read the script, she says.

Oh God. Really?

Dawn walks out. She doesn't look back.

A busboy cleans up her remains, takes the sardines too, smiles at us weakly, and I see she's actually female and Asian and our waitress.

Hi, I'm Grace, she says. You did not enjoy these fish?

No, says Will.

He's on his phone texting Dawn about a possible deadline for the trailer.

These fish are good with lemons, says Grace. You should take a lemon and squeeze the juice from it onto the fish, and then you will see how good the fish can be.

Will says, Thanks for the advice. Where's our bartender?

He went home. His shift ended. I will serve you, says Grace. May I recommend an *aperitivo*. A Negroni, which is gin, vermouth, and Campari and should remove any bad taste you might have on the tongue from the sardines.

Where's our pizza? Will asks. We've been waiting.

It will come soon, she says. Soon.

Then Grace scurries further down the bar. She wears all black with wobbly, high-heeled sandals.

Will whispers, Where the hell did she come from?

I don't know, I say.

She's kinda cute, Will says, putting his phone away. I love her bangs.

Grace mad-scientist mixes the Negronis on the far end of the bar away from us. She uses two glasses and eyeballs the levels.

Well, I thought our meeting with Dawn went better than expected, says Will. A trailer? Yes. Easy. We can pick up some footage on Cortes. I'll do the narration, and you can write some dialogue. We just need a short scene. Something sexy. Something that will sell.

We don't have a camera, I say. The Canon's broken and so is the Sony. And no actors either.

We have our iPhones and they will do just fine, Will says. It's a fucking trailer. Who cares?

We can rent a nice camera, I say. Maybe get some actors at the last second. Though it'll be expensive.

Forget that, Will says. We have us. We'll be in the trailer. It's going to be nice to put on the old acting shoes again, right? Me and you? Just like the old days. You bet. We're funny. Especially together, people always say that about us. "You guys are hilarious, but maybe don't drink so much."

I'm not sure that's a compliment, I say, finishing my wine. God, I'm thirsty today.

Don't sweat it, Will says. The *aperitivo* will be here soon. I can't wait for the *aperitivo*. I hope it's gonna clear my mind. We need to start planning shit in detail.

Grace drifts over with the drinks balanced on a tray and places them in front of us.

There you have it, Grace says. Enjoy.

Thanks, I say. They look fantastic.

I grab mine and sip it.

Will does the same, but grimaces.

Grace just stands and shuffles a bit.

Okay, okay. Where can we get a nice camera at the last second?

says Will. That's the issue facing us now. And somebody to shoot this shit. Somebody we can trust and who isn't very perceptive.

A moment as we sip and think. The drinks are totally, one hundred percent refreshing, and I suddenly feel quite brilliant and want to rework part of the script on my iPhone, especially the part on page fifty. Really.

I'm chugging this shit, I say.

Will doesn't hear me.

We don't need anyone who's brilliant, Will says. We just need a warm body. And a nice camera.

I have a camera, says Grace who has been hovering the whole time, but behind the bar. It's a Sony. I'm at Vancouver Film School studying to be an operator for the movie business. That's why I serve drinks here. To meet men of your calibre. Please drink responsibly.

Will blinks.

Me too.

Grace goes back behind the bar, nearly trips on the rubber mat. Gathering herself, she gives us a gracious nod. Then she picks up each wedge and holds it up to the light as if looking for imperfections. Grace knows we're watching her as she studies the lemons. Up to the light. One lemon wedge. Then another.

Wow, Will says. I just thought of something.

Will slides his empty glass back along the bar. It's a perfect push, and a perfect slide, with the glass stopping perfectly in front of our new server.

Have you ever been to Cortes Island? he asks Grace.

She wipes her bangs out of her eyes.

THIRTEEN

WE'RE ON THE FIRST FERRY of the three that it takes to get to Cortes. It's a huge boat. Cars and trucks are stacked three-deep. And the sound of the propellers churning up the Salish Sea behind us is strangely therapeutic. A throb. I have a slight headache, and my right thumb is suddenly numb. It's colder than I thought.

We sit facing the front window in the lounge where they have the nice buffet, watching the islands float by in green silence. They are stoic and very dark. Will has ordered us white wine. Grace pushes her full glass aside. She doesn't drink. I take it and down it. It's awful. Ferry wine is the worst. But it all helps with the journey.

This morning we piled into the old Honda and caught the early Sunday sailing to Nanaimo from Vancouver. Then we'll drive north to Campbell River and take another ferry to Quadra Island; then we take a small ferry to Cortes. The whole trip will take us over six hours. Maybe seven, depending on the weather.

We're going there to get back the memory chip that Holly stole. Unless it's been uploaded to the Cloud. Which I hope hasn't happened.

The plan is very simple, and now we have an assistant. What could be more innocent?

Grace keeps taking mini movies with her Sony, hoping that an orca will breach while she's shooting.

Will says, Look, why don't you take Grace up to the observation viewing deck and try out the camera? I'll hold down the fort here.

He pours himself more wine. He has some eggs sitting on his plate. They look fake.

Go, Will says. Go and have fun.

I grab Grace's hand and pull her out of the lounge and up the stairs to the top. The ocean grey gathers the fog like a forgotten childhood blanket, and there's a softness to everything and everyone on the outside deck, even the empty green benches.

Grace points to the water.

Look, I think I see a seal, she squeals.

And it is a seal, barely bobbing out of the water, watching our big hull slide by as if to say who cares, this is my world you stupid idiots, get lost.

I say this last part aloud and Grace says I'm funny.

You are funny, she says. Funny men must write funny things.

You'd think, I say. You haven't read the script yet, have you?

No, I haven't, Grace says. But I like comedy. I laugh at the stupidest things.

The seal isn't impressed. He ducks under the water. I study the heavy swells, guessing where he might show again.

Wow, Grace says. This is something to behold out here.

Grace wears a bright, neon yellow plastic jacket that has reflective strips down the arms. It's waterproof and windproof, but it makes her look a little like a mad ducker. She also wears a Chicago Bears baseball cap that doesn't quite look right.

That bear on your cap looks weird, I say to her while she snap snap snaps.

What bear? she says.

The bear on your cap.

That's a lion, Grace says.

Oh, I say, you mean the Chicago Lions?

What is the Chicago Lions? Grace asks, through her camera.

They're a football team, I say. Actually from Detroit, not Chicago.

You mean soccer? Grace says.

No, I mean — I think for a moment. This is stupid. Who cares about the cap?

I thought you were wearing a Bears insignia, I say, trying to put a capper on the cap conversation.

What is an insignia? Grace says. Look at that other seal. He is bigger.

Okay. Where did you get that baseball cap? I ask.

Vietnam, she says. Everything is so cheap there. It's beautiful. I want to pet that seal. He is so cute. Look at his eyes. He is questioning our adventure. Don't you think? Yes?

I look, but I can't see the seal.

Yeah, I lie. Nice eyes.

My phone shivers. It's Anna.

I answer.

What, love?

Look, Anna says. If you're going to go back to Cortes, make sure you walk along the shoreline.

I'm not walking the entire shoreline, I say into my cell. That's got to be eighty kilometres or so.

Haven't you heard of leave no stone unturned?

I shield the phone from the wind a bit.

Look, Anna. Sarah has never been found and probably never will be found. You have to let it go.

Never abandon hope, Anna sobs. Please. At least take a look where we came in with the kayaks. Can you do that for me? Can you? It's really important, Andy. Just go to the beach and look around. Just do it for me. Please.

Her sobs thin.

Okay, okay, stop it. I will.

Promise me you'll be responsible just this one time. Promise me!

I promise.

Okay, I love you.

Love you too.

I hang up.

Grace takes my picture with her camera. I wave it off.

Not now, not now.

Was that your girlfriend?

No, I answer. My wife.

Oh, says Grace. Oh. I didn't think you were married. That's good to know.

I shiver because the fog has somehow gotten into the crooks and crannies of my leather jacket and found my red sweater to be quite lacking. Seagulls follow the ferry without even trying. They keep ahead of our bow, gliding above it as if leading us to harbour. They probably ride the updraft coming from the ship's funnel. This is my theory.

There's an odd silence to our adventure. The slow throb of the boat's engine, the splash of the wake and slow, steady wind.

Nobody else is on the observation deck. Except for a very old, very tall man and his son. Last time I looked they were sneaking a smoke behind the clear Plexiglas windbreakers nearby. Not really a smoke, more like a toke. And when I saw his son's face, it was clear he could be an elf. Very thin and very white. I give them a wave, and they wave a tiny glass pipe back at me. Both of them wear blue jeans and blue jean jackets and cowboy boots, like they dressed together this morning.

They cough in unison. Wave.

Grace watches me.

Do you know them?

No.

They are breaking the rules, Grace says. I can smell that.

Yes, I say. But nobody is up here except us, and it's really getting foggy and cold.

Grace says, It makes for great movies. Look.

She holds her Sony up to my face, hits the playback, and I see she's got a great bit of footage on the seal bobbing on our wake. It's steady and clear and kind of professional. The fog is stunning.

Nice, I say. You're a natural.

Grace doesn't hear me, just hands over the camera. Then she moves to the rail and lets the wind hit her face as if trying to feel the fog, her yellow coat flapping like a flag in the slight wind caused by the ferry knifing its way to the harbour.

Instead of the shutter I hit the film button on the camera and watch her through the viewfinder as she goes all *Titanic* and stretches out her arms to feel more wind, her coat now a mini sail. Her yellow jacket contrasted by the passing green island, trees reaching out like cellphone towers.

I wave. Keep going, I say. Keep going.

Grace waves back at me and smiles.

This is the best, she says. The best day of my entire life.

She says this into the wind, and it sounds a bit funny. I get pieces of it in gulps. But I position myself further away to get another shot.

I can't exactly figure the camera out, and while I obsess with the buttons I feel someone approaching. Yeah, I feel the presence before the presence.

The old man walks up to me.

I put the camera down and look him over because he's doing that to me.

Hey, he smiles. You want me to take a photo with you and your girlfriend?

No, I say. She's not my girlfriend.

He looks me over. I think he hates my leather jacket or maybe my hair. It's then I notice he doesn't have teeth because the bottom of his face is sucked in a bit and his eyes are very, very grey.

Did you meet your wife in China? he asks.

She isn't my wife, I say, waving him off. She's my daughter.

I surprise myself with that one and decide I like it.

Oh, says the old man. I bet.

He grabs my sleeve.

Look, buddy, can you lend me a couple of bucks? he wheezes. My boy over there needs a hamburger real bad.

I study him and think about my options. His face looks sunken, and those grey eyes are deadly. No blinking, either. Just a gaze right through me.

Please, he whispers. Please. We could use it.

His hand shakes because his arm shakes. And I notice even his head does too. He's a giant bobble head. But a ghastly one.

Need some help, need some for sure, he barely says, then nods in the direction of his son, still hiding behind one of the windbreakers. The Plexiglas gives him a ghostly glow. He's hugging himself to keep warm, but it probably isn't working because he's too skinny and his jacket is ripped to shit. There are a lot of angles to his body, I decide.

The old man coughs to remind me he's still there, his hand outstretched and, of course, shaking.

Do you mind, mister? Do you mind?

I reach into my pocket and give him a loonie. Drop it into his shaking, withered palm. And he closes his hand on it like his life kind of depends on it.

He smiles.

Is that all?

I dig around and give him a couple of toonies.

And the ship's horn sounds.

And we have this moment where time doesn't count. A connection, I suppose, one old dude to another without really touching.

Thanks. Have a nice trip, he says.

The old man rejoins his son behind the plastic windbreaker and takes the glass pipe from him. They drift away down the deck like they have wheels for feet or they're spirits. Yeah. Something's changed about them and I want to believe my coins have done this — not because I'm religious or superstitious, but because really, inside I'm a good man with a good heart.

We are the only ones on this deck now. I walk toward Grace. I want to tell her we should head back soon.

Grace sees me coming and fixes her bangs.

I give her camera back.

Grace studies the footage I've taken.

Nice footage, she says. Too bad I look so ugly.

Then she throws the camera around her neck by the strap.

I notice she has tears in her eyes, just a little bit. She wipes at them with her sleeve.

You don't look ugly, I say. You look fantastic.

It smells amazing out here, like perfect freshness, Grace says into the wind.

It's a bit salty for me, I say. But the wind sure loves you.

Why didn't I know about this place before? Grace asks. Here we are crossing part of the ocean to reach a mysterious land I've only read about.

We're not going to Jurassic Park or anything, I remind her. It's just the Pacific Northwest. Maybe we'll see some deer. I'm hoping, anyway. Have you travelled much?

Not really, except to get here, Grace says. And I'm grateful for that. I am grateful to be here.

You're not scared, are you?

I see that she thinks hard about what to say next.

The way everything is, Grace asks, is this our existence? The journey so scary. And plus, the way we go through the fog and through these islands. Very beautiful. I can't believe we're going through this. It's amazing. What perfection. This world is.

I'm glad you like it, I say.

I realize how neutral and boring that sounds. I hear my father coming out of me in shorter and shorter sentences now. I don't know how to stop it. *Stop that nonsense. Grow up. Do better. Get smart. Andy.*

Grace has both hands on the rail.

Sometimes I think it would be great if my mother could be with me, she says. But she died when I was five years old, and I miss her every day and especially on days like this when there is too much beauty for just one daughter like me.

Wow, I say. I had no idea. Wow.

Wow is actually beyond the banality of what my father or uncle would ever say.

Grace does a movie spin.

Like something you'd do in a square in Rome or Venice or Paris.

Or at the top of any mountain.

Taking it all in, once around.

The carousel of wow.

And here it comes again.

Wow.

I prefer this to sunny days, she sighs. Don't you?

Well, I have this theory, I say, trying harder, that days like this you want to absorb through your skin.

Grace studies me then says, I have very thin skin. I wonder if it helps. I hope to write about this on Facebook so my friends can be amazed.

Right, I say. Right. But you can't copy this, Grace. You wouldn't come close. Its beauty is almost impossible to capture. Because it's so fleeting, I think. And so perfect. That's why you have to just embrace it, I guess.

What did you just say?

Grace suddenly stiffens, like maybe I've said something horrible by accident.

This moment here, I say. We are living it and everything around us … also lives. So, in a way, it's kind of perfect, right here, right now.

Yes, she says. That's exactly it!

Yes, I say.

Grace studies the water, looking for the seal. Something *should* break the surface, because it's almost like glass; a tired simile for sure, but it applies.

I step closer to the rail and study the water, and I don't know why I do that considering how terrifying it is. Death is a green-grey dragon beneath us.

There is this theory I have about life, Grace says. Some people are on this planet to give you joy and others will give you sadness. But almost everybody will give you inspiration. Even you.

Really, I say. Really. Yeah. Nice. Where did that come from?

I just thought of that, Grace smiles. We are saying important things today, Andy. About life.

Okay, I can't imagine what's inspiring Grace now. I mean, I don't even know her. And I've never had kids so I can't go by that. What do I know? She doesn't seem particularly keen on me or Will. We're obviously the crazy uncles. What else? Okay. She wears high heels to work and hates them, and now she wears expensive hiking boots. She's good with the camera. She loves the wilderness. Canada. Being here on the observation deck observing the observations and ...

Out of words. Out of the proper words. Shit.

I really wish I'd had kids. I say this aloud. And this just comes out of the blue. Or grey, in this case. I mean, why didn't I? We. What were we thinking? When we didn't.

Anna always said we needed to make a kid, but then we decided to focus on our careers for a bit, and before we knew it we were past the baby barrier, in our forties and childless, while our friends were already talking about grandkids.

Our big mistake, Anna always said after visiting nieces and nephews. Our one big mistake was we waited too long. Strike while the iron is hot, right?

If we want babies, we should really get some therapy first, Anna insisted. We're a little fucked up, don't you know.

I always thought she was intentionally being funny. But probably she wasn't.

Regret. Yeah, that one hurts, I would tell Anna after visiting her cousin's twin toddlers. Because Anna was a twin too. Although her twin died shortly after birth. Nothing like watching two little kids throw mashed potatoes at each other to make you laugh until you cry.

Are you okay? Grace asks.

She has her hand out like she's showing seats at the theatre.

You are okay over there? she says again.

I realize I'm still holding the rail with two hands and looking at the water. It probably looks suicidal, which to be honest, isn't a stretch.

Sure, I say.

I want to say something meaningful here. I should, because I'm in my fifties and I need to show some kind of maturity and depth. Two things that have been sadly lacking throughout most of my cheating life.

Sometimes I think we're all on a ferry and we're all lost souls, I say.

Exactly, says Grace. Exactly.

The fog thickens as fog will do. We're almost grey on grey on grey now; the sky, the sea, and the ship becoming one, and it's not clear what lies ahead. The ship's horn cuts through the grey like a low, guttural scream.

HELLO. HELLO. HELLO.

Grace doesn't flinch.

She looks at me.

I expected more of that, she says, grabbing my hand. What about you?

I hold her hand, and I notice now that she shakes too. It's different than the old man's shaking from earlier; these ones are full of sadness and loneliness and innocence.

That's not very scientific, I know. But I believe what I believe. And she does have those shakes.

Where do you think we will end up? she asks.

Nanaimo.

It's our first stop, I say.

I meant theoretically, Grace says. In life?

What?

Grace laughs. I didn't mean that. I'm so weird on boats.

Then Grace absentmindedly plays with the dials on her camera with her one free hand. I think she's blushing but it could just be the wind.

I don't know, I finally say. I really don't know.

I hope we never know, she says, now letting go of my hand. She moves away, toward the edge, and leans over the rail like she's a professional ski jumper from Norway. The wind parts her bangs. She grimaces or smiles or does both and lets the fog into her open mouth, swallowing the air with her eyes closed.

The camera around her neck knocks at her heart over and over again.

FOURTEEN

IT'S ON THE THIRD FERRY when things get weird. The one from Quadra Island to Cortes. It's much smaller than the first ferry, doesn't handle many vehicles (I count twenty-one), and has few amenities. Most of the patrons stand at the edge of the deck, looking out for humpbacks or orcas. Many are over sixty and some are in their eighties. I speak of the people. For some, this might be a last crossing, who knows. I seem to be the youngest on the ship, next to Grace, who has suddenly found a pair of aviators and now looks like a spy. She's positioned herself near the bow behind the fenced off area at the front of the vehicle deck, peering out at the open water with her Sony at the ready. She's a statue. There's a brisk wind, and the whitecaps churn the ocean into a slight frenzy, as if it's a bit pissed that we're all making this journey. Grace doesn't see the German Shepherd sitting politely by her feet, his leash leading to a slightly rotund woman wearing a huge, grey Tilley hat with a feather in it. It turns out it's Deborah, the same RCMP officer who helped us search for Sarah last fall. Off-duty, I assume.

I take off for the rear of the ferry and watch our wake mark our way. Seagulls catch free rides on our wake, and seals pop up as if finding our boat wrong for the water. There are a lot of seagulls on this crossing and almost all of them are angry. I decide to try to count them, but give up after fourteen.

It's around forty-five minutes into the crossing when I see Will sitting in the lounge with a glass of booze in front of him. Across from him with a taller glass of booze sits Deborah. They are in the middle of something.

I see you've met, I say to Deborah. Will is my friend.

Deborah says, Oh, we've met all right. He told me you were on board too. It's been a while, hasn't it?

Yes, I say. It sure has.

Deborah smiles.

We're having a fascinating conversation about the ancient Greeks, those inconsiderate bastards.

Will smiles. Aristotle writes in the *Poetics* that, in the beginning, tragedy was an improvisation, he says.

Deborah looks Will over; undresses him intellectually, I guess.

Is that what you're doing with your life, my friend? she says.

I believe I am, Will counters. That's why I'm having a drink with you, actually. I have no idea where things are going.

How terribly chaotic of you, Deborah whispers.

I shuffle my feet a little. My mouth feels dry, dry, dry.

Are you going back to Cortes on duty? I stammer.

No, Deborah says. Vacation.

She doesn't look at me, but stares at Will, who kind of beams like a kid who's just found a ten-dollar bill on the ground.

Anything new on Sarah? I ask.

No, Deborah says. Nothing.

It's been a while, I say.

It's been a while, she says.

Will says, I heard all about it.

I bet, says Deborah. I bet you did.

Then we sit and study the deck outside and watch Grace pet the German Shepherd. There's a tenderness to Grace's petting, like she's communicating with the dog, which she probably is.

She likes my dog, says Deborah.

She certainly does, I say. And your dog likes her.

Grace looks up at us almost on cue. Then waves.

Deborah has her foot out under the table. I swear it's up against Will's leg and neither one of them seems to want to say much so I excuse myself and leave.

I take the stairs down to the car deck, and the dog notices me first, gives me the once over before returning to lean on Grace's shoulder.

Hey, I say. Grace?

Hey, Grace says back. Isn't this the best thing ever?

It's great, I say. What are you doing?

Oh, I'm staring into the water, Grace says.

Anything interesting?

Grace touches the muzzle of the dog briefly.

We've decided that this world is perfect, Grace says. It makes me contented.

Okay, I say.

I've studied my surroundings, obviously, Grace says. This is my conclusion after careful observation.

You sound like a professor, I say.

Yes. I would do that. I would lecture students on how to be better stewards of the land, Grace says. Also, I would teach them about Sony cameras. And how to communicate with large dogs.

I wait for a couple of gulls to pass overhead. They're deafening.

I've never been totally contented in my entire life, I say.

Grace says, That's very sad.

The dog and Grace go back to studying the waves, although I'm sure her eyes are shut behind those aviator sunglasses. Sitting cross-legged, Grace holds out her hands to her side as if practicing yoga. The German Shepherd sighs as only German Shepherds can and leans in to peacefully rest his chin on her shoulder.

My father always told me that when animals are content their eyes narrow and they smile a little.

Like Prince. Right now.

I wander the ferry and look into the cars where the mostly old people lean back in the seats looking dead or very asleep.

I play sentinel at the back of the ferry when it happens. And I've been staring at the water for only five minutes or so.

I see it happening, and I can't believe it's happening.

It might be life-changing.

Here it is.

In the distance, barely visible, breaking the waves randomly but quickly, the fins of at least a hundred dolphins race toward the ferry. And behind them, a pod of orcas. As they approach the boat, the captain hits the horn, cuts the engine, and we drift. The dolphins splash into us, around us, quickly cutting in and out of the water like commas splicing a paragraph. People wake from slumbers, move out of the cars and SUVs toward the side of the ferry, most with cellphones at the ready. The dolphins pass, and the sound is incredible like I'm in a car wash. Then they move in unison in front of us where Grace and the German Shepherd stare at them spellbound. She fumbles for her Sony and hits record. The frenzy of the water subsides slightly. They move ahead of us. The dolphins leap, flashes of white from their bellies. And then, almost soundless, the orcas pass around the ferry and out in front; their bigger, more powerful bodies submarine the water as they close the distance on their prey. Eight of them — the biggest and oldest — in the middle, and others fanned out across the water on either side of us as the cameras click and people scream, Look at them. Look at that. Wow.

Killer Whales.

They close the distance without trying, smoothly and powerfully.

Grace strains to see where it's all going, takes her aviators off, and the ship's horn sounds again as we drift with the tide, engines dead.

The engines grumble to life, and we lurch forward and follow the killer whales and their prey into Desolation Sound, now beckoning us with a soft curtain of fog in the far distance. The sun at our backs still glinting off the windshields of the Hondas and Fords and Toyotas and Mazdas and BMWs parked on the deck, waiting to be disembarked on solid ground somewhere over there. We are all metal and rubber and bound by the rules of displacement and our movement is hardly graceful, more of a lurch than anything.

The fish, I think, are gone. Just like that.

Just like that.

I remember they are mammals.

We are all mammals.

Even the German Shepherd.

It's just that some of us are stuck on deck.

We are being carried away. To a specific time and place.

While those in the water are free.

I find I've struck a pose at the ropes at the front of the ferry, feet frozen to the floor deck. My lips are dry. My head hurts. My eyes run wet. I wander off to find Will. He must have seen this too. Climb the steps to the lounge, open the door and see him leave the washroom with Deborah in hand.

Did you see that? I say. Did you?

Sorry, Will says. We were taking a break.

And then I see Deborah fix her pants, button them more completely. Will's fly is open too. I'm embarrassed.

You missed the dolphins being chased by killer whales around our boat. Hundreds of them. Turned the water into a frenzy. It was a once in a lifetime event.

They look at me askance.

Trying to see if I'm full of shit or what.

I should leave before I make things worse, because sometimes you need to retreat to have a horrible sinking feeling by yourself.

By the time I get to the car the fog has us.

It's everywhere.

Settling.

Settling.

We are wrapped. Yup. Stifled, the 3D-white all around us, now, on deck. It's like a dream of grannie's cotton sheets, but somewhat fleeting. Yes, I feel it soften the cars while people retreat to their heated seats and steering wheels and iPhones. No doubt there's a lot of texting about what just happened. You should have seen the whales and dolphins. Facebook and Twitter light up with the fingers of the passengers. Photos race at the speed of light to other phones to other phones and so on. They were here, we say. They were here.

We saw them.

Everyone did.

The ocean was alive with them.

And we are changed because of that.

For good.

And that's the honest truth.

FIFTEEN

WE LAND AT WHALETOWN ON Cortes Island around suppertime. The narrow two-lane road — which is basically like a paved bike path — leads up the hill from the ferry and is packed with cars lining up to leave. A lot of people mill around at the edge of the little building where the ferry master — a cliché of his stature, complete with handlebar moustache — stands, in a hi-res jacket waving off the vehicles.

Will sits beside me in the passenger seat, and Grace sits in the back with her Sony at the ready. We barely move up the road following Deborah's white Ford half-ton, the German Shepherd in the back staring at us — maybe Grace in particular — and drooling.

We crawl up the slight hill. Where is all the traffic coming from on a remote island in the middle of nowhere?

A lot of delivery vans here, Will mumbles. And half-tons with wheelbarrows.

We pass several small trucks parked in the departure lane, service vehicles for a telephone company — upgrading the cellular service on the island, probably. The technicians stand outside the trucks while they wait and wave at us like we're neighbours. I count five of them, all men and all bearded with tattoos.

As the road cuts through the trees and winds its way up island, the number of vehicles thin out, and we're left with the occasional deer eating grass at the side of the road. I automatically slow down, not wanting to spook them, but they seem oblivious to us. At times, the trees darken the road, blocking out the setting sun behind us.

We pass signs that read No Thru Road on either side, their arrows pointing to narrow gravel lanes leading into even darker forest. Our windows are open; the air is sweet with moss and fern and evergreen. A tinge of saltwater too.

We still follow Deborah's vehicle. If any of us feels this is strange, nobody says so.

Prince is very happy to be on this island because of the smells, Grace announces.

He told you that? asks Will.

Yes, says Grace. He tells me many things.

Will looks at me as if looking for a sign. I don't give him one. I'm too busy scanning for deer, and there are a lot of them. I've counted six or seven already. Some drift back into the shadows of trees, while others ignore us and nibble at grass poking out through the concrete at the side of the road. They are nimble creatures who take two or three steps before kicking up their heels for a happy jump like they're studying for ballet.

The road goes on and on and isn't particularly smooth, with large parts of it patched over and sometimes full of potholes. After a while there's nothing to see but the rough concrete of the road and trees leaning in and over us. They aren't big trees, some deciduous and some fir, and as we move to the other side of the island, they get taller and thicker.

Will says, It's a witch's forest all right.

Grace looks through her Sony and gives out a wow or two.

This is beautiful, she says. Could you slow down, please?

Do you know where you're going? Will says.

There's only one way, I say.

Right, Will says. Right.

In fifteen minutes, we pull up to Holly's cabin. *Holly's Hideout*, a sign says. New since last year? I don't remember it.

Prince is already out of Deborah's truck, and Grace is out of our car. The two of them scramble into the forest to sniff ferns while I unload our bags from the trunk and watch Deborah unload a large backpack from her front seat.

Deborah waves at me.

You didn't tell me we'd end up at the same place, she says.

I didn't know, I say.

Back to the scene of the crime, she says.

What do you mean?

Didn't you hang out here while we were doing the search?

For a bit. Just for a bit.

I stand beside Deborah and study the outside of the cabin. It's all very neatly put together — expertly, I'd say. The windowsills are painted bright green. The door is red. It has a sign on it that reads *Come In, Please* in bold black and white. There's a deer fence around the house about seven or eight feet tall. Inside the fenced-off area, lots of tomato plants and garlic and kale.

There's a distinct natural feeling to everything, nothing complicated. Even the grass grows wild and is ankle deep. Dandelions everywhere.

The forest appears to be crying. Branches have droplets on them. So do the ferns and wires around the house. Tiny, perfect crystal balls everywhere.

No birds, though. Although I can hear crows call from the forest. Then nothing.

It's so quiet here I can hear my heart. I forget for a moment that Will stands beside me, also staring and breathing into my ear.

We can see our breath, the inside of us hangs around in the air as we stand there.

Cedar, says Deborah. I love cedar.

She's in front of us near the tailgate of her half-ton.

She smells the air like a llama.

And then out strides Holly. This time she's wearing a flowing black dress and cowboy boots, old-fashioned glasses that make her look like she belongs in the 60s — the 1860s. She strikes a pose beside the deer fence around her place and then opens the gate like it's a drawbridge. Hands on her hips now, Holly dares us to stare at her, which we do.

We stand there. Pretty much three abreast. Staring.

I'm so glad you made it, she says. I've been expecting you. All four of you.

Five, says Deborah, pointing to Prince sniffing the flora nearby.

I love dogs, Holly says. They love me.

Prince ignores her.

Come on in, she says. You must have some tea.

I have my cellphone out, looking for bars.

There's no reception right now, says Holly. You probably saw the cellphone vans on the way in. They're upgrading the system.

So … no email?

No, not for a while, says Holly. Not until the system is back up. And I don't know when that's going to happen. Oh well, you're stuck with me, I guess. Don't worry, though. I'll make you spellbound.

Then she turns on her heel and goes to the cabin door with the sign and holds it open.

Don't be shy, she smiles. I won't bite.

Then she hisses for some weird reason.

Yes, hisses.

Will looks at me.

You didn't tell me she was a witch, he mutters, moving past me.

I follow him in, but my legs feel heavy. And my eyebrows hurt.

WE SIT AROUND THE fireplace sipping lemon tea: Will on the couch beside Deborah, me on an antique wooden chair with a thin cushion for my ass, Holly on the floor poking the fire with a stick, and on a smaller love seat, Grace and Prince, his big paw in her hand, watching me squirm. The room smells like incense and not particularly good incense, but something weird, like tempura and vanilla.

I think it's grand that I have such a full house, says Holly. Look at you beautiful people. Look at you sitting here in my humble, little place. I don't often have a full house like this. It's a real treat.

Holly pushes at the pins holding her hair up in a tight bun, like they're holding the fuse of a hand grenade. She smiles at me. Lots of teeth flash.

And you, she says. Who would have thought I'd ever see you again?

Right, me too, I say. I know, I know.

Will notices that I avoid looking at Holly.

Deborah yawns. Will notices her yawn, too, because he's sitting right beside and probably had sex with her on the ferry.

Fate is so unpredictable, Will says, as if he thinks that will somehow help.

Stupid thing to say, I think. Stupid.

The whole plan to get the memory stick back needs to be rethought, I also think. We've planned to be here for a couple nights, but now I'm unsure how many of those will feature an RCMP officer as a fellow guest, particularly one with inside information about Sarah, the dead woman I made the sex tape with.

I love being off-duty, says Deborah to the room. I get to be with ordinary people who tell me ordinary things.

How's your back? Will asks.

I hurt my back on the ferry, Deborah explains to the room again. Probably when they cut the engines. I wasn't ready for the lurch. It got me. The lurch got me good.

Deborah blushes a bit as she says this, her face turning pink at the exact moment she pulls at her ear. It's uncomfortably quiet for a bit.

Then.

We certainly had a big lurch, says Will. Out of nowhere. Just like that.

They cut the engines for the dolphins, Grace says to Holly. We needed to let them come through.

Prince nods. Suddenly shakes like crazy, then pants like he's happy to just hang out with us.

So many dolphins swimming together, Grace says. It was magical. Except they were being chased by killer whales who intended to eat them. They were swimming very fast. So fast that the water was churning. I think there were hundreds of them, and when they jumped out of the water you could see how white their bellies were. But the killer whales did not jump. They looked like submarines and swam under our boat.

Wow, says Holly. I don't think I've ever seen something like that. And I've taken hundreds of ferry trips.

Grace says, It was a very significant moment.

Holly studies the room.

Did it change *your* life? she says to me.

Well, I say, it was something very special, that's for sure.

We sit there for a bit, and three of us sip tea at the same time. Then we clink our cups as we put them down.

Deborah leans over to look at Holly closely.

How did you get that fire going so nicely? she asks.

I coaxed it nicely, Holly says as she pulls off her old-fashioned spectacles and studies me intently.

I didn't know you could talk to fire, laughs Deborah. I'm in the wrong business.

I talk to fire all the time, Holly purrs. In fact, I play with fire.

Nobody laughs. And we have a moment big enough to drive a truck through. I study the ceiling; the cedar logs perfectly aligned about our heads, the flames flickering a bit across the walls.

It's cold for this time of the year, I say. Which isn't really true. But I know this is a weak, weak attempt. I have a tendency to try to fill uncomfortable pauses with drivel. A bad habit.

Holly says, Can I get you more tea?

She pretends to smile and pulls at a loose strand of hair.

No, I'm fine, I say. Just fine.

I'm so glad you decided to come back to visit me, Holly almost whispers. I guess I made quite the impression.

Will looks at me.

I look at him.

We have bundles of fake cash in the trunk of the car; most, but not all of it wrestled into a backpack. And we have two pills to roofie Holly.

What's your plan?

Holly looks at Deborah. She's asking her, not me. Thank God.

Me?

Deborah thinks for a moment, then straightens her hair, which I've just noticed to be a bit of a squirrel's nest and slightly greying at the sides. It actually makes her look handsome, but that's probably not a word she'd like to hear. My wife hates it when I say that.

Deborah studies the fire then says, Well, I want to hike through the old-growth forest and just get lost, I suppose.

What is old growth? asks Grace.

Holly turns to study her and when she does, the fireplace flames light her face red, making her eyes blaze.

Trees hundreds of years old, Holly says. Ancient trees so tall they almost block out light. So green and lush you can almost smell the elves and fairies.

Holly straightens her black dress so that it spreads around her like a pool of dried blood. She closes her eyes to remember this:

Over hill, over dale

Thorough bush, thorough brier,

Over park, over pale,

Thorough flood, thorough fire!

I do wander everywhere,

Swifter than the moon's sphere;

And I serve the Fairy Queen …

Everyone looks like they've been hit by a spell, none of us moving or barely even breathing. Even Prince stares at Holly and stops panting. Holly waves her glasses around the room, laughs a little, and we exhale into the magic. Oh, it's there, trust me. Hanging over our heads.

I'm always so dramatic, Holly announces. It's crazy how I remembered that.

Holly says that while waving her hands through the air; her fingers fluttering slightly.

Wow, says Grace. Fairies! What a surprise.

Holly continues to absentmindedly organize her black dress.

The forest where the fairies live, and it's right here, Grace says. That would make me very excited. I have an excellent camera.

You can never do it justice, says Holly. The Old Growth Forest is hard to capture … I have to warn you.

I'd like to try, says Grace. Plus, I have a good eye.

Prince gives her a lick and Grace doesn't flinch.

Thank you, she says to him. Thank you, my Prince.

Holly turrets her head back to me.

Can you place my little poem?

I think. Try to access my internal hard drive. When I do that I wrinkle my forehead and purse my lips. I get nothing. Nothing. University has failed me, all nine years of it. Normally, I'd google that shit, but I can't, the system is down.

Holly puts her glasses back on and with her hair pinned back she looks more and more like a librarian, although a very sexy one. She waits me out.

Shakespeare, Holly says. What do you think?

Yes, I agree.

Deborah snuggles up to Will even more.

How beautiful, Deborah says. How beautiful is that. Shakespeare.

Shakespeare, parrots Will. I knew it.

Deborah wipes at her eyes, trying to recover from the spell.

The poetry is within you. That's a fact, Deborah says. I'm glad I'm here. So glad. I don't think I've heard Shakespeare since high school. I was excellent in my English literature classes, and sometimes I wonder why I didn't become a writer. I guess I like solving crime better than iambic pentameter.

Deborah is the only one in the room who laughs at this joke. Then she stops.

We sit there for a bit, and I must say it's quite amazing what effect no TV or cellular service has on a group of bored travellers. We act like we're in the drawing room with Colonel Mustard or that dreadful old TV series *Downton Abbey*.

Our small talk is pathetic.

Will tries to clear his throat, but it's a weak attempt.

I can never memorize, Will says quite properly. It's not my nature. I am the forgetting type, I'm afraid.

You're forgetting, but not forgettable, says Holly. How about that?

I fidget because Will fidgets and he never fidgets.

Holly notices and points a bony finger at me.

And you. You. Yes, you. I could give you a personal tour of the beach near Squirrel Cove, she says.

That's okay, I say.

Holly winks at me while stroking the carpet underneath her. Of course, this is sexy. Of course, all the males in the room notice it, even Prince.

Will tries to get comfortable, but Deborah has his arm in a bit of a judo hold.

I blow my nose and then notice everyone staring at me.

You'd like that, wouldn't you, Andy? A private tour of eddies and tide pools and whatnot.

I put away the tissue and sip my tea. There's very little left, but I make a scene of it anyway.

I saw a lot of them last time I was here, I say. Up and down the shoreline.

Oh yes, says Holly. I almost forgot about that. Did anyone find anything?

Just a camera, says Deborah, then, thinking twice, turns professional very quickly. She squirms on the couch.

But you were there, weren't you? Deborah asks.

Yes, I remember a camera, Holly says. I certainly remember that.

It's an ongoing investigation, Deborah says in an official voice. And we'll keep looking until we get some answers.

Grace perks up, but doesn't say anything, just pets the dog and pretends to listen to his internal thoughts. Then she spots Holly's Mac sitting in the corner on a small coffee table. It's a laptop.

May I download some clips from my Sony on your Mac computer?

Grace gets up and stands in front of Holly like a sixth grader. She holds out her camera.

I should have some amazing footage on here, Grace says. Of the wildlife we've seen so far. It would look great on that display.

Holly looks her over.

Okay, but don't leave your files on there, Holly says.

I won't, Grace says. Promise.

Then she moves to the computer in the back of the room, and her face immediately lights up from the screen.

I stretch because I'm getting nervous and this is what I do.

How's your wife? Holly asks, lifting a leg as if doing Pilates. Has she recovered from all this tragic nonsense?

I don't know if Anna will ever be the same, I say.

Deborah says, You don't have to talk about that, if you don't want to.

She gives me a kind smile.

It's okay, I say. It's okay.

You might think it's okay, says Deborah, but inside you might not be. That's the nature of the beast.

Sure, I say. I guess.

I turn the handle of the teacup toward the fire and Holly and give my best fake smile.

It's been months, I say, so I've had lots of time to process things. You're never the same after a tragedy like that but …

He's had a lot of help, Will says. And support.

Deborah smiles and says, Let's talk about something else, can we? I mean, we're here for a good time, not a long time.

She probably doesn't know she's quoting rock lyrics. And let's face it, this seems like a really weird thing for a police officer to say.

Holly rests on her elbow, and I think she's actually levitating.

Where is she? Holly asks. Your wife?

Visiting her mother in Toronto, I say. She's eighty-six and has problems with the back of her neck so Anna went there to buy her a heating pad from Costco. Then she's taking her to a Blue Jays game, mainly the buffet, over centre field in the second deck. It's all you can eat. The cheese is from Québec, and there's a roast too. They call it an Alberta Roast because that's where the beef is from.

Wonderful, Holly coos. I love how caring she sounds.

She's like that, I say. I'm a lucky guy.

Sure you are, says Holly. Sure you are.

Will shuffles a bit.

He talks about her all the time, he says. Doesn't shut up. Happily married for how long now?

I think twenty-two years? I say. You would know just as well as me, you were my best man.

Oh yeah, Will says. There's that, isn't there? But I can't remember the year. Maybe I've just blocked it out.

Typical, Holly says. Men.

The women in the room chuckle a bit.

Different tactics are needed, I decide.

So, I say, we decided to come up here for the weekend to pick up some footage for the feature film we're trying to put together. We want to make a trailer to apply for some funding support.

Holly smiles, but it's clearly a fake smile.

What's your movie about?

Well, we're still working on the script, but it involves two men in their fifties whose marriages are falling apart.

Are they cheaters?

Holly uses her glasses to ask the question, pointing the ends like they're little knives.

Yes, I guess they are, I say. But that doesn't mean they're necessarily wrong. Or necessarily evil. There're two sides to everything, right? It's just a matter of point of view. It's completely made up.

You don't have to tell me, Holly says. My ex-husband just made up a story about his new girlfriend. Apparently, she loves all of him … not just a part of him. And she's more spiritual than I am. And she loves making him steak. Especially on weekends. When they have lots of great sex. Plus blow jobs.

The women chuckle again. Then fall eerily silent.

I clear my throat trying to signal Will. He fidgets.

Our characters. Our protagonists. Yeah. It's about their journey, Will explains. They're evolving. It's going to be great. Especially when they learn important life lessons about the true nature of love. And what it takes to actually feel something.

How's that work? Holly asks. I mean, are you basing this on your life or some asshole you know?

Wow, says Will. I didn't see that one coming. Asshole.

He's being serious. I think. And I can tell he wants to get up off the couch to flee, but Deborah still has his arm. He's stuck.

Holly turns her gaze on me. She touches her hair here and there and there as if pushing three distinct buttons.

And you, she smiles. What do you say?

Then she folds her hands like a funeral director. And waits.

I look around at the others, also waiting for me to reveal my stupidity. Or — and this is a long shot — my brilliance.

I'm making it up as I go along, I say. The script is in flux. Some improv will be included throughout. So … who knows what will exactly happen.

Why are men so flawed? Holly asks.

People are, Will says. People are.

I'm not interested in people, Holly says. I just want to know about your men.

Will shuffles.

Process, he says. Let's stick to process. Right?

Holly ignores him, keeps staring me down. Cracks her knuckles.

We don't want to give the story away just yet, he says. It'll ruin things. But what I can tell you is that this will be a very controversial picture because some women might see it as self-indulgent when actually it's about process.

Well, Holly pauses. I guess this is going to take some money, isn't it?

We have the money, I say.

Good for you, Holly says. Good for you. I would love to see it someday.

Then Holly lifts her teacup and pretends to toast us.

Cheers, she says. Cheers.

To your movie men.

I hope they find themselves.

Soon.

SIXTEEN

IN THE MORNING WE DISCOVER Grace's note, which simply reads: I'm exploring the island with Prince. I shall return within the hour.

She doesn't return in time for brunch, which we have outside. Heirloom tomatoes, local arugula, and goat cheese. Not tons of protein, which isn't a surprise: Cortes Island loves veggies and lettuce. In fact, kale is a major crop here.

That was a couple of hours ago.

Holly organizes a search despite our reservations.

It's only one, she's been gone since nine, Will says. No big deal.

You can't be too careful, says Holly. There's a windstorm coming in. It's a big storm.

Holly stands under her canopy of copper pots and pans near the counter separating the kitchen from the small dining area. She doesn't seem to care that the biggest frying pan in the world sways precariously above her noggin.

We could just phone her, says Deborah.

There's no cellular service, Holly reminds her. They're fixing it.

Holly's already in her searching clothes: a long grey dress with black lace and, underneath, her hiking boots. Her hair, that untamed grey and white tangle of mane, is turned up under a fedora of some kind — something from the 1940s. I'm convinced she has a collection of them. She also has a walking stick that could be from the set of *The Lord of the Rings*.

Studies us. Holly does. The three of us sitting on the far side of the nicely polished dark oak table, our hands flat on it as if trying to feel its breath.

You look ill, Deborah says to Will. Everything okay?

Did you take your blood pressure pill? I say to Will.

He shakes his head, which by the way, is even redder this morning than most mornings.

I figured all the calming dandelion tea we were consuming today would have been enough, says Will. So, I didn't take it. No way.

Deborah says quickly, Always take your meds, mister.

Will smiles. He likes being bossed around.

Holly stamps her foot.

Can we get our Gore-Tex on, please? she says. That storm is due in about two hours.

I feel her hand on my back as we get pushed out the door.

Watch yourself, she says to me.

Sure, I say.

Outside, the trees stretch and groan with the wind. There's a crash or two from deep within the dark forest where — I suppose — trolls live.

Holly equips us with small flashlights, and Will struggles to take his BP pill, leans on me to knock it back with a slug of water from his flask.

I look at him.

It's not water, he says. Irish whiskey.

Should you be doing that? I say. Mixing your meds?

What do you think? he says with a wink.

Deborah joins us. She wears what must be RCMP-issued boots. They look like they belong on a weightlifter. They're huge. She tugs at Will's sleeve and then disappears into the brush, walking into the green as if ready for an ambush.

Will says, She's great, isn't she?

He stares at where she went.

I want to shake him, but he shakes me off quickly.

Let's do this, Will says, then wanders down the path following her, flashlight in hand.

I follow them and Holly follows me.

After about twenty minutes, we find ourselves in the old-growth forest where the trees — mainly Douglas firs — follow a creek. Their sheer height and girth are astonishing. Every bit of branch, twig, and bough is embroidered in bright green. The path is strewn with mostly ferns and moss and everything in between. Everything moves with the wind. Everything ruffles as we pass underneath.

What is this place? I ask Holly, who turns to face me with a pained smile.

It's called the Children's Forest, she says.

Why?

Because it's so enchanting, obviously, she says. Then she shushes me.

Listen.

I listen, but only hear the trees groan under the wind.

Can you hear it?

Shush.

Listen.

Then I hear it, a bare sound like a whisper coming from somewhere deep within the heart of the dense trees ahead.

We move down the path, pushing ferns aside and using our ears like satellite dishes trying to fine-tune the sound.

Holly moves slower, holds her hand up like she's at a Baptist church waiting to be filled by the Spirit, and sways a bit.

Behind us, she says. Behind us.

We double back, down the path, across the log, through the bristling ferns, and around some Sitka spruce. I stumble and almost fall into some shrubbery when Holly grabs me and holds me. I notice how strong she is, like almost superhuman, and I want to thank her, but the wind picks up. She strains to hear above it, above the howl and holler, above the shush of branch sway and creak of boughs.

There, she says. There.

Holly stomps off, I follow.

We turn left through the brush, away from the path, downhill under three enormous Douglas firs so huge that light is almost blocked out, and there, sitting on a tree stump with Prince at her feet, is Grace staring up at the sky as if in a trance.

Grace, I yell as I stumble toward her. Grace!

She looks up as Prince greets me with a poke from his nose.

Isn't this perfect? she moans. Perfect.

Are you okay? I say. Are you?

I am in the best spirit, Grace says, holding out her Sony. I have captured such beautiful images for you. We must celebrate.

Holly looks Grace over, holds her face in her fingers like she's attempting to inspect for damage, but I can see she's worried.

The forest has her, Holly says. This might take a while.

I love this forest, says Grace, waving her Sony around like it's spreading magic fairy dust. I want to stay here forever.

Holly looks at me.

I look at her.

We need to get her back to my cabin ASAP, Holly says.

It's at that moment we hear a loud clap of thunder, and the ground actually shakes.

Grace squeals with joy while Prince cowers between my legs.

Let's get out of here, Holly says, pulling Grace down from the stubby stump.

I take Prince's leash and pull him out from between my legs. We turn to head back down the path, and it's then we realize we've lost Will and Deborah.

Oh no, Holly says. I thought they were right with us.

I thought we were following them, I say.

But they don't know where they're going, Holly says. Why would we be doing that?

Grace takes our picture.

Stop that, Holly snaps. Stop that at once. We don't have time for pictures.

Grace hangs her head.

I think this situation has given me unprecedented opportunities for photos and videos, she says.

Holly gives her the once over.

This isn't a normal storm for us — it's very, very dangerous. We need to get back to the cabin as fast as possible. Do you understand? There's a big storm coming.

Grace fiddles with her Sony and looks very sad.

I wish to experience all of nature, Grace says.

Not this time, Holly says. Trust me.

Some rain is hitting us, I notice — not much because of the canopy, but enough to know that out in the open it's most likely a deluge.

Why don't you take her back, and I'll head back into the really deep part of the forest and look for Will and Deborah. I mean, they can't be far off. This forest isn't that big, I say.

Holly nods. Follow this path on your way back — it leads right back to the road beside my cabin, she says. The trees are marked with orange tape — follow them.

I can't really see a lot of orange tape, but I believe her.

Then she takes Prince, pushes Grace ahead of her, and heads away through fern and forest toward the lighter trees.

I watch them until they disappear from sight. Prince turns and gives me a last look. One that says, You wish, don't you?

He's smiling. And I swear he winked too.

Then a gust of wind.

A shiver. Not sure if it's me or the whole forest, but it's overwhelming.

I turn and trudge up into the deeper part of the forest and turn my flashlight on. Not that it makes any difference. It's only around three o'clock, and the sun won't set for hours, but it's turning dark. The clouds are almost black. And the rain is becoming more persistent. Branches above me are excited or nervous, or both. They wave like maniacs.

I push through branches and complex spiderwebs and wander

among the trunks of giants that twist and grind in the gathering wind. I imagine this could be a tall ship in a storm, but I'm too grounded for that, so I turn off my flashlight and soldier on.

It's a slog. The path is rock- and root-strewn and greasy; the rain giving the mud a nice sheen. Puddles are everywhere. I need to concentrate. One foot, then the other. I catch my foot sliding. Concentrate. Move.

The path gets less defined the deeper I go into the woods.

When I hit a slight clearing where a ring of Sitka surround a small, fallen mound of twigs, I find Will leaning against a log. He's lolling and rolling, waving at the branches above his head like a cat playing with a mouse toy on a clothes wire.

Will, what the hell? I say, stumbling down the slight incline toward him.

I roofied myself, Will says. I guess I shouldn't have put those pills with my blood pressure meds. That was a mistake. Look at those branches. Look at them. They have fruit on them.

What?

Fruit, Will says. Right?

Where's Deborah, I ask. Where?

She went to get help, back to the cabin.

She abandoned you?

No, you idiot, Will says. She loves me and I love her and we're going to start a family.

Snap out of it, I say. You're too old for kids, and you're too bitter for love. Let's get out of here.

The world is shit, Will says. It's shit.

Come on, Will. This storm is serious shit.

Will lolls like the ship has just ridden up a wave. Isn't this just grand?

No, it isn't grand. Your so-called girlfriend has abandoned you to the trees and wind. We could die in here.

Hey, she tried to carry me out like she was a firefighter, but I was too heavy, and she hurt her knee tendon thing, Will says. Is it raining?

Yes, I say. Let's go before the shit really hits the fan.

I don't know if I can feel my legs yet, says Will. They're like pirate legs right now.

What?

Wooden, Will laughs. I'm hilarious.

I grab his arm, yank him up, and realize he is heavy like a body in a bag. He slumps, I slump.

Come on, I say. Straighten out.

This is as straight as I can be, Will says. Although get a few drinks in me, and you never know, right?

He laughs in my face.

Do you find me funny?

No. Now lift your foot and place it in front of your other foot.

He looks perplexed.

Really? I mean, really, Andy? That's asking a lot. I can barely feel my legs.

Come on, move, I say.

We're doomed, yells Will into the wind. We are all doomed, and life will soon end no matter what we do. We can't fight the end. We can't fight mortality. We can try to ignore it, but it won't matter. We are FOOLS. So, more wine, more wenches, more cards, and duels and feasts and lovemaking!

He spits the last words into the branches waving mere inches from his face, and then he grabs a nearby trunk and tries to spin around it but, failing, stumbles to his knees.

My kingdom for a horse! Will yells.

Come on, Will. Please.

More thunder. Closing in on us.

The wind lashes at us.

It's a movie out here, Will yells. It's a goddamn movie!

Come on! I yell, as I grab his waist and almost throw him over my shoulder.

I move away, try to spot trees with orange tape and then see one in the distance, plot my course with Will leaning on my right shoulder like a giant dead parrot.

There's the marker. Let's move, I shout above the wind.

What marker? Will shouts. Where is it? I can't see anything.

We stumble to the side, and the low branches of a fir tree catch us and push us back down the path as if shoving us back into the fight.

We try to balance, me holding Will, who now holds his side.

Let me catch my breath, Will says. I need to catch my breath.

Will's face is covered with my spittle or rain drops or sweat or all three, his forehead clenched up. Let's go, he yells at himself like this is his Olympic tryout and he's willing himself to coordinate his legs to do the old one-two. Let's go!

And we're in a drunk race. We meander, stumbling, through the maze of huge tree trunks, trying to keep our wobble from becoming a wipe-out, trying to not care that branches are falling around us with increasing regularity as the wind winds up.

Boom, more thunder.

A tree falls behind us.

No, we didn't see it, and yes, it happened so shut up.

There's a bright flash.

More thunder, almost instantly.

The ground shakes. Trees shiver and my hair bristles, arm hair electric, literally.

Will is on the ground — rolling around again, believe it or not.

What are you doing?

Will yells, I can't do this. I can't!

Yes, you can! I shout.

I stop for a second, prop him up against a mossy tree — the north face, of course — and hold my hand against his chest like it's a spear.

Look, I say. You got us into this mess, and now you're going to fucking get us out of it.

I just can't, Will says, as a branch or two crashes down behind us. I can't. It's not very fun being roofied, and I'm going to kill Dave when we get back. I will kill that bastard!

You did this to yourself, you idiot, I say. Leave Dave out of it, for God's sake.

He could have told me those pills look exactly like my BP pills, but he didn't, Will says. Dave is an asshole!

It's so loud out here I can barely hear him even though my face is inches away from his.

I don't want to get wiped out by a tree, I say. I don't. The forest is coming down around us — or haven't you noticed?

Okay, okay, Will says. Let's try again.

Come on, let's do it, I yell. Do it!

I lift him with my back and my left arm.

He's heavy. God, he's heavy. I adjust my posture, straighten up and hunch my shoulders.

Go, I say. Go!

And we lumber through the lumber cartoon-like, somewhat like two old dudes with bad knees. We stick to the path as sticks drop from the sky. The wind rattles the trees down to their winding roots. The ground itself pounds like a heart after sex, particularly in your fifties. It's exciting. It's dangerous. It hurts. There's a strange beauty to it all: us thrashing through the green, our bright red and yellow Gore-Tex the only other colours in the lush, lush forest; and everything beading off us, like we're impervious, I think. Follow the orange tape. Follow the tape. And once we burst through the forest and into the little trees, toward the yard and the deer fence, the lightning hits behind us with a sickening, bone-rattling boom and Will screams back at the trees: So long you fuckers! Live long and prosper!

Let's go, I say. Big finish. Big finish.

We stumble toward the cabin, the rain pelting our backs. We're twelve-years-old and yes, this is the three-legged race, everyone! It's the church picnic. Run like hell!

I fling open the gate to the yard.

Move it, I yell. Come on, you asshole!

Will's feet are practically dragging.

I actually feel pretty good, he says, his face inches from mine.

The ground shakes again. This time more violently.

BOOM!

I see a huge pine fall behind us. Smoke comes from its top.

Holy shit! Did you hear that? Will says.

Dead quiet.

We both stand there for a second and stare at the slow-motion fall. We wait for it to hit the ground, but of course it's caught by the trees that grow thick around it.

They don't want that tree to die, Will says. Do they? They're comrades.

Will salutes the forest.

I yank the cabin door open, and we fall into Holly's cabin like we've been shoved by an orca.

I can barely breathe, barely hold my head up, barely feel my arms or shoulders or even thighs. Everything burns including my eyes. I've ripped my coat somehow, and Will's face is covered in scratches.

But we're here.

And now we will operate like gentlemen, Will says with a wink.

Correct?

Correct.

So.

We brush ourselves off and take off our boots quietly by the back door. I sit on the steps. Will grabs the handrail.

Will chuckles. Fuck, that lightning nearly killed us.

Yeah, I say, throwing my boots down like they're cannonballs. They're covered in mud. Will pushes himself on me, his face still red and wet with bits of pine needle in his bushy brows.

Thank you, my friend, he says thickly.

No problem, I say. You're too close to my face. Back off.

The women must not know, he says, in an odd English accent. They must not, you understand, my friend, right?

About?

My dire situation, he drools. Right?

Right, I say, bracing myself as Will nearly collapses on me. He's a terrible, overwhelming drunk even though he's mostly sober and mainly drugged.

Always a gentleman, he whispers. Always. But from afar.

His breath smells like distant ferns and wild mushrooms.

Help me up the stairs, he moans. Help me, young man. You are my valet.

I push him up the two steps, and then, nearly sliding on the kitchen floor, I catch myself from falling by grabbing Will, who slumps against me all over again. I pull his arm around me and steady us. We teeter, but not enough to topple.

We step out of the kitchen toward the light.

Into the breech, Will mumbles. Into the breech, lads.

Shut the hell up, I whisper. Just shut up.

Inside the lovely, bright living room of the cabin we are faced with three women holding teacups like pistols. On the coffee table in front of them, in a green Chinese saucer, minus the cup, sits our last roofie. I'm sure it glows.

There is a moment of silence.

Then.

What have you got to say for yourselves?

I'm not sure who's said it.

But when I hear it, I drop Will on the carpet like he's a dead soldier.

Ouch, he says. Asshole. I'm not dead yet.

SEVENTEEN

I'M THIRTEEN. IT'S MY BIRTHDAY. My father holds his hands behind his back. He tells me, pick one. I pick left. I never go right. It's not my nature. He smiles. It's one of those no-teeth smiles, tight and nervous. Smokers have them. But my father has never smoked. He's a religious man. Very. He slowly brings out the left hand like he's an off-duty magician at a country bar. Wow. It's a large, heavy Bible. King James. Gilded pages. I feel sure it's even autographed. Presenting it into both my hands, he says to the room, an audience of four breathless siblings sitting on the reclaimed couch like frightened nuns, And you thought you were getting a hockey stick. Imagine that.

These are my thoughts as I orgasm into Sarah as I lie underneath her on a satin-covered, king-size bed from Sleep Country downtown.

Somehow, this is what makes me cum, not her breasts, which,

by the way, are out-of-this-world perfect. I won't dwell on them. What's the point? Nobody will believe me anyway.

Oh my God! Eww! She says.

With a little yelp, I suppose, Sarah collapses onto me, and our sweaty bodies meld into a fleshy, hot ... I don't know. Something. Stupid brain. I'm cold and numb. I try to catch my breath, and it's not easy. In fact, I sigh. I try to relax my toes, which strain to poke out from the too-tight sheets pinning me to the bed like an insect — a dead insect, obviously.

Sarah twitches. There's a quiver in her lips, and it's not all that attractive.

I close my eyes. The room smells like chilled lavender and warm beer. Why am I so tuned to smells after sex? What is wrong with me? Jesus.

She whispers, Wow, what were you thinking just then?

I think fast.

I was thinking about us, I lie.

Oh, so was I. So was I!

She plays with my ear, tweaks it, and giggles like a sixteen-year-old on MDMA.

This was awesome, she giggles. Awesome.

Yeah, I know. Awesome.

That's the exact word.

And it was. And we taped it. With her new waterproof camera perfectly positioned on the dresser across from us. Why? Because somehow in my deliriously deranged sex-mad mind I thought this would be a good idea. Memories, right? The good old days.

I think I need better internal thoughts, I think. Why can't I just be normal? Have I always been this ... stupid? Not stupid, rambling? Not rambling, inconsistent? Whatever. Fuck. Me.

Sarah gets up and turns off the camera.

I can barely wait to see how all that turned out, she says.

We'll watch it once, I say. Then erase it.

Absolutely, she says. I wouldn't want it to get out.

I know, I say drunkenly.

But you have some nice moves, Sarah smiles.

Do I? Do I? Nice moves? Really? Like what?

We'll have to see, Big Guy.

I think I have a good finish. I think I do.

Except for the face, Sarah says.

Except for the face, I say. All guys have that face.

Not all of them, Sarah says. Not all.

What?

She then plops herself back onto me in a sweaty heap.

I'm so into you right now, Sarah says.

Studies my face intensely.

Her breath is stale, but not bad considering what we've been doing for the last thirty minutes or so.

Wow, she says, sweetly. Wow, what a night this has been. Right?

Right, I say.

We've captured a moment, Sarah says into my ear. We've captured a beautiful thing. We can't let it go. We shouldn't.

I'd like to see the video, I say.

You're such a film buff, Sarah says. She kisses me.

I can't seem to take a deep enough breath.

I close my eyes. Breathe, I think. Breathe.

My right hand is trapped under her thigh, and Sarah knows it and now nibbles at my chin.

Guess what, you're my prisoner, Sarah says.

It's not the kind of thing any man wants to hear, naked in a near-stranger's bed at midnight on a Friday after several drinks and a very large joint. I'm paralyzed with post-coital relaxation and dope. Also, there was that fucking Tequila. And when Tequila gets into your head, you're mostly doomed.

When I first saw you, I knew we were going to end up together, Sarah says.

Fear in my eyes.

Her bedroom is much like an orbiting space station; the large windows beside the bed only show stars and half of the moon. There's a blue haze over everything, concentrating in a pattern along the ceiling, a reflection — I think — from the screensaver of her open laptop in the corner. It's the spiral called Random, comes with the Mac.

What are you thinking now? Sarah says, touching my lips now with her fingertip. Tell me or I'll scream.

I think I'm a flawed character, I say, trying to free my hand by wiggling it a little.

No, you're not, Sarah hisses. You're wonderful. It's just too bad your wife doesn't see this.

She might see this, I say.

No, she doesn't, Sarah says. And I should know; I'm Anna's best friend. She tells me everything, especially after I get a couple of Manhattans into her. And, let me tell you, all she does is bitch. Oh, I love your cologne … What's that smell?

Head and Shoulders, I say. It's a shampoo.

Wow, who knew, she says. It's awesome. But please don't tell me you have dandruff. I just bought these pillows at Crate & Barrel, and they're two hundred dollars each.

I don't have dandruff, I say. That's why I use that shampoo.

That makes sense, my captain, Sarah squeals. Oh, I can't believe how wet I am. This was the best sex ever, wasn't it?

I hesitate. And it's the hesitation that gets me in the end.

I know there's something going on in your head, Sarah whispers. I want you to tell me. I want you to be honest.

Okay, I say. Okay. I will.

Take a deep breath. Feel it. Feel it.

I'm not sure who said this. Doesn't matter.

I begin. Slowly.

Okay, I haven't done enough good in my life. I mean, God, I've tried to find the light. I mean, I've really tried. I'm a creative person, right, but it hasn't really paid off for me. Other than being really good with actors and spending a shitload of money on useless things. Yes, the people skills come in handy, but I can't maintain it. I can't. Maybe that's the human condition. We just can't do good for long; it's too hard.

Wow, Sarah says. That is some very deep shit. Wow. It's like a fucking monologue.

Sarah pulls herself off me, and our skins don't want to let go. When they peel apart, they make an awful sound in the process.

Why don't you see what we have, Sarah says as she sits up, pulling the sheets up to her chin. We have something here.

Do we?

Of course, we do, she says, trying not to cry. I mean, we connect and we understand each other.

I'm not sure that's enough, I say.

Enough for what?

For it to be something, I try.

It *is* something, Sarah insists. How can you not see that?

It's something, but not enough of a something to be really something, I say. Really.

Sarah tries a smile, but it's probably a wince.

I've tried to be a good person too, Sarah says. I know I'm not a normal person with normal thoughts. It's my brain. It's the way my brain is wired and I hate it. But that's the only brain I have, and this is the only life I have. And your wife is my best friend, and after I met her, I met you, and I thought why can't I have what she has? Why can't I be happy and normal and funny and outgoing, and why can't I be with the person that makes me feel that way because I deserve it? I really deserve it.

I'm sorry, I say. I didn't know.

What are you doing, Andy? What are you doing to me?

I think. I want to run, but my feet are like cement and my head hurts like I've just been swatted with a witch's broom on my left ear, which feels super red and hot. And raw.

I want to leave, I say. But I don't want to leave you alone, either. And, I want to be friends and have a normal relationship with you, but I can't. I know I can't. I've wrecked things. And even though I love — no, admire you, I don't want to be in a relationship with you. I'm sorry.

So, you're fucking me over, is that it?

The top sheet between us is now a sail, and it trembles as Sarah tries to stop herself from hyperventilating. She grabs it tight to her chest, almost to her chin. Very tight. I sit up, freeing both hands and feet from the bottom sheet. And then, for the first time, I also notice the scars on her wrist, both wrists. Sarah sees me see this and immediately hides both hands behind the top sheet.

Closes her eyes because I can't stop staring at her now, particularly the arms. I'm putting two and two together, and it's all kind of obvious. And really, really sad.

What happened? What?

I ask her this while also trying to keep my distance, and it's not easy since we're both naked and in bed.

The room is very blue.

You think I'm crazy, don't you? Sarah says, getting off the bed. She paces around the room. Actually, it's more of a stomp than a pace, like she's carrying two buckets of knives, one in each hand.

I watch her briefly from the safety of the bed.

I am not crazy anymore, Sarah says. I've dealt with my issues. It's taken me five years since my accident.

There was an accident? I ask and immediately regret it.

That's what I'm calling it, Sarah says. An accident. Do you want the fucking details?

No, of course not, I say, looking around the bedroom for my pants. I spot them hanging over the chair in front of her Mac. They look like dead man's pants.

Sarah walks over and pokes me, trying to be playful.

Or hopeful.

You think I'm normal, right?

I wouldn't be with you if you were crazy, I say. Would I?

I playfully try to dodge her pokes, but it looks calculated, fake, stupid. Like me.

Why did you marry Anna? Sarah says. What made you do it?

I don't know, I say. It was a while ago, and I can't remember all the details.

I say this without much thought because it's automatic, but also true.

She was different from all the other girls I was dating, I say, as if this has just occurred to me. Yeah, that's it. She was very different.

Sarah studies me like a plastic surgeon sizing up her next patient's face.

Well, you married her, and she's practically a psychopath, Sarah says, then arches her neck because clearly the room is spinning and she's trying to catch up or maybe she's moving evil thoughts around in her head and trying to spit them out, mainly at me.

She growls. Yes, growls.

I'm at the foot of the bed now.

We stand across from each other like we occupy separate tiny icebergs and there's a lot of cold water between us.

Her naked body looks strangely reptilian, her blue skin sinewy and throbbing like she's trying to cool down, which is probably exactly what she's doing.

You love me, right?

Sarah points at my penis, and I hope it's not intentional.

She says, Tell me you love me.

We hardly know each other. I mean, come on, Sarah.

Say it.

Okay, I say. This is getting too crazy. This situation. Right now, what's happening with us here.

I immediately regret saying crazy.

I move toward the desk and grab my pants, step into them; spot my socks lying on the floor, grab them too; spot my shoes, slip them on quickly because they are expensive super-narrow slip-ons I ordered online; and then telescope my head around searching for my off-black sweater from Eddie Bauer, grab it from the door-knob and throw it over my head. When I pull the sweater down, Sarah is out of the room. I spot her in her kitchen wearing a weird nightgown with a red Komodo on the back. She's totally pissed. The kind of pissed that makes you kick at cats. I can tell because she's grabbed a butter knife from the top of her dish-washer, and she waves it at me like it's Harry Potter's wand. At first

I think she's going to stab the camera she's holding in the other hand. But the knife, apparently, is just an appropriate prop for what happens next.

Fuck you! she says.

Fuck you for doing this to me! She throws down the knife like she's in drama school.

I'm sorry, I say. This wasn't what I wanted. I made a mistake.

I have my hands out like I'm guarding LeBron James. I move, shuffle, edge, sneak toward the front door; she sees me and moves faster, darting ahead and out the door, then slams it.

Fuck, she screams in the hallway. Then nothing.

She runs away. Yeah. Just like that.

What am I doing? What? This is nuts.

I stand in her condo, alone, the blue light around me. No sound. Not even a fridge running or a clock ticking or a mouse stirring. I've just had sex with my wife's best friend, and she's more than a little pissed, and I'm thinking this might be the worst thing I've ever, ever done.

Holy shit, I say to no one in particular. Holy shit.

I take the elevator down to the lobby where a weightlifter wearing a security uniform sits behind a chrome desk looking bored by his iPhone, and I ask the movie question — which way did she go, which way did she go — and he waves me off like I'm a street person. The lobby looks a little like it's been designed by someone from Mars; it's all glass and silver and red, and there's a fake couch made of twisted metal along the side with a strange small table, a prickly plant on it. It's cold in here, freezing, in fact. Blue bulbs drip down from the ceiling like Christmas lights from Canadian Tire. The walls are glass, like aquarium glass, thick and greenish on all sides.

I look outside, and there are a lot of people swimming around out there. It makes sense looking through all that thick green glass, their faces bloated by lensing or something, their limbs akimbo, which is not a word I use lightly.

I should not have mixed my drinks tonight. Really, I shouldn't have. I think I had tequila, then wine, then sparkling wine, beer, then grappa — which was probably the last thing I should have had after smoking a big joint on Sarah's balcony earlier.

You hurry, says the weightlifter. She very, very fast. Zip. Zip. Zip.

He has a Russian accent.

I spot her running between cars, moving cars, on the street, most honking at her and waving fists out windows. She's on a mission.

I push through the heavy glass doors and outside, and she's maybe eighty metres down the busy street.

Sarah, I yell. Sarah!

She pushes past people.

Sarah!

She stops for a second and turns around only to flash me quickly. Then she's off again, this time heading across four lanes of late-night traffic.

I cut between parked Smart Cars and chase after her, and I'm completely shocked by how fast she is in bare feet on cement.

Sarah runs past the ice hockey stadium named after a phone company and across a small park along False Creek where she mixes into a crowd gathering along the shore. Why are there so many people here? What's going on?

There's a bald man wearing a red Adidas tracksuit selling hot-dogs, and I run up to his stand beside the pathway beside the water.

Hey, he says.

Hey. What's going on tonight? I ask this trying to be nonchalant, but really I feel super sweaty and nervous like I've just come off a bender.

It's Australia tonight, mate, he says.

What?

Fireworks. Mate.

It might be the worst Australian accent I've ever heard; it's a little hard to tell with thousands of people murmuring over him.

Yes, it's a maelstrom of murmur.

I look around. Rows of people along the shore, somewhat loosely organized on blankets on the grass. Families and dogs and glow sticks, little kids with headsets on either dancing or trying to stomp on bugs. Everyone gathered around the water as if waiting for the mother ship, eyes to the sky, anxious for the show to begin. There's a hush to it all. Planes blink above.

And then there's a pop pop pop, and the sky lights up with glorious red and green and white bursts of flaming electric colour, which drift down over the heads of the thousands and thousands of people lined up around False Creek. We're all lit for a moment, all gloriously lit, like angels looking up at the sky watching for the Promised One to descend. And I hear "Clocks" by Coldplay start up, bouncing off the mirrored, crowded water and the crystal condos around me and then BOOM, silver with red tracers form flower tendrils above my head. Look up. Look. BOOM. It's amazing and beautiful and, okay, visually arresting, what the hell.

BOOM.

And a cheer goes up. The crowd, as one, reaches up.

I look for the music.

I look across the water.

I lose track of the red Komodo. And Sarah. Crazy, crazy Sarah.

Frozen now. Held to the spot and all that.
Aware only of my beating, shrivelled heart.
The explosions I can feel through my chest.
Boom. Boom.

EIGHTEEN

SOMEONE'S TRYING TO KILL ME, obviously, says Will, facing down the three women sitting across from him on the big couch, and yes, they have their arms crossed.

Deborah finger-pokes the roofie that sits like an after-dinner mint on the Chinese saucer. She's an expert.

I'm an expert, Deborah says. I've seen these pills a lot. And it's lucky I found it on the bathroom sink before any more damage could be done. It's a roofie.

My head hurts, Will says.

That's normal, says Deborah.

And my eyes are itchy, Will says.

Also normal, says Deborah.

I didn't know that was a roofie, says Will. I thought it was my blood pressure pill. I wasn't wearing my glasses.

It's okay, sweetie. Everything's okay, Deborah says.

And with that the cat is out of the bag.

Am I to assume you two are in a relationship? says Grace, petting Prince, who sits in front of her like a panting statue, his ears erect.

No, says Will.

Yes, says Deborah.

There's a moment when we look at each other in disbelief. Holly gets up and off the couch like she could easily levitate, but decides not to and instead gets a kettle.

More tea, anyone?

I stretch out my legs, my wet jeans still sticking to my thighs and covered by pine needles. My hair hurts because, it seems, I've got twigs in it. Lots of twigs. I want to leave the cabin. I want to go back to my boring life in Vancouver. I want to make my movie and spend all my money and become a famous writer slash director and do the festival circuit and answer questions from the audience about my non-existent feature film budget and how I dealt with temperamental actors who hate filming on remote islands. But I'm in the middle of a very bad scheme, and it's only getting worse.

Who would want to give you a roofie? says Deborah to Will, who apparently thinks his flask of whiskey will clear his mind.

That's what I want to know, Will says, pointing his flask at her. What's left of his hair is plastered to his head like he's been standing in a shower.

And why would there be a roofie sitting on the sink? Deborah asks.

That's what I want to know, Will repeats, now waving his flask over his head in mock surrender.

Holly watches us from behind the counter like a very pissed-off judge in juvenile court. I think she thinks she knows. And she probably does. I fidget. She parts her hair, and I can see how intense her eyes are, like they're about to pop out of her skull.

Thunder.

And not normal thunder, but BOOMING consistent thunder of ripples. Fixtures throughout the cabin rattle, and the lights blink off and on quickly as if we've been hit by a torpedo.

A flash from outside the windows temporarily turns the panes into plasma TVs with nothing to show.

Holly doesn't blink.

What do you want in your tea? she says, pointing a very witchy finger at me. What's it going to be?

She has a sing-song voice, the kind of voice that hides behind anxiety or anger.

Andy Man, she says again. I'm talking to you. Look at me. What do you want?

Nothing, I say. Just plain. Just normal.

Holly sighs and wheels around to fill up the stainless-steel kettle from the tap. We don't say much for a second. I can hear Will breathe very deeply like he's walking to shore carrying diving weights.

Wow, he says. What a trip this has turned out to be.

Good material? Deborah asks.

What?

Good material, Deborah continues, for your movie?

Oh, yes, I say. Yes indeed.

I study my jeans and how the wet blotches look like Australia. Why are my knees mainly dry, but not my thighs?

What's your story? Deborah asks.

I pull a twig out of my hair and place it on the coffee table in front of me beside the roofie.

We haven't figured everything out yet; the script is still in development, Will says to the room.

Does one of your characters get roofied? asks Deborah. Then she winks.

No, I say. I don't know anything about that pill.

I didn't ask you that, Deborah says to me quietly. Did I?

Holly comes from behind the counter wielding a large soup spoon. She stands in front of me on the other side of the coffee table.

Was that pill supposed to be for me? she says.

Why would you ask that? says Deborah. And for once I'm glad she's so cop-like.

Well, says Holly, it was on my bathroom sink, right?

You don't use the guest bathroom, do you, Holly? Deborah scans her, studying her face carefully. She's in full investigative mode now, and I bet she has a photographic memory.

Have you used drugs in this place before?

Deborah leans forward after her question as if waiting to pounce.

Holly taps the soup spoon against her thigh, one-two-three times. She's seething. Clearly.

Obviously, a guest has left a pill in one of my bathrooms, Holly says. Obviously.

Deborah now gets up and straightens her bra, looking around the cabin as if searching for evidence.

Who were your last guests? Deborah says.

Telephone guys, Holly answers. They were the ones updating the cell service on the island.

Well, says Deborah, could it have been left by one of them?

No one says anything. The wind picks up. It sounds like it's turbocharged.

Anything is possible, Holly says, just as the kettle starts screaming from the stovetop. I wouldn't put it past my guests to be assholes.

She wheels around, steps on my toes, pulls the kettle off the stove, and efficiently lines up our five cups on five saucers, none of them matching, then throws in five teabags quickly and starts pouring.

Deborah paces like Columbo, the TV detective from the seventies, and shoves her hands deep inside her dark blue cop pants. The pockets.

One must consider, she begins, who would want whom to be rendered senseless? And for what purpose?

Will says, I love watching you think.

Thank you, Will, Deborah says. It's what I'm built for.

She throws her shoulders back and her breasts pop out. I pretend not to notice. Will nods as if keeping beat.

Grace has her camera up and is shooting us, particularly Holly, as she places teacups on a tray and carefully puts it down on the coffee table. Nothing spills. Then, with a slight finger wag, Holly quickly reaches over and pushes the Sony down.

Don't shoot me, Holly says. I don't have my face on.

Prince growls slightly, and everyone is surprised.

I guess he doesn't like me anymore, Holly says to the room. I wonder what happened?

She retreats behind the kitchen counter with her teacup in hand.

We listen to the wind for a moment, the howls rising in pitch.

I'm curious to know why someone would intentionally leave a roofie on my sink, Holly says. What kind of man would do that?

What makes you think it was a man?

Deborah asks this from across the room, looking out the window at the branches waving like drunken sailors coming home from an Australian tour.

Don't be ridiculous, Holly says. Why would a woman have a drug like that around?

There's plenty of anecdotal evidence that women have used roofies too, particularly lesbians, Deborah says. Then she wheels around.

But you're not one of those, are you?

Holly just shakes her head and mouths *unbelievable.*

I sip my tea and taste it for poison.

Will pours the contents of his flask into his cup, pockets it — the flask — and then tentatively tastes his tea.

My Earl Grey is perfecto, Will says to the room, then slugs it back. The wind suddenly dies down and rain stops hammering the roof.

My head is starting to clear, he says. Thank God … I thought I was Alice in *Alice in Wonderland*, and, let me tell you, it wasn't a good trip. I saw gnomes and fairies and wee folk sitting in branches with pointy hats and green fucking faces. Not a pretty sight, that's for sure. I guess I better stick to alcohol, preferably a good Merlot.

He laughs. He's the only one. So, he stops.

Holly sweeps by and sits on the couch with Grace, then straightens her dress, still muddy along the bottom edge from the forest walk. She sips her tea like a queen taking a break from beheadings.

I'll tell you what I think, Holly says to everyone. Someone had plans to take one of us to dreamland — why?

I've already been to dreamland, Will says. I wouldn't take that trip again if you paid me.

Usually, people use roofies for an opportunity to commit sexual assault, Deborah says. She holds her teacup away from her body as if it's filled to the brim with contraband. So, the question becomes, who among us was the intended victim and why?

Wow, says Will. You are the best cop I've ever met outside of film and TV. Brilliant.

It's then I notice Deborah has Holly's guest comment book in hand. She pages through it slowly, then stops.

I see Sarah stayed here, Deborah says.

Who's Sarah? says Holly.

Sarah is the woman who went missing while kayaking in the fall of last year. You helped look for her.

Holly bites her lip.

She didn't stay here, she had brunch here.

Deborah walks over to Holly and places the book in her lap, as delicately as if it were planked salmon.

Deborah says, Read it.

Oh please, do we have to be so theatrical?

Read it, insists Deborah.

Holly gives a thin smile and reads it.

I like this place, sweetie. Let's stay in touch. We'd make a lovely combination, that's for sure. Sarah.

Holly slaps the book shut.

So what?

So what, Deborah says. "Sweetie?" "Combination?"

Holly sighs. She studies the ceiling. Look, she says. Lots of people eat here. It's no big deal, but most of them stay at the yoga centre in town; that place has a bunch of rooms and a huge dining room. Sarah stayed there once. She stopped in here for something to eat with her friend Anna. We hit it off. She calls everyone "sweetie." She also thought we were a lot alike. We both hate men, for example. Especially those who cheat.

Holly directs the last part of that at me. She's a cannon of innuendo. And she hardly ever misses.

My wife, I say. She stopped in with my wife?

Holly looks at me.

Wow, I didn't know you were so married. Did you ever mention that?

I'm sure I mentioned it when we did the search for Sarah along the beach with you. You know, me and the woman who was my wife? The one with the diamond ring whom I referred to as "my wife?" You know, the one called Anna. My wife. You fucking met her.

Well, you could have treated her with more attention and not like she's just another woman, Holly spits.

We were looking for a body so I was a little preoccupied, okay? I yell.

That silenced the room completely.

I have a lousy memory, Holly says. Why are you getting so mad? You got something to hide?

Just my true anger, I say. And, trust me, you don't want to see that.

Oh, grow up, Holly says.

Okay, okay, says Deborah. Let's not get caught up in semantics. I think we should plan a visit to the yoga centre.

What exactly are you investigating? says Holly. I thought you were on vacation.

You think me showing up here was just an accident? I'm not really on vacation. I'm working.

Deborah says this to the room, and the room is very quiet now.

She looks at me as if I was in on it all along.

I say wow.

The RCMP is smarter than that. I'm here because I'm working on a case, and that case is the disappearance of a woman while kayaking. Obviously. But I'm human too. And I can't deny feelings or connections, can I?

She walks over to Will. Touches his face. It's romantic.

Nice, says Will. I love watching you figure shit out. As long as it doesn't involve me. And, by the way, I'm completely innocent of all charges.

Then Deborah kisses him on the forehead just below a dead patch of skin.

Will turns very, very red.

Oh boy, he croaks. Oh boy …

Time and space stretch out slowly.

Thunder in the distance, perfectly timed.

Will wipes the spot where Deborah's lips were.

He reaches in his pocket and pulls out a blood pressure pill. While everyone stares, he throws it in the air like it's slow-motion popcorn and catches it in his mouth. He swallows with a pronounced gulp.

What?

Will looks around at us, mostly because our mouths are open in surprise.

NINETEEN

WE MAKE CAMP AT BLISS Landing. It's maybe ten kilometres from Cortes Island. There's nothing here but rock and trees and maybe some eagles, but it's got a nice beach where we can run up the kayaks and pitch our Canadian Tire tents with ease.

I can describe the place as typical because a lot of things look the same in these waters: lots of very green and spindly fir trees, lots of off-white rock, lots of grey water. And starfish. A lot of them are dead; not a good sign.

Once the kayaks are in, we walk around to look for solid ground to peg up the tents. We want somewhere toward the shelter of the trees, away from the water. I don't really walk; I mainly limp — my legs are cramped from sitting in a stupid kayak and paddling for three hours across open water. My feet feel like cucumbers. My breath smells like cheese or moldy bread. I'm dying for a sandwich.

I walk with Sarah because she walks with me, and I notice she's not really looking for a place to put up her tent; she just wants to talk things over. With me. I really don't encourage this.

I want to talk things over, she says to me.

Are you vaping?

Yes, don't tell the others, Sarah says. I've been dying for a smoke for the full five days now. I can't believe we've paddled for that long. My arms are ready to fall off. And my neck feels like someone ran a cheese grater over it.

Stop vaping, I say. Others will notice. I mean, what is that flavour anyway?

Maple, Sarah says. Maple walnut.

No, it's not, I say. What is it really?

Sarah says, Can I give you a suck? It's fucking delish.

No, I say. Look, we're looking for a lookout so we can look out over the water from our tents. So look out for the look out.

Say that again real fast three times, Sarah laughs, then grabs me by the arm and turns very serious, very quickly.

If Anna and I were both drowning at the same time, who would you rescue?

Drowning? How?

Like we fell out of our kayaks because of a big wave, a freak wave, Sarah says. Or maybe the wake of a passing oil tanker has dunked us. And there are sharks, baby. Sharks everywhere.

No sharks, Sarah.

I notice how serious I sound.

I look back at our landing party, around sixty metres back where the rocks meet water. Count nine kayaks pulled up. Colin, the voice actor with the crazy eyes and red helmet, is still on the water, about twenty metres out. He's looking at the starfish near the big rock with Rastafarian seaweed guarding our beach.

They're mostly dead, Colin yells. What is going on with the starfish out here? They're dead. All dead.

His voice carries like it's been aided by a megaphone, but then, he's a professional.

The others wave at him to come in, including Anna, who has removed her yellow waterproof jacket and who I now see is searching for me. I wave a little when I catch her eye, trying to point out a flat patch of ground to pitch our tent on about thirty metres from the shore.

What makes her special to you? Sarah asks. What?

We do a lot of things together, I say. And she's up for anything. We're a team.

That's not a real reason to be with someone. That kind of sounds like a line-mate, Sarah says, picking up a small boulder nearby and weighing it as if it were my brain. She tosses it aside.

What makes it work for you? she says. You think?

I don't want to answer. Instead, I try to move branches from the hard ground and toss them back into the trees to clear the place for the tent. Tufts of long grass stick out from the sandy ground. I rip some out.

Well? Sarah pokes me.

I think whatever you're getting at shouldn't be gotten at out here, I say. I mean, it's bad enough you've planned this trip with my wife after what's transpired between us.

And exactly what has transpired between us? Sarah asks, blowing vapour directly at my face.

Don't be an asshole, please, I say. I'm allergic to smoke.

This isn't smoke, Sarah laughs. It's all in your mind. By the way, what's going on in yours right now?

I study the trees. Behind them, the rocks pile up to a small hill rising up maybe fifty metres or so, as if some giant wall of ice pushed them away at some point. The rocks beyond the trees are covered in lichen and look slippery. The whole beach might be two or three hundred metres across. The rocks cut the wind.

I can tell Sarah watches me. But I ignore her.

You thinking of an escape? Sarah asks.

No, I say. I love it here, really I do.

But I don't.

Sorry about saying suck to you, Sarah says. But you know what I mean, right?

Right?

Anna joins us, and she's very limber for someone who has just been stuck in a little boat with her legs half-bent for a very long time.

Hey, she says bouncing up and tossing her mousy hair. What's up?

She then touches her toes effortlessly.

Isn't this just the best trip ever? Anna gushes. Then she stretches out grabbing at the sky.

Everything out here is so fresh and innocent, she adds. Don't you think?

Where did you go? I ask. You're supposed to be picking out a place for the tent.

I was taking a pee, Anna says, then adds, I like this spot for the tent. Right here. Perfect.

Sarah wipes at the hair sticking to her mouth, and I notice the vaper thingy is gone.

Sarah says. What do you think? Should we sleep together?

Yes, Anna says. We could put your tent right next to ours. As long as you don't mind me snoring. I tend to do that when I'm in the great outdoors. Plus I sleep on my back because my right shoulder hurts too much so there's no spooning going on whatsoever.

Oh, I love spooning, Sarah says to the world. I just love it. Are you good at it?

Are you talking to me? I ask.

Yes, of course I am, sweetie, Sarah says, grabbing Anna's arm like they're pairs figure skaters now.

So?

Yeah, I say. I love spooning. It's so intimate and everything.

Who do you think would be a better spoon girl?

Sarah poses with Anna and both stick out their boobs. Then they both laugh.

Oh, this is so funny, Sarah says. We're competing for your love.

That is funny, I say backing away slowly.

I walk away to the kayaks because this is getting too weird too fast. And this has been the pattern for the last five days and counting. I knew this trip was going to be a nightmare from the start — and it became a much bigger nightmare when Sarah showed up at the departure gate with her paddling gear in tow.

I go back to the landing spot. To the beach.

My kayak smells like plastic and tuna and it's not pleasant. I pull off the gear from the straps and fish around for the packed tent. I straighten up for a minute to rest my back, and I see the other paddlers, all shouting and pointing to Colin, who is slowly beaching his craft.

Behind him, maybe fifteen metres off, a large orca dorsal fin cuts through the surface.

Emma, our fearless leader, holds her paddle above her head as if to silence us. And we are silent. Colin isn't aware of what's going on, but he knows something is amiss. Just as his craft scrapes the rocky surface, he turns around to see the very large killer whale skim by like a Japanese mini-sub, soundless and slow, its dark, shadowy shape just under the surface.

A gull screams.

Holy shit, Colin says. Holy shit. Somebody help me get out of here.

I do a zombie walk down to him not taking my eyes off the water around him, scanning for other orcas because they travel in pods. I don't see anything else, but it doesn't matter. Colin scrambles to get out, awkwardly wobbling his craft so that it almost tips over. The water around the kayak shivers. I wade out down the slippery rock and reach out my hand to help him. It's then that he flops out and lands on his ass hard and almost up to his waist in the cold water.

Shit, he yells. Get me out of here!

Emma reaches down, paddle in hand and pulls on me pulling on Colin, and we yank him up onto the rock just as the orca glides by for a second look. All three of us are now sitting on the rock, our toes barely in the water. One of us might be crapping his pants.

Everyone stay calm, Emma says. You might want to take some photos to post on Facebook. This is amazing.

Colin looks at me. He's shivering and cold and scared.

I think I may have soiled my trousers, he says with a stiff British accent.

You're lucky then that you fell in the water, I say.

My dear friends, I didn't think this trip would be so life-changing, he says. Carry on. Ignore the trousers, if you can.

He announces this to the whole group in an Indian accent now so I shove him back in the water a little, and we both laugh like robots. Then we stop laughing and look out at the water. We see fins.

Yikes, Colin says. We're being hunted, you know. Not nice. Not nice at all, fellows.

The orca drifts toward the big rock guarding our landing spot. Then with a flash, it's gone.

We both stand up and inch back away from the water.

Maybe it's a sign, Colin says.

Of what?

That Mother Nature is watching us, he says.

Why, I ask. What did we do?

Take a look around, Colin says. We're warming the planet and killing off species. I think it's obvious, old chap.

We're not doing that personally, Emma says to Colin and the group. We're here to preserve nature. To enjoy it.

And only three grand each, Colin mutters. It's a steal of a deal. Look, all I'm saying is humans are ruining everything for future humans. I have four boys. You think they'll come out here in the middle of nowhere to find themselves? Not if we keep doing what we're doing. They might as well stay at home, drink beer, and watch Netflix.

The others perch on several large boulders around the rocky beach, still wearing their life preservers and helmets. No one talks, but some check their phones to see if they got that special shot of the swim-by.

An eagle passes soundlessly overhead and heads to the trees where Anna and Sarah speak in hushed tones, trying to start a fire inside a ring of rocks. Nothing is happening, and it's getting dark fast, the sun now behind the horizon and the wind picking up.

Colin notices I'm still holding his hand. Weird. He pushes my hand away.

It's then we both notice a looming oil tanker along the horizon. It's red and belching black smoke.

Where did that come from? Colin says.

There seem to be more and more of them all the time, I say. Why are they here?

Why am I here? Colin says. That's the bigger question.

He digs out his camera and starts filming the oil tanker, zooming the zoom until he can't zoom anymore.

Proof, he says under his breath. Proof. There you have it, mister.

I back away, pick up my gear and head back to Anna and Sarah. The others around me go back to unpacking too. Some people are very excited, and others are a little scared. Faith, a rotund psychologist from the University of Texas, says, I don't think we're in Kansas anymore.

She says this to her somewhat rotund daughter, Kayla, a teenager with the biggest, brownest eyes I've ever seen, and Kayla just nods. She's never been outside her state until this trip, and she's never seen fish as big as that orca. She shivers so hard it kind of looks like she's an unbalanced clothes washer.

Anna waves at me to come to the tent.

Behind the tents is an incline of boulders that goes up sixty metres or so. A small knot of stone, a grey bundle of watch your step.

Sarah stands there in her yellow Gore-Tex, hands in her pockets, her eyes watering over. Her matching yellow gumboots, lined with mud, tremble.

There's something wrong, Sarah says. We shouldn't be here.

I look around.

We're safe here, I say. Orcas can't walk. They haven't evolved enough.

I think this is a fine joke, but Sarah isn't happy. Her face is red in places where red normally doesn't go: her chin, her neck. It's then I realize she's cut the tip of her chin and blood drips down.

What happened to your chin? Anna says, wiping Sarah's neck with a tissue.

I fell, Sarah says. I fell in those rocks.

She points behind us to the knoll of boulders, and then she's off, stumbling up the hill, one stone to another, picking her way up.

What are you doing? Anna says. Where are you going?

I need to go, Sarah says. I need to leave. Now!

I look at Anna, who looks at me.

What did you say to her?

I didn't say anything, I say. I was watching the killer whale troll Colin until he crapped his pants.

What did you say to Sarah today? Earlier?

I didn't say anything, I say. I was busy paddling.

You must have done something. What did you do?

I have no idea what's going on, I say. I've been in my own head all day.

Anna goes after Sarah, picking her way up the stones, hopping one after another, pausing briefly between hops to pick out her landing spot.

Where are you going? Anna yells. Sarah?

Sarah ignores her, quickly making her way up, much steadier on her feet than I would have imagined.

Emma, our group leader, wanders over.

What seems to be the problem?

Nothing, I say.

It doesn't look like nothing, Emma says.

Look, I say. We're all tired. We've been paddling for hours today and everybody's on edge, that's all.

Then Emma goes after Anna, who is falling behind Sarah quickly. I can barely feel my feet — only my heels have warmth, my toes are still numb. Colin joins us.

What's going on?

We have a train of climbing women, I say.

Why?

I don't know, I say. But it seems urgent.

We follow the gaggle of gumboots, picking our way up like we're doing crosswords with rocks. Above us, Sarah is out on a ledge looking like a superhero about to fly. Her jacket flutters like a buttoned-down cape. She throws her sunglasses off, but since they're tied around her neck with a rubber cord they just bounce back.

I catch up quickly. Colin huffs and puffs his way past me and says, Blimey this is hard.

With an accent, of course.

I almost bump into his smelly ass because he's slower than I thought and he straightened up unexpectedly to catch his breath.

Watch it, he warns. I'm not as spry as I once was.

Move it, I say. Come on, that's my wife up there, and she's on the edge.

I see Anna as she coaxes Sarah down from the ledge. Or tries.

Come down now, she's saying. As if speaking the obvious will lead to obvious decisions.

But it doesn't. Obviously.

Sarah isn't listening to anyone right now. Instead, she holds her hands out as if testing the air around her, feeling for something indelible. And it's true, there is something in the air tonight, ask Phil Collins.

I tell this joke to Colin and he stares at me.

This is not the time to try to be funnier than me, he says.

Sarah now waves her arms. She's in a giant blender, apparently.

What are you doing? Anna shouts now.

Sarah, what are you doing?

This is the way it ends, Sarah says cryptically. Out here in the middle of nowhere with everybody watching and nobody really caring, this is the way it ends.

It's not going to end, Anna says, waving at me with one finger.

I push aside Colin and Emma and move toward the ledge where Sarah stands poised to take flight.

Hey, I say. What do you think you're doing?

Sarah looks at me. It's a dead, empty stare.

You of all people know why I'm doing this, Sarah says to the whole wide world.

What does she mean by that? Anna asks. What's going on?

What's going on is she's obviously having a breakdown, I say. Come on.

This is all your fault, Sarah screams at me. Fuck you!

I freeze. I'm maybe three body lengths away from her now on the same ledge, but Sarah has managed to creep closer to the edge, and the edge leads to a drop of thirty feet down. I know I'm mixing up my measurements here, but I can only think in metres and feet, not metres and centimetres. It's a product of transitional education; when they made the switch to metric in school and it confused the shit out of me as a child. Beneath us, lots of sharp rocks and a few lonely spruce. Or firs. I don't know.

Do you know what the fuck you've done to me? Sarah screams at me. Do you?

I look around at the others, thinking that maybe one of the group will save me. It won't be Colin, I just met him. And he's a wise-ass. It can't be Anna; she never saves me from anything. Suddenly though, Emma steps onto the ledge beside me and bless her for being my angel, bless her for saying something nobody thought of until this very moment.

Sarah, honey, Emma says, what were you taking before this trip that you're not taking now?

A moment as we all realize what's being asked.

I notice the rest of our group gathered at the bottom, a small Gore-Tex murder of colour along the pale grey of the rocks. Some stand with paddles still in hand; others sit like they're Roman gladiators on individual stone seats to watch us send somebody to their death. Some of them have their smart phones out and are filming vertically and this irritates me. I want to tell them to please shoot horizontally like you're supposed to. Idiots.

What were you taking that you didn't take with you on this trip? Emma says again.

Sarah looks around wide-eyed and, naturally, desperate. It's the look of a fawn after stumbling onto a highway in the winter. Motherless. And cold.

There's a part of me that wants to grab Sarah and jump over the edge too. Maybe aim for a tree and hope for the best. But there's also a part of me that wants to run to my kayak and head out to open sea never to be seen again.

Sarah? Emma pleads.

The wind pushes Sarah's hair back from her face. She looks like a nine-year-old who's playing dress-up with her mother's clothes because she actually shrinks a little, gathers herself in like a turtle and closes her eyes to think and then very clearly answers.

Lithium.

Fuck.

And for the first time in my life, I know what it's like to be very happy when someone's actions are roundly dismissed as obviously crazy and not your fault. *My* fault.

Even though deep in my soul I know it is.

What kind of person does this? What does it take to betray your wife with her best friend and confidante?

Emma now moves toward Sarah and calmly puts her hand around her waist. She wipes a strand of hair away from Sarah's face.

That cut must hurt like crazy, Emma says. Maybe I can put a Band-Aid on it. You've lost a lot of blood. You must be dizzy.

I am dizzy, Sarah says. I'm very dizzy.

Sarah tries to right herself using her hands as stabilizers in the air. It makes her look like she's suddenly about to fall, and that's when Emma steadies her.

There, there, she says. There. There.

Emma guides her past me, her arms around Sarah like she's an ocean buoy and the waves are huge.

Watch your step, Emma tells her politely. You don't want to trip and fall.

Sarah nods.

But you already did that, right?

Sarah nods.

Does your head hurt?

And Sarah nods as she passes me, and when she does, I notice the back of her head. There's a small gash at the top of her skull, and blood is mixing with blond hair, streaking it. I realize her fall was bigger than anyone thought.

When did you fall? Emma asks.

When I went to pee in the woods, Sarah says. I didn't want anybody to know. I was squatting down and then I fell, and when I tried to get up I sorta fell again.

How awful, Emma says, moving Sarah gingerly down the rocks, picking her way carefully, past Colin who looks slightly dazed, past Anna who looks fairly pissed, and toward the rest of the group now mobilizing to gather poor Sarah up. Some of them are holding their arms open as if hugs will solve everything. They form a doughnut of sanity around Sarah, some of them now with hands on her shoulders as if trying to keep her from bouncing away. Sarah bobs slightly in the middle like she's being juiced with tiny shocks from a used car battery.

This is not normal for me, everybody, Sarah says. Can we not make a big deal of it? Please!

And then Faith, the psychologist from Texas, begins the diagnosis earnestly by asking about the dosage of the lithium and then finding out Colin, our group comedian, also happens to be taking the same drug. The trick was the dosage, it seems.

I'm on very little lithium, Colin says later around the fire. Like the same dosage you'd give a child. And I only take it once every two or three days if I remember. But I can't drink wine with it … especially Merlot.

I'm not sure I'd give lithium to a child, says Faith. But without knowing the exact dosage I'd be reluctant to give Sarah anything more than the bare minimum.

The others around the fire murmur in agreement. And Sarah is given a glass of Canada Dry Ginger Ale and a small, salmon-coloured pill from Colin's precious stash of lithium.

To your health, Colin says, handing the pill over.

Cheers, she says, gulping it down and then hiccupping horribly.

Sorry about all this. You must think I'm crazy, Sarah says to the group.

We eat a dinner of the fried salmon we caught earlier in the day. Emma found wild rosemary, and we're using the branches as skewers. It's all very civilized even though we are three hours away from any physical help and probably ten hours away from any psychiatric help and probably a lifetime away from any spiritual help.

I feel completely stupid about everything, Sarah says. I don't want you to worry about me. This isn't anything new for me. And, it will pass for sure. It's just that I hate the wide-open spaces in particular, and it fucks with my mind, you know? Especially being out here in the middle of nowhere, and you realize how small you are and who your best friends are. And, some of you know what I'm talking about, right?

My face feels hot — but then, so must everyone else's.

The flames paint our faces an awful orange, as if we are savages, but in really nice gear from Mountain Equipment. Nobody wants to talk except for Sarah, and she's just getting started. The rest of us? Mostly we dip our empty skewers into the fire and watch the cackling flames lick at them until smoke hits us. A few of us cough. It's a bit chilly, but not so cold because of the dense, low-hanging clouds we can barely see above us. When the moon shines through, we understand how small we are on this tiny beach, this Salish Sea, this little blue planet third from the sun.

Faith watches Sarah carefully, trying to judge the limits of crazy. I know this is not a good way to describe mental illness, but, on this trip, I've become much more hollow and less sensitive, not at all what my wife hoped for. I've been disappointing her for decades. Two of them.

I'm aware of her at my elbow, sipping on lemon-infused tea from the foldable metal cup she purchased at Canadian Tire along with her waterproof and insulated Patagonia Torrent-shell Jacket and her Outdoor Research Carrie Beanie.

While she is pleased with her purchases, she is not pleased with me. I'm Metro Marvin to her Wilderness Wanda. You want proof? I'm wearing cotton jeans made in Vietnam; she's wearing reflective, waterproof pants from Germany. I've brought along a cellphone that needs recharging; she has a Leatherman that can saw down small trees. I brought six cans of Coke Zero with me instead of a proper filtration system for locally sourced water. And for snacks, I filled my pockets with Mars Bars while she has waterproof plastic bags of trail mix you have to order special from Hawaii, and, yes, the nuts are wonderful and delicious — I've been stealing them all trip. So far, a few days in, Anna regularly poops on bark or small stones and then flings her feces discreetly into the ocean without getting any human discharge on her. I've been crapping on the beach using logs as toilets.

Anna is in her element when she faces extinction in the wilderness. I'm good at theatre openings when my ex shows up. I'm good at picking out the right wine for dinners with poached trout and rocket salad, and she's good at hugging unemployed environmental activists going through trauma over pipelines. And dogs. She's excellent with dogs. And old people. Like really old, old people who just want to hold your hand and talk a lot.

You're such a nice, nice girl, they all say.

Now, with the flames dancing on her giant cheekbones, Anna honestly looks happy, even though her best friend has sort of lost her mind.

One more day out on the water, Anna announces blissfully to our group.

One more day, others murmur back. Some of them raise their metal mugs. Some just grunt. It's a little medieval. We have the dirt on our faces; we have the scars and bandages; the sore arms from chopping at water; and we have very sharp knives on our belts, purchased at our local Home Depot.

Beside Anna, Sarah hums. Not a song. Just a mindless tune like a nervous American golfer who cheats on his income tax, hanging over a four-foot putt. She's kneeling and rocking, eyes closed.

She tries to straighten out the song. Give it melody instead of chaos. But it's a process and it sounds bad. And given my sexual history with her, it's a dreadful thing to hear. Dreadful. It's definitely the calm before the storm. And really, really off-key.

Betrayal, Sarah snorts suddenly, her eyes wide open and blazing like lasers. Have we talked about that yet?

We all look at each other. Somebody please take this on, each of us thinks.

Have we?

Sarah looks at me fiercely.

Have we? she asks again.

Anna says, Maybe you want to handle this one, Faith.

Faith sighs.

I really didn't think I'd need my thinking cap on this trip, Faith says.

Colin farts a little. He apologizes.

Betrayal, Sarah now shouts. We're talking about betrayal, right?

I think we can all agree that we're here to have fun, Faith says. To enjoy the great outdoors and to let this natural energy fulfill us. I'm not sure we want to get into the canyons and crevices of betrayal, Sarah dear.

Here's the thing, Sarah says. When you trust someone with your heart and soul, when you become intimate and vulnerable and give away your secrets, what do you expect back?

From whom?

Faith holds up her skewer like a question mark. It's bent, obviously.

From the person who loves you.

Sarah looks around as if to study our lying faces, only to affix her gaze on me.

I pretend to think of an intelligent answer, but I've got nothing.

You're such a fake, Sarah says suddenly.

Of course, I'm a fake. I produce and direct TV ads, I say. That's the nature of my business. But I'm also a storyteller, and sometimes stories have sad endings because betrayal makes it so. And, betrayal is the fundamental cornerstone of every great story. Ask Shakespeare. Or Mamet.

You know what, Sarah says. This is not a story, and we are not characters. We are real people on a real fucking journey. And real people have real feelings. Don't pretend that you don't know what's going on here.

Sarah stands in front of the fire now as if she is our tribal leader. She has her hands on her hips. Faith watches her carefully and picks up Kayla's Thermos and then gets up and walks over.

Drink this, she says.

Why?

It'll help calm you down, Faith says. It's valerian root tea.

I don't drink alien tea, Sarah says pointing to the sky. Keep that shit away from my lips, all right?

It's not an alien tea, Faith smiles to the group. It's my daughter's. She finds it helps her sleep at night because her dad left us without saying a word last Christmas right after we opened our gifts in the morning.

No one says anything.

It's special tea. And you should drink it. Now. Please.

A moment under the stars and cold, stretches.

Into.

A.

Pause.

Even Sarah looks surprised. But then recovers slightly, takes the Thermos and slugs some back like she's in a saloon.

Yeah, it's good, Sarah says wiping her mouth. Those Valerians know their tea. I like it, but it could use some Scotch.

Colin raises a plastic Scotch bottle.

I have bloody good Scotch, he says with a Scot's accent. Glenlivet. Twelve glorious years old.

And you're not sharing until now? I say, laughing a little too loud.

You pretentious asshole, Sarah says to me. Unbelievable.

The group laughs a little now, not realizing it wasn't meant to be funny.

Sarah slugs back more valerian like she's a deep-sea mariner on a bender in Calcutta. And then, argh, throws the Thermos down and lights up a vape pipe. She throws back her head as if loosening the grip of a hidden octopus. Then shakes her head like her eyeballs might pop out if she tried hard enough.

Fuck me, she says.

Anna says, Come on Sarah, everything is going to be okay. Just relax.

Sarah backs into the flames a little too close. A big log has caught flame, and it licks up at the night sky like a fiery lizard.

Faith intercedes.

Would you like to sit down over here away from the flames? Faith asks. It's safer.

Faith gets up gingerly and moves toward Sarah. Faith's hands are open and at her sides. She smiles a little. It's like negotiating with a cat.

Please sit with me. I sense your frustration. And it's okay to be frustrated.

You have some concerns that we should discuss as a group, Faith says. Right?

I don't like you, Sarah says calmly, but I appreciate your connection with the Valerians. They're good people wherever they're from. But here's the thing, I come to you with a heavy heart, obviously, and one that makes me question the tenets of love.

We all question love, I say, then instantly realize I've made things worse, much worse.

Sarah turns to me slowly, like her head is the turret of an Abrams battle-tank and with the fire now smoking hugely it's like a movie effect — in fact, the whole scene has a big-screen feel to it out here in the middle of the ocean on a tiny, rocky beach.

This is what I do for distraction, but it isn't —

You piece of shit, Sarah screams. You lying, stupid piece of shit!

Then she lunges at me from across the fire pit, knocking Anna flying into Kayla, who has only now picked up her empty Thermos, and it's only because Colin stands up to put away his Scotch that he manages to catch Sarah in mid-pounce.

Whoa, he says. Gotcha girl.

Sarah tries to ward him off, but he's a bear of a man and wraps her in his arms like she's his long-lost daughter.

Don't, he says. Don't do that. Please.

She tries to knock his head off, but can't free her arms.

Let me go!

And then the group closes in around Sarah, who kicks and flails, screaming at us to fuck the hell off and to then to fuck ourselves or vice versa. I just sit there, watching the madness unfold like a poker player with two red queens down, waiting for the river card.

Fuck you all, Sarah screams as they haul her away to her tent.

I take three or four very deep breaths and shudder.

My eyes water to the edge.

My hands glued into my pockets.

I'm a shit. I'm a shit. I'm a total shit, and it's all coming back to haunt me like I knew it would.

Like I knew it would.

Fuck. Me.

I hate kayaking.

I hate myself.

How did I get this way? What was it that made me a total shit? I mean, even JFK had affairs, and Alec Baldwin screams at his daughter, and I'm sure my wife has thought about cheating on me. Isn't that just as bad? I mean, what if our life is just a journey of ups and downs and good and bad decisions? Why should we be so hard on ourselves? Why? Aren't we supposed to experience the most our short lives can provide? Isn't it important to forge as many important relationships as possible? Doesn't the wide range of life experiences make us more complicated and artistic humans? Are we really built to be monogamous? I don't think so.

I hear Sarah scream FUCK OFF!

It's not something you hear a lot of in the middle of nowhere, but there's something profane about swearing that loud in a world this perfect.

FUCK YOU!

They take Sarah to her tent. They guide her, I guess. No, they drag her there. It's slippery and Emma falls down and swears.

Shit!

Can we just slow down, please, Emma says. Can we slow down and take a second? It's slippery out here.

Sarah tries to slap somebody, but can't free up an arm because two people on each side of her hold them like they've studied bouncers at Guns N' Roses concerts.

Faith tells us not to say anything.

We understand you're having a difficult time, Faith says. You're doing the best you can, right? We want to make sure nobody gets hurt, that's all.

Nobody should get hurt.

Please.

They pop her into her tent like a bagel goes into a toaster.

And that's that.

We take turns guarding Sarah's tent.

Anna and I take the second shift after Sarah begins to quiet. We have a little candle to keep us lit and somewhat warm. Occasionally, the breeze picks up and threatens to blow the light out. But it doesn't. It's probably one a.m. or so before one of us speaks.

What did you do? What did you actually do? Anna asks.

Anna looks me over carefully. Her hands cup her face because she sits cross-legged on a very flat rock easily and rests her elbows on her knees. Four years of Pilates has made her incredibly flexible.

I didn't think it would come to this, Anna says. I thought we were ...

She trails off, and I think I know where she's going with this.

I decide the best defence is a good offence.

You had a relationship with her, didn't you? I ask.

Anna looks me over trying to decide whether I have inside information or whether I'm just playing out the hand.

She holds her fingers above the slight wavering candle as if trying to catch the flickering heat between them or feeling for truth.

There's obviously more to this than you can imagine, Anna sighs.

I have a fairly robust imagination, I say, trying to be clever.

I didn't intend for anything to happen, Anna says. It was never supposed to be that way.

But it did.

Did you initiate it? I ask.

Anna thinks about her answer now. She looks over at Sarah's tent, then back at the wavering candle.

Not really, Anna says. It was a bit of a surprise when it went that far. And, here's the weird thing: it kinda happened in the middle of an argument about you.

I feign surprise.

Me? That's weird, I say. Wow.

I sit on a makeshift wooden stool we found behind an abandoned canvas tent nearby earlier. It wobbles slightly because one of the legs is too short. But I like the sound it makes when it moves against the rock. It's a nice way to dissipate anxiety.

Tap-tap, tap-tap.

Anna reaches out and steadies me.

You know what I find strange, she says quietly.

What?

That you aren't more upset, dear.

I feel Anna's grip on my arm tighten. I hope for a squeeze of forgiveness, but I don't get it. I get the vice instead.

Anna studies my face now. I don't like it when she does this. Not at all.

Look at me, Andy. Look at me, she says into my right ear.

I look. Anna's face is kindly. And in the candlelight, even slightly angelic. It's maybe ten inches away from mine. Wow, are her lips red, I think. Blood red.

What did you do to Sarah that got her so upset tonight? Because that was some weird shit that came out. At you. Specifically.

Oh boy.

I try to think of the right words. Or wise words. Actually, any words.

All I come up with is …

I thought we were friends and … and … I'm a …

Anna waits for me to finish, but I'm spent. I don't have the energy. I can't find a complete sentence to save my life. I'm a coward. Really, when you think about it, I'm a fucking coward.

I might have actually said that aloud.

Coward. Part. Yeah.

There you have it, I guess. There it is.

That's it, Anna asks.

That's it, I say.

Wow.

So, we sit there, watching a tiny candle flicker inside of a tiny can — a Tim Hortons coffee can actually — on the rocks, listening to the steady breathing coming from Sarah's tent beside us, under a somewhat cloudless night in the middle of nowhere, hoping no more hurtful words will land.

The candle threatens to die, but it defies the odds and stays lit even when the wind suddenly picks up from behind.

Anna takes back her hand.

My arm hurts where she grabbed it.

Then our shift is over, and Colin takes over wearing new pants.

And when morning breaks one of us notices wolf paw prints in the sand all over. Like everywhere.

Wolves, Emma tells the group as we gather for morning coffee. They've been watching us. Watch your backs.

Emma has a stick and pokes the footprints tenderly.

A whole pack of them, Emma says. Probably six or seven, at least. And this one is a big fella. Look at the size of his mitts.

She bends down to study them, her red rainproof jacket catching the wind.

Look.

We cluster to view in an ad hoc grouping and cluck our tongues. A group of terrified humans is not a group you want to be in. People don't breathe right and suddenly you're aware of sweat. And it smells.

Wow, Anna says. They've been here the whole time. Wolves. Weird. How could we not be aware of this?

Kayla looks around.

I didn't see them, she says innocently. So maybe it didn't happen last night. Maybe we just didn't notice the paw prints before.

Emma looks at Faith — Kayla's mother — weighing what to say next.

They were always here, Emma says. And they knew we were here. But let's not forget that wolves are just about the smartest predator out there.

Faith says, I'm not sure that makes any of us feel any better, Emma.

Colin stares at the prints and shakes.

I'm not a wolf man, he says. Not a bit.

He says this in the voice of an old vampire. And no one laughs. I'm keeping score; I know. Some things just aren't funny. Wolf packs, for example: not funny.

Then Sarah comes out of her tent looking like a movie star; makeup on, her hair gloriously radiant and bouncy like she's been in a shampoo commercial. Even her pants look pressed. They're light brown and look like the kind you'd wear on a horse ride through the oaks with Englishmen and beagles.

Hello everybody! Hello!

She waltzes over, happy and excited, and sashays to the beach. She's crossing a ballroom before the band begins to play and doesn't care how weird this all looks. Stops. Looks around. Kicks at some pebbles and washes her hands in the cold, cold ocean. Stands and holds her red, dripping hands out to the sea, measuring its beauty I suppose, but it also seems like she's dreaming of being a surgeon.

What a morning. What a beautiful morning!

She twirls like she's doing a triple Salchow, looks around at us perched on the rocks, coffees in hand, shivering and not talking, and staring at her.

Did you have a good sleep, everyone?

She laughs and pulls out a vape and poof, her head disappears in a cloud of white.

TWENTY

WE HEAD OUT TO THE yoga centre on foot — so many trees were knocked down during the storm. They litter the roads. It's as if the forest has imploded. We pick our way through the green debris led by Holly, who wears a long, Gandalf-white coat that flows behind her. It's dirty along the bottom and slightly frayed. She also carries a staff. But I doubt there's any magic in it.

Holly stops ahead of me after we turn a corner. I can see a very large tree across the road. Huge.

Obviously, we need to climb over it, she announces to the group. The group being me, Will, Deborah, Grace, and Prince on a leash. It's warmed up a little. The sun peeks between clouds overhead. Steam comes off the road making everything look like a stream bed in *Jurassic Park* starring Jeff Goldblum, my favourite cheating-bastard movie star. I've always wanted his glorious life of bedding beauties. Also, I've been to the Garden Island of Kauai, and I've walked that same stream bed from the movie. This road with all the debris mostly looks the same, minus the raptors.

Am I dreaming? Will says. Look at this. I mean look at how wondrous everything is. Total destruction. Beautiful.

You get used to it after a while, Holly says. I know I did.

We can't take it for granted, Will says hoarsely. We can't.

Okay, Holly says. I won't.

Holly says this with the tiniest scoff.

Come on, she says. Let's get over this.

So, we take turns crawling over the giant cedar tree. It seems to be hollow inside, but I'm not sure that has anything to do with it falling over. It's fairly massive. I grab for Holly's hand as she hauls me over the trunk. My face hovers close to hers, and she looks at me very closely.

I hope you brought the money, she mumbles.

It's in my backpack, I say quickly, pointing to my back.

We need to be alone, she says.

I agree, I say. Soon.

Then I move on, jumping down from the log and over to the other side.

Deborah jumps on the log quickly.

What did he say? I hear Deborah ask Holly, in full-on RCMP officer mode.

He's tired, that's all, Holly says, as she guides Deborah to safety.

Careful with that branch, Holly smiles. She holds the stubborn arm of the tree down with the heel of her big boot.

Then we move on, down the road, the six of us winding our way through the mess like we're survivors of an apocalypse. We have our supply of water and Clif Bars, we've got cellphones that don't work and our weatherproof jackets of various Crayola colours. It's a three-kilometre hike. I can't believe the number of trees flat on the ground. The forest huffs around us as if recovering from a beating, but it's just the wind, just the wind.

Wow, I say to nobody in particular. That was some storm. Yikes.

Yikes, says Grace too. And I can tell this is a new word for her.

Yikes.

Grace grabs my hand briefly.

If I shoot this, nobody will believe it, Grace says. It's like the end of things. Like God has acted upon us.

I don't believe in God, I say to Grace. Sorry about that.

That makes me sad, she says, dropping my hand quickly and moving ahead to join Holly, our fearless leader.

She pans the scene with her Sony, careful not to trip on the branches littering the road.

I don't notice any birds, which is weird. My nose itches. And my ears are hot. There's a stillness to my world right now. I'm aware of how warm my hands are, and I can sense the forest, how it hurts. Or it could just be me. I'm months away from being totally bankrupt and living in some warm country like Belize with other middle-aged men with aspirations to be with women half their age who are into a nice brie.

I nearly trip on a branch because I'm not watching my feet.

I need to stop daydreaming. And stupid thoughts.

Holly points to favourite trees as she leads us. That one I've named Edna, she says, pointing with her staff. She's still standing, thank God. My. Favourite.

And that one is Violet. She's almost two hundred years old, a teenager in tree years.

Grace films them with her trusty Sony.

Beautiful, Grace says. This is beautiful.

Grace turns slowly, like she's a human tripod.

And there's Rachel, Holly says. She's the queen of the forest. A cedar tree over four hundred years old.

She leads us into the darkness of the forest, away from the road, and as we study Rachel, I notice notches in the trunk.

You see the notches, don't you?

I nod. Yes.

Holly looks us over. They tried to take her down, but she was too demanding and so they left her.

Who left her? I ask.

The men who wanted her to become a house or a barn, Holly says. But she's the queen of the forest, as you can see. Like me.

We are all a few steps away from the road edging our way into the actual forest.

Grace circles with her Sony, trying to capture the essence of Holly who pretends she isn't aware of the camera.

Nobody owns the forest, Holly says directly to the camera. Understand?

She swings her staff around trying to conjure a spell, then decides to jump up onto a nearby fallen tree for a better angle.

Grace follows her every move with the Sony.

This is my world, Holly says. My world. Mysterious and dangerous and exotic. And nobody owns me. Nobody.

Deborah laughs. That's what I call a metaphor.

Then Deborah grabs Will and moves away.

If you're the queen, Deborah says, then I'm a fucking princess.

Deborah says this over her right shoulder, and I notice that she doesn't really walk away but marches. Maybe because she's been trained that way, but probably because she's always been driven to succeed. And I know she wants like hell to solve the disappearance of Sarah. Not just because it's her job, but because she's taking it personally. On one of our quieter encounters at the cabin, she told me she's never had a murder case before, to which I said I didn't think this was a murder. Then she studied me and said you seem to make a lot of assumptions for an innocent man, to which I said yes, that is the whole point of being innocent. I assume.

Deep inside, though, I know what kind of flawed human I am. Well, mostly on weekends or Friday nights after work. And vodka is involved. And rum. And then Riesling. And really, who said you get wiser with age? I think having too much money negates any wisdom you might have achieved, too. And I think working with actresses makes things worse, particularly young, ambitious ones. I used to idolize Jack Nicholson too; now, apparently, I've turned into him.

Also, just like him … I love golf and sarcasm.

And my hair is thinning.

Let's move out, Deborah says to the group. Come on, it's not far.

We go back to the road. With all the steam coming off the blacktop it's very foggy and there's a stillness to the air. Yes, the kind you get after a storm.

Will says suddenly, I have a feeling we're being watched. Does anybody else feel that?

I grab him by the arm.

You're still recovering from that drug, I say. From being roofied. You need to just take it easy out here.

No, I'm serious, Will says. I feel we are being watched and judged. How about it, everyone? Are we being judged?

Will stops and waves his arms around like he's batting away bats.

Holly, a few feet ahead of us, turns around dramatically. She points with her staff.

Come on, let's go, Holly orders us. Let's go.

I beetle over my third or fourth tree trunk, following Holly who suddenly stops and raises her hand like she's leading a troupe of marines on a secret mission.

We all stop in our scuttling tracks.

In the slight fog, foraging on young ferns, are six or seven deer; I guess you can call them a herd. I don't know. Beside the road. They lift their heads, sensing something isn't right. I can feel myself breathing. Will, beside me, pulls out his cellphone to snap some shots. Behind him, Grace pans the scene with her Sony.

Beautiful, Grace says. Amazing.

Prince sits, and for once, he stops panting.

Will holds out his arms as if balancing. The deer watch us with a slight what-the-hell, but it's not much of one. We exist. They exist. There will be no trouble.

What is happening to us? Will says in a low whisper. What is happening? They are here.

Then the deer decide we're completely harmless and all go back to doing what they were doing before: having lunch. Heads down, they munch on the green stuff left by the storm. A couple of them drift back toward the forest, and I see how their tails twitch nervously.

Deborah says, They're a nuisance. Let's keep moving.

We do, but slower, not to disturb their meal. They watch us watch them as we move away down the road. Grace backs away shooting the scene and zooming out trying to get perspective.

They're mainly oblivious, I say to Will. We're nothing to them.

They mean something, Will frowns. That's why they're here. Don't you get what's happening? Don't you?

The biggest one decides to stare us down, refusing to chew until we stop staring.

He's got many points to his horns, and he knows he looks majestic, so he continues to stare at us, perfectly still, a very muscular statue amongst the ferns. I'm pretty sure he's about to kick our ass, although I'm no deer expert.

Watch it, I say. Watch it.

Will stares at the deer and the deer stares back. Neither blinks. Will's having a moment. No one but me seems to notice. He reaches out both hands as if to calm either himself or the beast. He then closes his eyes and his lips move. For a moment, I honestly think Will is talking to the animals. In his head.

What's happening? Grace asks. What's going on?

I'm not sure, I say. Will? Will?

He doesn't move. The deer doesn't move. It's a standoff.

They are nearly head-to-head and inching closer.

Holly turns to us and says, The big one you want to watch; he's a nasty shit. The one with the big rack.

He's got a huge head of horns like a Russian chandelier, I say.

I call him Igor, Holly says. He ripped up my roses and ate my kale. He's an asshole.

And then with a jolt, the deer disappear, just like that.

And the road ahead of us clears.

Will snaps out of it. He looks around anxiously, wanders toward the edge of the blacktop to peer out into the maze of trees.

What happened there? Will asks. Are they afraid of us all of a sudden?

Will looks around like he's just been transported from the bridge of the USS *Enterprise.*

This is weird, Will says. They know! They fucking know!

They must have heard something that spooked them, Holly says. That's all.

What is it they sense? Will asks. What?

Relax, Holly says. They're much more afraid of us than we are of them.

They know something, Will says. They know what's happening.

Deborah takes Will's hand gently.

Let's go, Will. Let's keep going. Please.

Will nods slowly.

Yeah. My apologies.

In the fog ahead, I see dark shapes I imagine are wolves.

Wolves, I say under my breath.

Holly stifles a laugh. Wolves? Don't let your imagination get the best of you. Holly pats me on the shoulder. It's me you should really be afraid of.

Then she moves ahead.

Deborah, with Will now in hand, walks up to me.

She leans in.

Don't worry, she whispers. I'm armed.

Then, for some reason known only to himself, Will breaks away from Deborah and climbs up on a downed tree — to get perspective, I think. But then brushes his pants off and faces us like a lost, desperate Greek philosopher.

People of the road, he starts. My friends. Fellow travellers and explorers. I would like to say something here. He takes off his Toronto Blue Jays cap and holds it against his chest like he's at the funeral of a best friend.

We're here because we're here. Our very existence has resulted in a plundering of the planet. What you see before you is Mother Nature's way of defending herself. That's right, take a look around. We've exacted too much of a cost on the planet. We've loved it too much for too long. This is not a healthy relationship. We're abusive. We're demanding. We're absent. We're wrong about almost everything. We can't keep denying it.

Will stops. He looks like he's about to weep.

They've been following me. This whole trip, animals have been watching me and pressuring me to do some goddamn good in this world. But I didn't want to listen. I couldn't. I wasn't in tune with them.

Deborah looks at the rest of us, sees that we are gape-mouthed and speechless, and decides to take charge.

Will, she pleads. Please. We're almost at the yoga centre. Save it for the people who meditate. Come on.

This is meant to be funny, obviously. But Will isn't laughing. He wipes his mouth with his sleeve and continues.

Human beings — we're here for such a short time, he says. And we're not such great inventions, are we? I mean, we cheat, we manipulate, we lie. We're abusive and negligent and short-sighted and reckless and cowardly. And we're destroying the fucking planet.

Will looks up to the sky now.

This is all our fault. It is. I mean, here we are. Time marches on. We can't … we shouldn't … we're fools. We are complete fools.

His chin drops. A tear trickles down his cheek. I'm not sure he's sober, but it might not matter.

Yes, I'm a total fuck up, Will says. There, now I've said it. You heard me. All of you. I'm a total fuck up, and I want to apologize right here and now. I'm sorry. I'm sorry …

Deborah reaches up, holds out her arm like she wants the next dance. For a moment Will hesitates. He looks around at us. Grace has lowered her Sony. Holly lowers her staff. I see the deer returning from the dense forest. Most of them have tilted heads. They are quizzical, no doubt about it. Prince studies the deer.

The thick clouds above us part, and for the briefest of moments, the sun shines, mostly down on us and mostly down on Will who looks angelic, majestic, and sweaty all at once. And he basks in it. He lets the rays melt into his forehead like he's a receiving dish. Starts to raise his hands as if to levitate. I look around for the sound of trumpets.

Then the light goes away.

Grey is grey and we're in it, our futures fuzzy with regret, no doubt. The wind picks up and blows shit around.

Fuck it, Will says. I'm just saying.

He grabs Deborah's hand and hops down from the fallen tree and moves to the other side. They walk down the road together.

Will rubs his head over and over again.

Fuck me, he says, ahead of me. That was embarrassing. Wasn't it?

He snaps his lid back on, his Blue Jays cap slightly askew, an aging director looking for a lost headset.

Jesus, he says. What's wrong with me? I mean, seriously?

Deborah holds Will's hand. He apparently likes it. I notice a slight limp, like he's afraid to step hard on the road with his left foot and, in fact, he is listing.

I watch him try to correct his walk with the help of Deborah. Mostly they succeed. But it looks weird. I'll be honest. They are an ungraceful pair, but they seem to be perfectly at ease with that.

Holly motions to Grace and me. And the dog.

Let's go, she says. The centre is just over there.

We follow Will and his newfound love down the messy road. Down the road to the yoga centre that appears up ahead in a clearing.

Yes. Magically.

It's aglow with positive vibes. And a neon sign that reads OPEN YOUR MIND. It's in red, of course.

And, yes, there's a yogi sitting out front on a mat, meditating. Just sitting there cross-legged, his hands on the tops of his thighs, palms up, as if hoping to cup rain. He is very peaceful.

Unaware of us stomping toward him.

TWENTY-ONE

THE DIVORCE KAYAK.

That's what Anna calls the two-person kayak.

It's months earlier. Before I made some very questionable life choices. I want to blame alcohol and my penis. But I'm not going to. Not this time. It's just too easy.

I sit in a shiny, two-seater kayak in the back of Canadian Tire near a wall of green-and-black tent gear and sleeping bags.

Anna sits in the front seat.

Raj, our sales attendant, stands in front of us, arms folded, waiting. He has the blackest hair I've ever seen, slicked back with something greasy, but fashionable. Red shirt, black pants, and Adidas. Pencil behind his ear. He's tiny, but in fantastic shape, like he runs a marathon every other day. Very nice cheekbones. Thick eyebrows. Hairy arms. Beard. Trimmed.

He's too peaceful, I think, for someone so young. And expressionless. Even for a sales representative. I wonder where he comes from. A slight undeniable accent.

Nine hundred dollars, sir, and you can paddle out of here, he says quietly.

You need to take a right at Cambie Street and go toward the water by the Olympic site. There's a ramp there. Very nice. All super.

Anna winces.

Don't talk to him, talk to me, Raj. I know more about our funds than he can imagine.

My apologies, madam, Raj says politely. My mistake.

Anna pretends to paddle the floor, swiping at it expertly, then leaning back as if she is floating under the stars, while staring up at the fluorescents dangling like icicles from the distant ceiling.

Would you like to hear a joke, Raj?

Anna turns around awkwardly in her seat.

I used this one when I went to open mic at Yuk Yuk's.

Knock, knock.

Who's there?

A Canadian.

A Canadian who?

A Canadian Tire.

Raj's face is made of stone.

Super, he says. Super, madam.

Anna continues to improve on her stroke, moving her powerful shoulders like she's punching the shit out of the air or trying to generate laughs in an empty high school gymnasium.

There's an efficiency to her actions, each stroke effortless and controlled. Calculated.

Which, of course, she is.

Anna is exact and often very demanding. She insists I succumbed to her vast and infinite allures, which, she reminds me, are in ample supply every passing minute. That's why I love her, right?

Despite my flaws.

And she loves being loved.

I have to work at that.

I do, because, essentially, I'm a prick.

I bite my lip to buy some time here in this overly bright store because I actually knew it was going to get ugly. I could tell. Honestly. That's one of my superpowers next to avoiding eye contact at red lights and identifying rare dog breeds in city parks.

Anna looks back at Raj.

That joke killed at Yuk Yuk's.

Because why?

Because Canadian Tire comes out of nowhere, Raj. It's unexpected.

I always expect the unexpected, madam, Raj says unblinking.

A moment.

About the kayak, madam, Raj says. About the kayak. You need outerwear to go with it.

Yes, Anna says. Outerwear. Perfect.

Preferably impermeable, Raj says.

What the hell is that? I ask.

Sir, you need protection, Raj adds. From the elements.

Do you have anything like Gore-Tex, but isn't Gore-Tex, but works like Gore-Tex?

Anna smiles, then says, We're on a budget so …

Wait, I say. What's wrong with just wearing a garbage bag? Or a cheap plastic covering like the ones people use when they go to football games?

Raj smiles.

Clearly you are not familiar with paddling in the wilderness, are you? The Gore-Tex is breathable.

Look, I say, I don't care about how I'm waterproof. It doesn't matter to me. I can handle it. Okay? I'm a grown man.

Raj does a slight bow.

It's much healthier for you to allow moisture to dissipate or else you will feel colder and less able to react to the elements positively. I speak of the material. The nature of it. How it works to be breathable. As a human being. Of course.

Raj brushes off the tops of his hands like he's just performed sleight of hand. And then waits me out.

Anna watches for more.

There's waterproof and then there's really waterproof, Anna finally says with a quick laugh. Guess which one we're getting?

I shake my head.

This is going to cost me, I say. It's really going to cost me.

Raj shuffles his feet.

I think with the Gore-Tex and the proper kayak you two will have an incredible time in any conditions and in any water you choose. It will make the trip very memorable. I think so.

He somehow manages to magically produce a mobile credit card machine, probably from thin air. He holds it in his left hand.

The choice is this, Anna mumbles. Then waves at her mousy hair that always seems to be in her eyes or caught in her lips. It's not easily tamed.

The choice is this.

Anna gathers her thoughts, then continues, One-person or two-person? One means independence. Two means anything can happen, but you're trapped with that. You are always together. That can ruin any fucking relationship.

To be honest, Anna doesn't use that word often. Fucking.

It comes out like a Baptist preacher said it behind the church during a smoke break.

Raj smiles. Yes, he says. The woman always knows.

He taps his pencil on his credit card machine.

Wap wap wap.

Let's move things along is what I get.

Anna twists at her waist, pretending to look for seals behind us in the Christmas decoration section; upon spotting none, she rests her paddle on the bow of the red kayak.

The kayak wobbles a bit on the floor. Grinds a bit. As if there's sand under us. It's irritating.

Then.

She pulls out her cellphone and checks something.

This is the part I dread.

Raj shuffles his large feet. He looks around, maybe searching for another customer to save him from what is about to happen.

Anna gasps.

Yup, she just checked our bank account.

I hold my paddle up, stare at it, and feel the back of my back, where my sweater touches my body, start to heat up. And get wet.

What the fuck happened? Dear?

Anna rises from the kayak like she's able to levitate.

She might be, from the sheer energy of the anger building up under her.

Raj takes a step or two back as she swivels to face me.

Where's the money, dear? What the fuck have you done to my money?

She flares a quick, fake grin while tucking the paddle back like a baseball bat.

I feel slightly small at the back end.

A coolness to the atmosphere, as if a ghost has appeared in aisle four under plumbing.

Anna doesn't blink.

If you drained our savings account to shoot your stupid movie, I will shoot you. I will go to the gun department and pick out a handgun and shoot you in the head. I will, and I don't care how much it costs.

We don't sell that kind of handgun, madam, Raj says tentatively. But you could put out his eye with an air gun.

Then I will put out his eye with an air gun, Raj. Whatever that is. I will.

I try to stand, but Anna pushes me back down with her the tip of her wooden paddle.

Did you or did you not do what I think you did?

I lick my lips.

I think I did, I say.

UGH!

Anna takes a seal bashing stance, paddle raised high. The kayak wobbles mightily again, but then stops. She closes her eyes, perhaps envisioning my brains splattered across the life jackets on the nearby shelf beside us. Perhaps envisioning her life without me, she alone out on a kayak under the stars, not sharing the experience, not saying how wonderful it all is.

I might not be worth it.

And that is the damn truth.

I am deeply, deeply flawed.

Raj clears his throat intentionally.

One might surmise that love conquers all, he says. But what is love really? It's an agreement, in my humble opinion. Between two parties. Between ships passing in the dark. To journey together, no matter how rough the water.

He taps his credit card machine again.

Slower than before. And louder. And calculated.

It takes a long, long moment for Anna to lower her paddle.

You're lucky I love you so much, she says, in one breath. You big dumb … lunk.

Lunk. Yeah. A controlled put down.

Which is just like her.

The control.

Which is something I do admire about her. No matter what happens, she is able to control herself. That's why most of her closest friends are all crazy. They are drawn to her. Her stability. Control. There's balance.

Two kayaks it is, she says to Raj. How much is that?

Raj punches out the numbers on his machine quickly.

Fifteen hundred, plus tax.

Not counting the Gore-Tex.

TWENTY-TWO

OUR YOGI'S NAME IS NORMAN. He lived in Vancouver for a while before having a breakdown and moving to India for six months to study under a guru who didn't cut his fingernails for ten years and needed to be fed by nubile young women barely out of their teens and who, oddly, didn't like his lentils. The guru's lentils, to be clear.

Norman is whippet-thin and has a small shock of white hair that stands up on his head as if he's put his finger in an electrical socket. His fingers are bony and his nails are also untrimmed, but since he has only been growing them out for a few months they kind of look like they belong on a fashion model. He's clearly proud of them and waves them around like he's doing a TV commercial for soap.

His face is very wrinkled. Crow's feet surround eyes a very deep blue. His gums are grey. He smoked for twenty-five years before a heart scare made him throw his last carton into a dumpster. Then he jumped in and retrieved it and smoked those sons-of-bitches before stopping cold turkey. He talks a lot.

Let me tell you about our little community, Norman says. Can I do that first?

Our conversation goes on for a while so this is all a summary because I zoned out for a lot of it.

I love people, he says. To a fault. And that's why I provide this service to the public. Also, it's a very profitable business these days with the politics to the south, right?

He nods and nods.

He wears designer frames that give him a very hip, professorial appearance like he teaches drama at a hip school, which I later find out he still does. Takes a ferry in once a week, but only during the summer months.

The designer frames are off-white.

But not grey.

And thick.

After this rather long preamble about his history and the centre, Norman takes stock of us. Of me, in particular.

He does this by pointing at the top of my head. Maybe because I'm the tallest of the group. Maybe because my head is overly large. Maybe because I have a bad haircut.

I've been expecting you.

Why?

I say that.

He looks at me and takes off his hip glasses.

Well, Holly phoned me, so that's why, Norman says. But ask any question you want. We may not have the answers, but the questions are important. They always are. I hope I didn't bore you with my introduction, but I feel my clients should know everything about me right away. It's a trust thing. Isn't it a wonderful day? The calm after the storm? It's my favourite feeling, by the way. Like we're survivors. And we are, aren't we? All of us here. We're living in hope.

Deborah doesn't look like she's in any mood for further bullshit.

Do you have a guest book I can take a look at?

Who are you? Norman asks.

I'm with the RCMP, Deborah says. And I'm investigating the disappearance of a woman.

Sarah. Oh yes, Norman says. From last year. I remember. It was a sad day for everybody on the island. She stayed with us, of course. And we all found her to be wonderfully opinionated and outgoing.

Norman gestures like Gandhi, his arms outstretched, and it's then I notice the loin cloth thing he's wearing is barely covering the essentials. I avert my eyes.

Grace stops filming.

It looks like it's one floor, I say.

It is one floor, Norman says. We have a large banquet room and a spa, too. Ten meditation rooms, a few one- and two-bedroom suites. Office space. Some small cabins in the back. A special garden. The whole centre is powered by solar panels installed three years ago. We're off the grid. The toilets are composted, and we use our poop on our tomatoes and collect rain water. The floors have mats made by local Indigenous peoples. The walls are covered with paintings by local artists. They are all available for purchase in our gift room at the back.

Then Norman takes Deborah inside to look at the guest book. Holly gives me a look before following them.

We should connect soon, she says.

I nod and take off my backpack.

Will wanders inside like he's entering a spaceship. He takes baby steps and deep breaths. I start to follow.

Holy shit, he says. Holy shit. Anybody else feel that? Weird.

He moves down the hall like he's seeing invisible birds fly around his head. I notice Grace isn't following, so I go back to her. She's sat herself down on a bamboo bench with Prince beside her on his leash.

Don't worry about me, Grace says. I will be fine here. It's warm out now. And there's an eagle up there I would like to study.

I look up at the surrounding pine trees and, indeed, there's an eagle up there watching us cautiously. Grace has her Sony pointed at it now.

I enter the centre.

It takes a while for my eyes to adjust to the light. All the lightbulbs are red, giving the whole wooden structure a feeling of being a Finnish school of prostitution — particularly when our guide, Kerry, approaches. Wearing a tight-fitting, white T-shirt and pants, she talks with her hands and almost twirls. Very excitable.

We get a lot of tours here, Kerry says. Particularly because of our unique gardens outside. There's a lot of flora and fauna native to our Pacific Northwest, and people from all over are always impressed. We even try to grow kiwi fruit. But they rarely ripen enough to eat raw so we make jam out of them.

Will wanders back from the darkened hallway. His eyes are glazed over.

Do you have an empty room for me? Will asks.

Kerry looks confused. Do you want to meditate?

Yeah, let's say I do, says Will. I need to fucking meditate. Fast.

Oh. Okay. I didn't expect you to swear inside here, Kerry says.

Yeah, okay. Surprise, Will says.

Kerry blinks. And blinks.

Because certainly that's what we're all about here at the yoga centre. That's our reason for existing. We treat the mind, body, and soul. Gwyneth Paltrow once came here because she needed to cleanse herself, and she brought six friends from Manhattan and —

Will stumbles toward her, and I worry about him toppling for a second, but he manages to right himself, grabbing Kerry by the waist.

Sorry. I just feel like I want to get right with the world in my head, Will says. I've had a rough couple of days, you know what I mean? But I'm a huge fan of Gwyneth Paltrow, just so you know.

Yes, by all means, Kerry points to a doorway. It's only fifty dollars an hour and well worth it because we call this The Room of Discovery.

Thanks, Will snaps.

Will shuffles in and closes the door. I'm left with Kerry.

She smiles, but I don't smile back. Her hair is pulled back so tight her eyes are narrowed. We stand for a minute, one of us at least feeling awkward and silly.

You may look around, Kerry says, pointing down a long hallway.

She disappears behind a beaded doorway, red and white glass beads sounding like chattering teeth.

I wait a moment, inhale deeply, and notice how everything smells like mossy tree trunks and mushrooms. My toes sink into the floor mat — woven out of tree branches, I assume.

I make my way down the corridor, backpack in hand, past the red lights on each doorway. I hear music coming from — where? hidden speakers? Oddly, it's "Yesterday" sung by a choir without music.

I walk on, passing rooms with different-coloured Tibetan prayer flags on the outside and words like *Lucky*, *Serenity*, or *Providential* painted by hand near the door handles. In red and black. Why does that sound familiar? Hmm.

The music gets louder as I walk on.

I'm curious.

At the end of the long hallway there is a big banquet room, and in the middle of the room is a men's choir led by a tiny bald man wearing a black turtleneck, waving a large baton. The choir sees me watching, but doesn't stop, finishing the song beautifully and only then does the choir leader turn to me to say, Please, nice comments only.

It's beautiful, I say, standing in the doorway. Beautiful.

He nods, Well, not quite, not yet. But we're close, right gentlemen?

The choir — made up of the most handsome, clean-shaven men I've ever seen — nods in agreement. All twelve of them. And all of them wear plaid shirts and blue jeans with Birkenstocks.

Are you a choir? I ask stupidly.

You bet we are, says the director.

Wow, I say. A choir.

You're welcome to stay to hear "Walkin' on the Sun" by Smash Mouth. It's our best song, says the director.

Thanks, I say. I'm just killing time.

The choir looks at me as if hoping for a yes.

I wrongly think they might be military men, what with the nice haircuts.

I turn to move back toward the entrance, and it's then I run into Gili wearing a white dress and what I assume are operating room slippers.

Gili stares at me, pushes me against the wall so that we're out of view from the choir.

What are you doing here?

She says this with a bark.

What are you doing here? I ask.

I'm studying to be a yogi, goddammit.

You're what?

Gili crosses her arms and pouts. You don't think I'm yogi material?

No, it's not that. I'm just surprised to see you here.

Are you stalking me?

No, I say. I'm here doing some research.

For what?

For the feature I was telling you about. You know, scouting locations and everything.

I'm in it, right? Gili says, pushing her dark hair around her ears. Because I think I know what part I'll play. That script needs a way better ending.

You read it?

Mostly, she says. I skimmed the bad parts.

It's a draft, I say.

The ending is awful, Gili says. With those stupid kayaks. Jesus. Talk about cliché. Please tell me you're not staying here too, Gili says, punching the wall a little.

I'm staying at Holly's Bed and Breakfast down the road. I had no idea you were here.

Holly? Gili looks troubled. She bites her lower lip.

Yes. Holly.

I hope to God *you* didn't sleep with her too, she says with a low growl.

Why? What's going on?

I don't know if I can tell you, Gili says. I just don't know.

Uh-oh, I say.

Yeah, she's a complete weirdo who nearly wrecked my family, but luckily we're still friends. She recommended this place so I can become whole again because you nearly ruined my life.

Me? I'm aghast.

Gili leans against the wall looking seriously perturbed. It might be a pose.

Well, thanks to you and that stupid car commercial I have PTSD and need to get my shit together, if you were wondering, Gili says. That's why I'm staying here.

Well, good, I say. Good. Can we get out of the hallway, please? The choir guys are very loud, and I hate Smash Mouth.

We listen for a second. They work through the song and stop and start, and I hear the director yelling, Please stay on key, Rodger!

Follow me, Gili says. We better get further away before they start practising Celine Dion. They do that song from *Titanic* like a hundred times a day. It's fucking crazy.

Wow, I say. What are they doing here, anyway?

Well, Gili says, I think that's obvious — they're practising away from all known humanity. I hate choirs. Come on.

Gili drifts ahead of me, her white dress swishing behind. I smell a touch of smoke.

We head down the hallway to the second door on the right, and Gili uses her electronic key to gain entry. Inside, there's a large futon bed — white — a writing desk — also white — with a fruit bowl — also white — and white walls with Tibetan prayer flags over the doorway to the washroom — also white. This room could be used for interrogation in North Korea except for the prayer flags. No, that would just be ironic.

The choir fades.

I'm aware of my own breathing.

I bump my backpack with my left knee and pretend to take in the room, but really I'm looking for an escape. My shoulders hurt. And my neck. This room smells. It could be her perfume.

You want to put that down? Gili asks.

Yes, I say. Yes, I do.

I'm sweating. I can smell myself.

Not pleasant.

It's warm in here.

I say that aloud and smile weakly. Do you find it warm in here?

I've centred myself in the room under the ceiling fan. If I were a foot taller it would behead me.

What part was I supposed to play again? Gili says, circling me now.

A good part, I stammer.

Like what?

How about a student? I say.

Do you think I could actually pass for a student? Gili says quickly. Do you?

Is this a trick question?

Cute, Gili says. Very cute. But it better be a good part. I'm tired of doing one-liners for stupid American producers who come up from L.A. and wear sunglasses with trendy New Balance running shoes. You know what I mean? Grow up, douche bags. Grow up and stop chewing gum during my fucking audition.

Gili wipes her hands off on her white dress, but then I see she's actually digging around in a side pocket.

Sure enough, Gili lights up a smoke. A cigarette package has appeared from the right pocket of her dress.

You smoke?

Oh. Don't be so disappointed, she says.

She drifts to the washroom and flicks the match into the toilet. She draws in the smoke and lets it linger in her lungs before blowing it out toward the single bare lightbulb hanging down from the centre of the room under the fan.

If I want to smoke, I'm gonna smoke, okay?

You can do whatever you want, I say. You're the practising yogi.

I'm taking a break from all that shit, Gili says. You need to do it in phases because it's so intense. Or it might be because I'm Jewish.

I look around the room, at the ceiling in particular.

I'm not supposed to smoke in here, Gili says. Obviously. So, I removed the batteries from the smoke detector, if you're wondering.

She blows smoke at the smoke detector above her head and smiles.

This centre is very strange, I say. A men's choir? What else is the place hiding?

Then I push the backpack behind me. My feet are now playing guards. I pull on my eyebrows.

Gili continues to smoke and stares at me.

I avoid looking back.

You want to tell me what's going on? Gili asks.

It's just advance scouting, you know, shooting some footage, that kind of thing.

I look around for a place to sit. There's the futon bed. I go for it even though it looks moldy and the white spread has a weird carpet thing on it.

Gili's eyes narrow.

You know how I know you're full of shit?

No, I say, sitting stiffly.

You pull on your eyebrows, she says.

Okay, okay, I say. Nice job on that.

You've been to Cortes before, Gili says. Right?

Oh yes. This island seems to have me, I say. I guess ever since Sarah's disappearance.

Yeah, I bet she disappeared, Gili says. What did you say to her? What did you do to her?

I didn't do anything, I say. Why does everybody think I had something to do with Sarah's fucking disappearance? Can't people just disappear on their own? We were in the middle of the ocean.

Right, that totally makes sense, Gili smiles. You were in the middle of something, that's for sure.

Oh Christ, I say. Come on.

She stayed here, didn't she? Gili starts to pace like a gunfighter. Is that why you're here? Is it?

Gili stops pacing and sucks on her cigarette. The room, I notice, is turning film noir, light seeping in between the slats of the window blinds.

Reaching up to pull on the cord, Gili switches on the fan attached to the bare lightbulb in the centre of the room. It speeds up, moves through the cigarette smoke like a propeller which is a totally obvious comparison to make, I guess. Creaks and whines. Sounds like a baby crying from downstairs. Or way over there, past the trees and down near the river. It picks up speed. Then quietens.

You look nice, I say.

Fuck you, Gili says.

Typical, I say.

Who cares, Gili says.

Are you happy?

Are you?

You look very attractive still.

Still? What the hell?

I try another weak smile. My legs hurt from all the tree trunks I've clambered over today, and it's only now while sitting I notice how stained my pants are. The sap from trees makes it look like my pee has frozen on the outside.

Gili leans against the desk and watches me. She's wearing lipstick, but it's a dark shade of red that makes her thin lips look somewhat black. She has a tiny cold sore on her upper lip. She sees me notice it.

So? Whose life are you about to fuck up now?

She asks this, of course, without batting an eye.

Look, I say. The accident with the car was an accident despite what the court decided, and I'm just trying to find a way of doing some good, you know, doing a feature about finding love and losing it, or the other way around. Yeah, the other way around.

Gili cocks her head looking for a close-up. Just so you know, my life is totally fucked up. I can't sleep. I haven't had an audition for months, and I'm totally haunted by the little girl I nearly killed with the Smart Car … what's-her-name.

Kiddo.

What?

No, not you, I say. The kid. We called her Kiddo.

Don't you think we should remember her name considering we nearly killed her? Gili asks. I mean, that's so impersonal.

Listen, she had a pre-condition or something, I say. It was a bump. You bumped her and she fell over. Then she bounced up again, and we finished the shoot, remember? She was fine. Her mother said she was fine. We had no idea. About the pre-condition. It was … it could have happened at any time, but it happened then. She recovered. Right. She's fine now. Really.

So now you're a medical expert?

I'm just telling you that it was an accident, and you shouldn't let it stop you from acting or doing what you love. You're going to have to rise above it. We all do.

That's a dumb thing to say, Andy, Gili says, blowing smoke in my hair.

I close my eyes.

Her name was Quinn, I say. Quinn. And that's why we can't remember it, because it sounds like a dude.

Quinn?

Her mother called her Kiddo on the set, I say. But in the court it was Quinn.

Quinn? Are you sure?

I nod.

Fuck, Gili says. What a horrible name to get a brain injury with.

She blows smoke at the ceiling fan.

I sense you're angry, I say. For sure.

For sure I sense you're right, Gili says. And now you're involved with my father's ex-lover. Holly.

What? Ex-lover? No. I'm not involved. I'm renting a room from her. What the hell. Where did that come from?

Gili's futon bed is very uncomfortable. I grab the pillow and shove it under my ass. Gili notices.

How long was your dad seeing her? I ask.

Sixteen years, Gili says. Give or take.

Wasn't Holly with Todd the Mormon then?

Yes, Gili says. She certainly was. But that didn't stop them.

That's a long time for an affair.

I didn't say it was an affair, Gili says. They were lovers until my mother found out. I was caught in the middle. Holly was my friend. Is my friend. Why do you think I'm on Cortes?

The men's choir passes by in the hallway then, some of them laughing and the last one singing "Yesterday."

There goes yesterday, I say to Gili.

But she isn't talking.

The smoke in the room is now overwhelming. I feel it in my clothes and hair and covering my skin.

Wow, Gili says. It's bad enough you've destroyed my life. Now you're complicating my past. This could get ugly.

But I didn't know about your past, I say.

You never asked, Gili says.

She stamps her foot, but because she's wearing a medical slipper thing it sounds like a tiny bunny thump.

Just how is it possible for you to have sex with me and not know anything about my past? Gili asks.

I do it all the time, I say. You probably do the same thing. I mean, what do you really know about *my* past?

I know you're married. How about that particular past?

Gili puts her smoke out on a banana in the white fruit bowl on the white table. Then she shows her teeth. They are nice teeth. She wallows in her broadside. I blink it off. Crack my knuckles and rub my eyebrows which are really bugging me right now.

You really shouldn't put out a cigarette on fruit, I say. What if somebody picks up that banana and wants to eat it? It looks bad with the burn hole on it, like you're into torturing fruit.

Nobody cares about what I'm doing with the fruit in my room, okay? Gili says.

I kick at my backpack and notice that it's open a little, and I can see the bundles of fake cash. I zip it up quickly. Gili watches me, then picks up the banana and peels it seductively.

She throws the peel into the garbage bin near the futon and puts the naked banana back in the fruit bowl.

Happy now?

Sure, I say. Whatever. Jesus.

I sit and study the Tibetan prayer flags and then the bed covering under me which also has a Tibetan design on it of some kind. Diamonds. Blood red. Repeating.

Look, now that you're here we might as well just clear the air, Gili says. Can you do that? Can you clear the air?

Why are you wearing operating room slippers? I ask.

Because when I go barefoot my feet get dirty in here. If you haven't noticed the floors are covered in shitty mats made of stupid little branches, and the cafeteria has an Afghan rug in it from the nineteenth century and probably hasn't been cleaned since then either. The dude that runs this place is pathetic. He's a total stoner. Do not smoke hash with him; he'll show you pictures of his Corgis on his cellphone, and you'll never get back those two hours.

Gili plops down on the bed beside me.

Don't get any ideas, she says. This bed is covered with a Tibetan prayer blanket or something. It's sacred ground, okay?

She takes my hand and holds it tightly.

Look, I feel you've ruined my life, she says quietly. And I want things to be normal again. I want to go home and get rejected at auditions and work at a bar serving drinks to middle-aged men who all tip nice because their marriages are falling apart, and I want to feel like I'm beautiful again and wanted and important.

And I want to get rid of my guilt. I need to feel whole again. Do you understand what I'm saying? Do you?

She holds my hand too tightly. My fingers are turning pale at the tips. They look like white asparagus.

Don't look at our hands, Gili says. Don't do that. Look at my face. Or do you have issues with that?

I stare at her face, but slowly feel my face getting drawn in by it. Those eyes … I can't describe them … those lips … yes, I'm six inches from her lips when Holly walks in holding a spare electronic key.

What the hell? Holly asks. What the hell is this?

Then she screams at me.

TWENTY-THREE

WE SIT IN THE TRUTH Room, the four of us: me, Holly, Gili, and Norman. There's one bulb on and it's red, of course. Candles are lit on tables around the room, mostly at the back. The sound of wind is piped in through hidden speakers. It's supposed to relax us. We're around a Tibetan table made of IKEA wood, which is essentially pressed cardboard painted piss-yellow and beaten with dog chains to make it look old and weathered. The candlelight makes silhouettes on the wall, our heads hulking black potato heads, unmoving and stoic. The place smells like mint. It might be the tea on the back table.

No one speaks; we are taking a moment to consider our lives, Norman says. We are taking stock of things: the way the world swirls around us, the rhythms of life.

I wonder how I managed to get here in this stupid meditation centre in the middle of the Salish Sea with two women whom, yes, I apparently slept with and who are somewhat related, and tons of fake cash in my backpack, which is safe between my legs on the floor made of reclaimed lumber from an abandoned silver mine somewhere to the north.

I know Holly wants me to look at her.

She's willing me to throw her a glance. I refrain. I need to be strong.

Everyone breathing? Norman asks the quiet room.

I think about a smartass answer, but just nod.

The others probably think the same.

We all nod.

And we all breathe.

Good, Norman says. Very, very good. We're all in a terrific place then.

I notice that when Norman talks, his facial muscles barely move, almost like he's been reanimated by Disney on *Star Wars*. You see it a lot in hospital wards for the elderly. Although, to be fair, Norman isn't much older than sixty, I'm guessing. Only a few years older than me.

He has laser-blue eyes. He may be made of ice, too, his whole body slightly frozen.

Norman raises a pale, bony finger to his blue lips.

Shh, he says. Shh.

The room turns cold. Instantly.

I hear my father's slippers now sliding across linoleum.

It's Christmas Eve, and I've just knocked over the tree.

He's coming for me. He's mad as hell.

All right, says Norman. Let's begin.

He lays his hands on the table, flat, as if to smooth out the dents hammered into the fake wood by some poor IKEA worker in rural China.

There is a matter of an exchange that must happen, Norman says, slowly and deliberately. We have one person who is willing to let go of something in order for someone else to let go of something too.

Holly takes his hand and squeezes it.

Norman, she says. Let's be clear. This is simple blackmail. I want cash from this cheating husband in exchange for a sex tape I found on his dead friend's camera.

Well, actually *I* found it, I say quickly.

Well, I took it, didn't I, Andy? says Holly.

It wasn't yours to take, I say.

It wasn't your affair to take, she says. Was it?

Of course, it was, I say. There's nothing wrong with having sex with another person even if you are married to somebody else. It may be slightly immoral, but it's not like stealing — which is what you did.

I'm not stealing, Holly says. I'm protecting your poor wife.

You have a funny way of protecting, I say.

I'm the Robin Hood of blackmailers. What can I say, Holly smirks.

Look, Norman says with a frown. Look, can we be civil with this transaction?

And he slept with me, Holly says.

I definitely have that proverbial blank look on my face.

You just don't remember because I roofied you with magic mushrooms, Holly says.

Holly leans forward in her chair.

Was it good for you? Was it?

Norman waves her quiet.

Please, we need to focus, he says. Who cares who slept with whom and why?

Gili says, Gee whiz. Thanks. That really helps.

Gili shuffles in her seat and then sighs and gets up and moves to the table in the back where Norman has three kinds of tea set up: mint, green, and turmeric glow.

I say, I just didn't expect tea.

Norman smiles. It's by donation, he says. From the centre.

Then I get up and wander across the room to help myself to the tea, trying to stall for time. I'm elbow to elbow with Gili.

How could you? Holly? Gili whispers at me. With my father's former lover?

I was drugged, I say. You heard her.

Just so you know, Gili says, pouring milk into her tea, if you hadn't been a famous director, it would have been a stupid one-night stand I would have forgotten about by the next morning.

Ouch, I think.

Then she returns to the mediation table where Norman sits unblinking like a statue of himself. He's heard us. I know it.

I pour myself some turmeric glow and hold it up to the dim, red light. Then I shuffle back to my spot at the table and sit down beside my backpack.

Give me the money, Holly says. Then get off my fucking island.

Norman pretends to wince.

Look, he says. I want you people to relax. We need to get

along. This is what our centre is all about. Peace and meditation. And wholeness.

I sip my tea, then move the cup out of the way and throw my backpack on the table.

You give me the memory card from the camera, and I give you the cash. That's how it works.

Norman reaches out with a bony hand and takes the backpack. He pulls it toward Holly, but when she goes to grab it, he frowns and pulls it away.

No, he warns. Please. What do you offer?

Holly digs around in her wallet, which looks handmade by an eight-year-old at Girl Guides camp and pulls out the chip like it's a rare diamond, holding it up between her index finger and thumb.

You better not be screwing with me, Holly says.

Likewise, I say.

She gives Norman the chip, and he gives it to me. I immediately pull my laptop out of the backpack and plug in the memory card.

It doesn't take long for the dirty images to disgust me even though it's mostly my own naked body doing the disgusting. I pull the memory card.

Then Holly pulls out the packs of cash. She doesn't actually open any of the bundles — which is a very good thing for me, considering only the first few bills front and back are actually bona fide twenties. The rest is paper with the same-coloured edges.

Norman picks up a bundle, looking us over while rifling through it.

Then there's the question of my fee, he says.

What? I say.

What? Holly says.

You don't think I would mediate this transaction for nothing.

Norman reaches into his breast pocket and pulls out a joint, then another one. And another one.

We must smoke together and consider our options.

I'm not smoking dope with you, you lunatic, Holly says.

Tut, tut, madam, Norman says. On Cortes Island we share.

Gili grabs a joint.

Then the candle.

Fuck this, she says. Let's do this. Things might improve. Who knows?

Look, Holly says, I hate to break up the party here, but just so you know, it would be stupid for me to have just one copy of the sex tape.

Well, Norman says, that would be unfortunate for all.

His voice has become deeper and more sinister, particularly as he relights the candle, his face looming over it. He uses an old Zippo.

Gili takes a deep puff from her joint and holds it in her lungs, and when she speaks, the smoke speaks too.

This is getting weird, she blurts.

Lovely, Norman says. Lovely sentiment.

The room has slowly shrouded itself in smoke.

Holly looks me over and says, You've made a fine mess of things, haven't you, Andy?

Why does everybody think I'm an asshole? I ask. I'm in process, right? That's why I'm going to do my feature here on Cortes. It's going to be therapeutic.

Holly laughs softly through a puff or two.

That's rich, she murmurs. Rich.

We sit there.

Norman clears his throat.

Is there a part for me?

What? No, I say. Why would there be a part for you?

Norman says, I mean, I'd assumed you'd heard of me through IMDB.

What? Why would I?

Well, if you'd come to Cortes without knowing I spent five years on *Stargate* as the untrustworthy American general who worked for the Edorans, I would be sadly disappointed, my friend.

My brain races to think of when I might have seen him.

Stargate?

I look at his — my — bundle of cash. He looks at me looking at his/my bundle of cash.

He clears his throat.

Norman finishes the joint, then licks his lips, and I see how they belong in a Western, along with his face, which is begging to be brimmed by a cowboy hat — a black one, preferably.

He looks at me like he's holding a shotgun and I've got a little knife.

Yes, one could assume I'm just a little famous, he says.

Well, I've never heard of you, I sputter.

What? What did you say? Norman says very slowly.

Yeah.

There's a movie moment in this place, sitting at this stupid, fake wooden table in this fake meditation room with my fake money in front of us like a prop, which is sort of exactly what these bundles are, and everything I've done to get to this point has been fake. But maybe that's what happens when you lie and cheat and have no moral standing. Maybe that's what happens when you have sex with your wife's best friend and she then disappears on your kayaking trip. Maybe that's just how it goes when you're a loser and you can't seem to understand what it means to be whole and not just an asshole. Maybe it all ends here. In the meditation room on Cortes Island smoking dope with three lunatics. Four, if you include me. And you should.

Norman picks up the bundle of cash and smells it like it's fish that's been sitting out on the counter for a day.

This transaction needs to be authentic, he says to the room.

Norman reaches out and unlocks my one hand from the other. I've been squeezing my hands together for the last ten minutes.

Look at me, he says. Look.

And I do.

His eyes, those dead pools of blue lit by the candle, seem to flicker too.

What?

Don't you want to feel authentic for once in your sad, disillusioned life?

Yes, I say. I do.

And truthfully, who wouldn't say that?

My ears hurt because I can hear my heart pounding. It's not a good pounding. My ribs ache.

We're in the same boat, Norman says, now patting the backs of my fingers. I would like to make a proposal. I propose we give back these bundles of cash.

What? Holly stands up. Why would I do that?

Norman stares her down calmly.

Because this man is about to do something authentic, aren't you?

I lick my lips and now feel my eyelids starting to pound too.

What is it I'm about to do? I can barely get the words out because I feel like crying. Pot does that to me.

Norman says, I'll articulate it for you. First, you will take this cash back and deposit it in your bank. Second, all of us in this room will sign an official contract with you. For me, it's a starring role. For Holly, it's for her location rental. For Gili, it's for a major role as well. Maybe as a love interest.

I'm not interested in being a love interest if you're my interest, Gili says to Norman. I have high standards, okay? And you're old enough to be my father.

Wait a minute, I say. What's in it for me?

A legitimate write-off. Plus you keep the money and not get blackmailed.

Norman holds my hand up like I've just knocked somebody out.

Look, Champ. For tax purposes, it's important that everything is legitimate and authentic and proven. You need to leave a proper paper trail for a proper business loss. And. We're in it for artistic reasons. Right?

Norman grabs Holly's hand too.

I'm listening, Holly says, leaning forward. Their heads are inches apart.

It's free advertising, isn't it? Norman says. Free.

Well, I say. Not exactly. I mean, it's not free for me, is it?

He drops our hands gently.

What's the total budget of the film? Norman asks. Is it the normal range?

Depends on what you think is normal, I say.

Let's blue sky it, Norman says rubbing his nose. How about eight million?

How about around two hundred thousand? I smile. Because

really that's all I have, and if I'm spending that amount right now to you people, what does that leave me with to pay anyone else? Like real talent? Nothing.

Gili sighs.

Oh Jesus, she says.

You really think you can make a movie for that paltry amount? Norman looks around the room and stifles a giggle.

I mean, come on, don't be naive, he says. Quality costs money. And just to get into festivals will cost you an arm and a leg. Then there's Errors and Omissions insurance. That's twenty or thirty grand right there. And you need a good band for the soundtrack. That's going to cost you another twenty or thirty. And postproduction will cost a fortune. And getting a full crew up here … well, that's bloody expensive.

Where am I going to come up with millions? I ask. I couldn't raise that kind of dough if I tried.

How about a million?

No, I say. I don't know anybody with that kind of cash, and all of the funding bodies already turned us down. We happen to be middle-aged, white dudes, if you haven't noticed, and we're making a movie about middle-aged, white dudes who cheat on their wives. It's a fucking dramedy of epic proportions.

We sit there bathed in silence.

I love it, Norman finally says. Honestly. This is right up my alley.

Norman picks up his phone from the table and texts somebody. He holds up a finger.

Wait for it, he says. Wait.

I wait, but I feel the sweat running down my pant leg and my wool socks start to itch. I'm hot and the room starts to spin. A little. What was in that joint?

Norman clears his throat. Does anyone want a bagel? We've got some rosemary rock-salt ones fresh out of the oven. They're wonderful with a little organic butter and honey. We have a lot of busy little bees around here.

A little knock on the door. Kerry walks in, now wearing what looks to be a sharp business suit. She has a tablet in front of her like she's using Google Maps. She navigates to our table quickly, her face lit by the glow of the screen.

Hello, dear, Norman says.

Kerry smiles.

Hey. What's the plan?

How about a million? Norman says to me.

Kerry smiles.

I can have contracts printed within the hour, she says. I love working on features.

Wonderful, Norman says. Now, about the script …?

Gili and Holly and Kerry all look at me.

My eyes itch. My hair hurts. I need to floss.

What is this? I ask. What exactly is going on?

It's a corporate take-over, Norman says. But a friendly one. I've been looking for a project to run my fortune through ever since I left the industry for the safe confines of this so-called yogi centre, and now I think I've got it. I have a production company, and we produced a couple of shorts that CBC aired years ago. They were about my life as a hermit on this beautiful, pristine island. But now this island has a chance for a starring role. And that, my friend, might just create enough publicity to stop the oil tankers from going through.

Norman pauses.

Come on, everybody knows about the oil tankers. They come

through here four or five times a day. And one spill will change everything. One spill and all of this will be gone. Can you fucking imagine that?

We sit there.

But you don't know anything about the project. I mean, not really, I say.

Is it about a disillusioned man about my age?

Norman prods me with a finger.

Look. Is it about a man about my age trying to find meaning to life?

It is, I say. In a way.

I have friends in high places, my friend, Norman says.

Norman went out for drinks with Billy Zane last month on his boat, Kerry gushes. A forty-seven-footer.

I did, Norman says. We drank Campari all night. And in the morning, we had flapjacks with real maple syrup. We were so hungover. But what a charmer. A keeper. Billy Zane is a mensch. He really loves sea otters.

Seals, Kerry corrects him.

Seals, right.

Billy Zane? I say. Wow. That's amazing.

Gili clears her throat.

I can tell you it's a great script because I've read it before. There are so many great lines, and the characters are amazing, she says in her usual smoky voice, like she was raised in some jazz bar in Chicago. And there's a kayak trip.

Gili is acting now. And doing a great job of it.

Wonderful, Norman says. So. That does it, then, doesn't it?

This is a moment that feels filmic. It seems defining for me. I wrinkle my brow as if to corner doubt. I mean, I've just doubled my money, haven't I? Actually, quadrupled it. Right? Shit, I am stoned. Really stoned. Did I just lose control or earn a seasoned partner?

Norman reaches out again, and I'm shocked at how long his arms look right now — serpentine, actually — and he makes this sound with his tongue between his front teeth like a hiss, but not a hiss.

Yes, he says. Yes.

Let it go. Let it go.

My friend.

A moment. Close my eyes. Think. Wait for some peace — after all, this is a meditation room — or divine guidance or something.

Okay, I can send the script, I say, fumbling for my phone. But I'm not sure you guys have internet service yet, do you?

Everything's back to normal, Norman says. Send it.

I hit send on my phone, then slam it down on the table for effect.

Norman gathers up the bricks of fake cash and pushes them back into my bag.

We don't need to talk about what just happened here, do we? I mean, I didn't see any cash, did you?

I shake my head slowly.

Gili and Holly follow suit.

I feel the air come out of me. It makes me sad all of a sudden. But in a good way.

Norman leans back and crosses his spindly arms. He does the head turret thing and takes in each one of us momentarily: Gili, who smiles weakly; Holly, who crosses her arms; and me, I think I'm drooling.

Yes. Drooling.

Now, Norman says quietly. When can we start?

TWENTY-FOUR

WE SIT OUTSIDE IN THE sun and wait for Will and Deborah. It's hot. Like we're suddenly on a tropical island and the heat settles around us like a hoop dress. Norman fans himself with some of the contracts from the pile on the stool in front of him. He's drinking a martini. Grace and Prince play with a shredded tennis ball on the neatly manicured lawn along the front façade of the building. She has the dog doing tricks, figure eights around her legs and jumps and crawls. It's all very impressive considering none of her instructions are in English.

When Will wanders out into the sun with Deborah beside him, I see he looks different, almost like he's emerging from a tent revival meeting in the 1930s and he's been converted. He's been on the hallelujah train. Amen and amen. His eyes look puffy, and he's got a silly-ass grin. But he looks peaceful, particularly because the top of his head has a white rim around it from where his cap usually is. It's the only part of his head that never gets sun, I guess. It's clear he's now Friar Tuck, not Producer Will.

Hey, he says to me.

Hey, I say. Everything okay?

Oh, yeah, he says. It is. Everything is really okay.

Have you been crying?

Yeah, maybe. A little.

What happened in there?

It just hit me, he says. The whole enchilada.

Wow, I say.

Mind blown, he whispers. Mind fucking blown.

Deborah wanders up to me. She looks like she's found something. And she has.

Holds out an envelope with Anna written on the front.

Hand shakes.

A little.

Here, she says. I'm sorry.

Uh, I say. What's going on?

We found this in a drawer in of one of the rooms back there, Deborah says. Obviously, it's for your wife. Poor thing.

From —

It's from Sarah, Deborah says.

It is?

Yes, Deborah says. It's like a suicide note, but it's more of a goodbye, I suppose.

You found that in there? For my wife?

Yes, Deborah says. In the room where Sarah stayed. Before the accident. We found it in the bottom drawer under a Tibetan prayer cloth thing.

Why would she leave it here? I ask.

I don't know, Deborah says. Maybe she didn't intend for it to be found. Or maybe she forgot about it. Maybe it was a practice letter. A rough copy.

Oh, I say. And, you read it?

Of course, I read it, Deborah says. That's my job. But I don't need to keep it. Your wife needs it.

I hold the envelope like it's a dead butterfly. I don't know where to put it, actually.

Deborah puts on her sunglasses and watches Prince play on the lawn.

Wow, she's got that dog going good, Deborah says. He loves her. Look at that weave he's doing between her legs. When did he learn that?

She's good with animals, I say. Evidently.

I fold the envelope and put it in my shirt pocket, patting it after to make sure it stays there.

Norman wanders up to me holding contracts out.

I need Will to sign, he says. Then it's off to the races.

Will wanders over.

Sign what?

Norman is going to produce our feature, I say. He's investing in it.

And starring in it too, Norman says. I just read the script and it's brill. Absolutely brill.

Thanks, I say. I wrote it. Mainly.

Norman smiles like a tiger. Lovely work. Lovely, my friends. But less monologues and more snappy dialogue and "Bob's Your Uncle", right? Sign please.

Will puts on his hat.

I'll sign. I don't care, he says. I'm out anyway. I really don't give a shit.

What?

I grab him by the shoulders. What?

I've had ... I went through something in there, Will says. I mean, what is my special purpose in life? What am I supposed to be doing? I don't have a lot of time left.

You have plenty of time, I say.

Nope, Will says. Nope. I do not.

You're supposed to make this feature, I say. You're supposed to help produce and direct our feature. What the fuck.

Not anymore, Will says. I'm going to become a conservation officer.

What are you talking about, Will? Snap out of it. Jesus, I say, shaking him a bit.

One of my degrees is in Criminology, and Deborah said they are looking for people up here. I just want to protect and serve this area, Will says. I mean, look at this place. Look at it. It's amazing, and it's all around us, and pretty soon, if we're not careful, it will all be gone.

Will holds out his hands as if pretending to be a human barometer. Or something.

But what about our movie?

It's all yours, Will says. All yours. Have fun. I mean, if I can help you out when I'm not on the job, I will, but nature calls. And I might be out on a boat. In the middle of the Salish Sea. Protecting a pod of orcas that claim this sea as their territory. Or maybe I'll be collecting abandoned baby seals or something. There's a lot I can be doing. I'm not going to stand around anymore. Not a chance. I'm on a mission.

Are you nuts?

Have you noticed all the tankers? Will says. Have you? It's time we reclaim the sea for nature again and live and let live.

You're quoting Bond films, I say. Are you high?

I over-shake Will. Not fun. Will wobbles.

Deborah wanders over with Prince on his leash. Hey, you. Stop shaking my fiancé!

What?

Will smiles, saying, Yeah, big surprise on that one, for sure. We're getting married in four months, and we're going up north to Bella Bella for the honeymoon. Her ex-husband — Vern — has a fishing lodge there, and we're getting a week free in the Halibut Room.

Are you … wait, I stutter. This isn't you.

I know, Will says. I've changed. This place, this trip has changed me. And I have you to thank for all this.

Please don't thank me, I say. Please.

Look, you can produce it all yourself now, Will says. Have fun. Even though you have no budget and nobody in it.

Norman pushes the contracts in front of Will.

Well, he says, I think that's all changed. I'm in it. Billy Zane is in it, and the budget has just climbed to three million. Billy loved the script. Absolutely loved it. And he's dropping a million or so into it too. He wants to play the part of the other cheating bastard husband and feels it might be a breakthrough part for him.

Will looks like I just shot him with a bean bag. Then clears his throat. Looks around him at the sky and trees and dog playing and Deborah waving at the dog and …

He smiles. It's a rather toothy, lame one — the kind you make at awards presentations when you walk away with nothing, including your pride.

Doesn't matter, Will finally sighs. I have my freedom. I have made my choice and I feel good about it. Life is good. Life is very good. Life is grand.

Deborah wanders over, cellphone in hand.

I feel good, Will repeats to her. Right?

Of course, you do, sweetie, Deborah says, grabbing him by the arm and dragging him toward a police cruiser in the parking lot where a super tall Mountie with a neat beard stands guard.

You're going to make one hell of a conservation officer, Deborah says. We need good men like you.

Will turns around and waves at me weakly.

Peace and prosperity, my friend, he croaks.

What are you doing, Will? The cops are taking you away, don't you get it?

I hope you find love too, Will says. It's a beautiful thing. Maybe having a good cry will help you. You need to change, bro. Stop fucking around. Life is too short. Okay, bye.

Then he gets in the cruiser with Deborah and Prince, who bounds into the back hatch-door opened by the basketball-player-turned-Mountie. He gets in after tipping his hat at me, and they leave quietly.

No lights flashing.

Just a quiet escape into the trees and gone.

I can feel the air coming out of me.

I want to collapse, but it's no good. I can't.

I see Norman playing with Grace's camera while she sits in the shade of the lone pine on the front lawn looking depressed and holding the ragged tennis ball.

Wandering up to Norman in this heat, I feel like I'm pushing all the air in front of me to get there. Eventually I stand next to him, both of us breathing into the back of the view screen.

This footage is amazing, Norman says. We need to use it. Who took it?

I take a quick peek, and it's all of Prince jumping in slow motion, happiness in sixty frames per second.

She did, I say pointing to Grace. She took it all.

Grace says, That's my new Sony. Excellent camera.

I hired her for this trip, I say. She's learning as she goes. Still in school, but when she graduates lots of people will want to hire her. She's fantastic.

I suddenly notice how hollow I sound. Words come out of me like I've been cast out of bronze. A shell of bronze. A shell of a man.

Norman turns the camera over like it's treasure. He plays with the buttons.

Well. This is amazing stuff; she's a real pro. Maybe we can get her on the second unit to shoot pick-up stuff, location shots. She's got a beautiful way of composing shots, don't you think?

That's why we brought her, I say quietly. She's a talent.

My eyes still throb and my throat feels scratchy. I'm coming down with something.

Love it. Just love your work, Norman says, giving the Sony back to Grace. I notice suddenly that she wears a long white dress over her jeans, too. Why didn't I see that before? I wonder. It's completely out of character for her.

Where did you get that dress?

Grace points back to the centre.

They asked me if I wanted it, and it fits so I am practising wearing it.

We have a lot of white outfits in there, Norman says. It helps with the meditation.

Norman looks around, suddenly deciding to end our meeting.

The sun suddenly lights the top of Norman's grey head, and he ducks away quickly to remain in the shade. I think I see steam coming off his forehead, but it might be smoke.

Grace stands up with her camera now around her neck. I decide that the dress looks good on her, although it doesn't go with the Sony.

I have footage of the storm, Grace says. The one that knocked down trees. It is my best footage. Trees fall. Lots of trees fall. And it's not expected.

I bet, Norman says, turning back from the safety of the shade. You rock, young lady. I'm impressed.

He flashes a Hollywood smile.

It's then I notice Holly standing under the awning at the front door of the centre, talking to Gili. From a distance, it looks like they could be siblings. I know they're talking about me because they see me looking at them and then lean in to whisper.

Norman sees me see this and moves closer like we are secret sharers. He smells like organic aftershave, whatever that might be. Maybe apples? But he also has the mouth smell of a secret smoker.

We both stare at them, and it's clear we're thinking the same thing.

They are wonderful women, he whispers. Beautiful creatures. But watch yourself, my friend.

Then the two women march in unison toward me.

Norman excuses himself.

You three obviously have a lot of catching up to do, he says. I'll have my assistant call you when Billy gets his schedule clear for the shoot. And I'll email you the signed contracts and some information about where we'll do our banking, that sort of stuff. Let's make this happen, my friend. Let's do this!

He does a circus clown bow and gives me a grin where I see he has extra teeth, mainly in the front. I'm surprised by the toothiness of it all.

You will absolutely love Mister William Zane, Norman says. Trust me, he's a real mensch.

Then he leaves, perfectly timing his exit.

I dread hearing the words I know Holly is about to say. Dread it. But here they come.

We've been talking, Holly says.

She points the bottom of her walking stick at me, and I can tell it's sharp because there's a leaf impaled at the end. Trembling.

Holly hesitates briefly, sizes me up.

I have a hand to my head shielding my eyes from the brightness of the day.

Holly takes a deep breath.

We've decided that despite the fact you're a complete douche bag and not to be trusted, we're going to work with you because the money is good.

Gili chimes in, Yeah, the money's really good now. Thanks for that and thanks for the part.

Right, I say. No problem. Thank Norman.

We also think we know what's in that suicide note, and that's going to be enough punishment for you, I'm sure.

Holly says that. And she says it with no apparent irony or humour. Just a matter of fact.

What are you talking about? I say. Come on.

Lesson learned, don't you think? You already look like a changed man.

Not sure who said that. One of them did.

My hand slowly goes to my heart.

Okay, I say. Thanks. I think.

I shuffle my feet. I'm hoping to feel different. But I don't.

We can walk back with you and Grace so you can make the last ferry, Holly says. You have a few hours before it leaves. But you better be on it or else you'll be trapped on this island forever.

She laughs.

Oh, I will leave, I say. I don't have to be here any longer. Not a chance.

Holly smiles.

Good, she says. Happy trails, I'm sure. Right?

Right.

Gili pretends to clear her throat. The pretense is very obvious. She has very rosy cheeks right now, like she's been breathing in too much fresh air and eating strawberries.

She does a pirouette. Not sure why, but I think it's because she likes everything around her.

This place is starting to grow on me, Gili says. It might be the air. It might be the trees. It might even be the water. But I know I love this place. I love it!

She stops mid-spin and looks at me — hoping I'll say something embarrassing, I'm sure. Not this time, I think. Not today.

Gili reaches out, I think to touch me on the cheek, but instead pulls a small twig out of my hair.

You okay in there?

She leans in and leans in, rosy lips and everything. Her eyes are brown and catch light, blink, blink.

There it is. There it is.

Hey, Gili repeats. What's going on?

I really find this island strange, I say. Don't you?

I can tell neither one of them will agree.

Holly bends on her stick and stares me down with her pale blue eyes as I try to loosen my neck muscles and lower my blood pressure.

I rub my forehead, hoping for a magic thought.

These two women have amazing eyes, I think instead. Amazing. And they're so fit. And so attractive.

What am I thinking? I say that aloud, obviously.

You're just shocked because your best friend in the whole world has decided to choose true love and commitment instead of whatever it is you're always choosing. Isn't that right, Andy?

Holly says that.

Then Holly grabs Gili by the arm.

I'm staying with Holly for a couple of nights, Gili says. We have some catching up to do.

Holly, Gili, both stand in front of me with crossed arms. They wait as I wait. Gili bites her lip. Holly raises an eyebrow.

Okay, I say. Let's go.

I walk back to the front of the building and grab my backpack. It feels lighter. Before I can turn around, Norman grabs me and pulls me into the shade of the front door.

I've kept the paper, the fake money, he says. You really shouldn't have tried that idiotic scheme. Fake money? It's really, really stupid. Amateurish, in fact. But it makes me happy to know how sneaky you are. You're a real producer, all right. We are going to work wonderfully together. You're like my evil twin. Don't you think?

How did you know? I ask.

My friend, that trick was so obvious and so old I'm surprised you weren't found out earlier. It's from the 1970s. Nobody really thinks that kind of bullshit works these days, but your cover is safe with me. So far. I had Kerry dispose of the blanks. We'll use them in our compost pile for the tomatoes.

I see Kerry, still dressed in black, sitting on the desk in the lobby, legs crossed tightly. She points at me with her finger and makes it go off. BANG. BANG.

Then she blows pretend smoke away. Smiles and points to the stack of contracts on her lap.

See you soon, cowboy, she says. Then she gets up from her perch and disappears into the back, toward the sounds of the men's choir singing "Get Lucky" by Daft Punk from deep within the belly of the meditation centre.

Her ass is …

Hey. She's my daughter, Norman says. Don't ogle her. You're far too old for that kind of shit.

I'm sorry, I say. I wasn't doing anything.

Yes, you were, old man, Norman says. You were. Grow up. We have a lot of work to do if we're going to do justice to cheating husbands in this feature, or anywhere for that matter.

Then he leaves after slapping me on the back with an open palm. It hurts, but then, that's maybe what he was hoping for. I wouldn't have thought a man that skinny could slap backs that hard. But apparently, he's had practice at it. Hollywood. Where backs get slapped a lot and other parts get screwed.

Norman slithers away, arms akimbo and legs stiff like celery sticks. I honestly don't know how he does it, but there's a jerkiness to his motion like travelling on this earth has always been tricky for him, and he feels better seated in the lotus position.

He gets to the entrance of the meditation centre and then, quite deliberately, folds in half, kind of sits down exactly how I found him when I approached earlier in the day: cross-legged and with palms up, barely breathing.

Six big crows walk across the lawn to perch around Norman on the porch, three on each side.

They ruffle their feathers in unison.

The world spins around him.

I catch myself saying …

Whatever.

I put on my Maui Jim sunglasses, adjust them on my sunburnt nose, and head out into the light where Gili and Holly await.

I'm aware of their teeth, which catch the light.

Holly grabs one arm and Gili grabs the other. I'm in the middle, feeling a little like a nine-year-old, which might be entirely appropriate for this threesome.

Let's go, someone says.

When we hit the pavement, I notice that the fallen trees have all been removed, cut and set aside into rows like gravestones.

The setting sun makes the blacktop glow.

Golden.

We leave Oz for the dark cabin with the sun at our backs.

Behind me, Grace.

TWENTY-FIVE

THE FERRY RIDE OUT OF Cortes is almost uneventful. We see some kayakers. A cruise ship. One humpback. The second ferry ride is short and boring. Nothing happens except a quick cup of really bad coffee. Only half full. The last ferry passes a whale-watching boat that capsized the week before; we take a circuitous route around booms set up to contain a growing oil slick. Only the tip of the boat is visible; a shark's fin of metal that catches waves, including our wake. The accident claimed the lives of three tourists from the Netherlands when the overloaded boat flipped over from a rogue wave. They had been all standing on one side of the top deck, watching seals, and when the wave hit it didn't take much — over it went. Unbalanced, experts said. Top-heavy. If it wasn't for the Coast Salish fishers who witnessed the accident, more tourists would have died.

Fished out the Dutch like they were big trout.

Halibut, Grace corrects me.

Sorry, I say. I thought trout sounded funny.

Not so funny, Grace says. Halibut though … is somewhat humorous. Because of the "but".

Great, now you're telling me what's funny and what's not.

That's the story, Grace quips. Perhaps you need some help.

Yeah, right. I laugh. I need help. Ha.

I zip up my windbreaker. Dusk now. Cooler. The air makes my hair stand on end. A bit here and there so I got the Stan Laurel look going on.

I say that aloud and into the wind.

Who's Stan Laurel? asks Grace. Does he play for the Canucks?

Yeah, that's what I get for standing by the rail not being funny.

I also get suicidal thoughts. But that's another thing, I say.

Grace laughs. That's funny, Mister. Good one.

She drifts away from me. Pulls her bangs out of her face.

Grace has her Sony out and takes a movie of the wreck. Most of the other passengers hang out along the rail and do the same thing. The slick is endless, and as we float past the last of the booms, it continues marking our way back toward civilization with the last of the sun, the water and oil now a mirror to the sky.

It's a fluorescent rainbow, but without depth.

Look — where it goes … we go, Grace says. What do you think that means?

I don't think it means anything, I say. It's just shitty. Very shitty.

I want to go in and have another coffee, but I notice another oil tanker in the distance; the red and white navigation lights warning others, I suppose, of its looming presence. The hull now so dark and low on the water it looks like a croc sliding by.

Grace sees it too.

Another one, she says. Six, so far today. Six.

Let's go inside. Come on, it's getting cold out here.

We turn at the same time, bump into an old man — a very old, very tall man — and what I think at first is his daughter. And when I see his daughter's face, clearly she is a he, exceptionally thin with long, blond hair — he could be an elf. They wear matching cowboy clothes, and I'm sure I know him somehow.

Things repeat. They do. A pattern to life.

Hi again, says the old guy. You're back.

What?

You're back with us, he drawls, then takes a drag on the tiny pipe which has been in his spindly hand the whole time.

Yes, I say. Going home.

So, he says. Good journey?

Yeah, I say. Interesting.

I'm trying to place him.

I want to push him aside. I see Grace give him and his son a coin or two.

What are you doing?

Grace looks at me.

I pay this time, she says. Come on. Let's go.

Spindly cowboys stare at us.

Is that all?

Look, guys, I say. We're done.

The two of them block my way. They have their arms held stiffly at their sides as if ready to reach for six-shooters. Their jeans ragged and lived-in with matching ragged blue denim jackets. And they have the biggest shit-kickers on I've ever seen. Dark brown.

Where do you think you're going?

I don't know, I say.

Cowboy son closes his eyes; his blond lashes quiver. He holds out a bony hand, reaches out toward my heart.

What's in there? he whispers. What?

Grace takes a quick shot of him with the Sony, and for the briefest of moments, he's illuminated by the flash.

Bang. But not a bang. A quick bolt of light, I guess.

Zap.

There. Like that.

They are lit up. Again. A second flash.

The cowboy son. He recoils. Staggers two steps back, his hands over his eyes like a vampire seeing the sun.

Crazy legs as he completes his slight stagger. A moment as he catches his balance.

Good one, he says, rubbing his eyes. You got me.

Sorry about that, Grace says. Sorry.

Then she pushes past the cowboys and into the belly of the boat.

Excuse me, I say, brushing past them too. When I pass, I notice how much they smell like sulfur, like they've been smoking since birth.

Have a good trip, says the older one, smoke drifting from his pipe.

I stop for a second and think of a reply.

You bet, I say.

I grab the door to the inside, yank it open, and walk in, carefully stepping over the ledge.

Warm inside. Half full. Mostly retired people, I suppose. The seats are somewhat purple. The floor, too, purple. But darker. Some kids play on a heavily carpeted area at the front where they can run around and fall without a care. There's a little yellow slide set up where a young, blond mother holds her two-year-old at the top and the father, a bald guy with a goatee wearing a Harley Davidson black leather jacket, crouches at the bottom saying come on, girlie, come on. Be brave. Let go. Let go!

And she nods with tears in her eyes while Boney M plays from somebody's phone nearby.

We survey the room carefully before we choose seats near the door where nobody is behind us. We take off our waterproof Gore-Tex jackets. It's like we've removed chain mail.

I decide against having another coffee. Instead, I pop a Tylenol and swallow it dry. Do I have a slight headache? Yes. A little. I put the pill vial back in my bag and kick it under my seat. It isn't very heavy because there's very little in it now: my computer, some underwear, some rocks I found on the beach while waiting for the first ferry on Cortes. They are skipping stones, smooth and flat.

Still standing, I look out the Plexiglas window, scan for the cowboys, their denim.

They're gone, Grace says, sitting nicely. Gone.

I sit down stiffly. Grace pulls out her phone and starts playing with it.

Now I remember. They were on our other ferry, the one on the way here, I say to Grace.

I know, Grace says. Weird.

A lot of the other passengers have ear buds in and most play with their phones like Grace does, but some are asleep, heads leaning on windows or other heads as the powerful engines shake our spines. We're moving steadily; the boat has a belly full of cars and trucks. We humans are the crumbs.

Grace puts her phone down on the crappy, stained seat, screen-side down.

I got a nice contract to shoot some footage, Grace says. From Norman.

Great, I say. Perfect.

So, now I can stay in Canada, Grace says. I am legal.

You weren't legal before?

No, Grace says. I worked at the bar, as they say, under the table. But now, starting in three months, I will shoot this movie. Your movie. Wonderful opportunity. I think.

Three months? Is that what Norman said?

Yes, Grace says. We will go back.

Okay. Wow.

The shoot will last four weeks, and then I will have enough money to last for a long time.

Grace wipes her bangs out of her eyes.

What are they paying you?

She grabs her phone and holds it out, and I see the number, a big number. Some people make that much in a year.

A soft whistle from me. All earned.

I think it's fair, Grace says, now putting her phone inside her jacket near her heart.

Sure, I say. Absolutely. You deserve it.

Grace squeezes my hand for the briefest of moments, then pushes back her sunglasses with her thumb. She stares out the window at the islands and boats that pass us by.

I look around at the old folks falling asleep on seats too small for a curl up because of the arm rests. A lot of necks look broken and white heads everywhere loll awkwardly. Disconnected, I guess. Aren't we all?

We sail back to the city half asleep, half aware, half dead. The shore is surrounded by shadowy mountains. Shapes I can only imagine, the dark getting darker.

Grace yawns.

I just need a place to live, she says into her fist as if stifling a cough. I gave my notice. And now there is nowhere to rent. The city has a big problem that way. So, after this week, I will probably need to sleep under a bridge. It will be my fate.

She's trying to be funny, I think. Smile a bit. Let her know. Funny.

It's not funny, Grace says then, reading my thoughts, obviously. She pulls on my sleeve just a little. I need help, mister. I do.

Right, I say.

Then I sit there for a moment. Just sit there.

You have a nice place? Grace asks.

Yes, I say. It's a house in the east end. Three bedrooms, two bathrooms. Big yard because of the dog.

You have a dog? Grace says as she looks me over.

She pushes her bangs apart. I can tell she's excited.

Yes, I say. She's an Australian Shepherd. Nine years old. Very smart. Like a German Shepherd. Only smarter. She's actually my wife's dog. She's the one who looks after it. She's a lot more … attentive.

I know the breed. They are active. Like me, Grace says.

You should stay with us, I say. We have lots of room.

Thanks, Grace says. I accept.

We sit with the slow throb of the big ferry engines tickling our butts through the ferry seats. Watch very dark clouds pass by, caught by the row of endless windows port side, a gull moving through each frame like it's 35mm. Then gone. Gone in an instant.

Light. Then gone with the wave of a cloud shadow. Black top meets black water. We're in it, though. Big time.

The water has us.

The ferry horn sounds, and the old folks momentarily lift their heads.

In unison. They look around for no reason, ignoring the fact that others also look around. It's a choir of What the hell was that?

I touch my wedding ring and twist it down away from my knuckle. It itches. Right to the palm.

I love dogs, Grace says.

Really?

I think it's obvious, Grace smiles. Don't you think?

TWENTY-SIX

LET ME FIRST BE CLEAR about kayaking: I don't like it. You're at the mercy of the sea and when the sea is angry, you're just a bug to it. One misstep and you're in the drink. People die all the time doing this. But I'm doing this to save our marriage.

It's fall. And the water is colder than we thought. Rougher.

But Anna insisted. It was our chance to reconnect, she said, because I've been so preoccupied, first with the impending lawsuit over the kid and then with the feature. Although I was released early. Relegated to a co-writer credit while Billy Zane directs and Norman stars with Gili who's turned out to be a great foil to his cheating bastard. What a character. Really, who cares? She's a great younger woman. Plays one perfectly. Takes shit from no one. I lasted four days on set and then felt my spirit getting crushed after Billy "Zany" Zane started rewriting my feature to make it darker and more relevant. It's too nice, he yelled at me. You're too nice, he said. Don't be such a Canadian. Let's find the heart. We'll find the fucker. We need more drama. Come on. Let's work together, people. Dammit. Where's the grip? And what's with all this fucking rain?

My source now is Dave, who got the lighting gig and sends me text updates from the location, which is Holly's cabin. Yeah, she's making six figures too because she also got a part. Turns out she's a natural at playing somewhat evil. A natural femme fatale. Also turns out she's going out with Billy, who by the way, is charming as hell.

We're going to make magic out of your crap, he said to me before I left. You leave out the drama and you leave out the transformation and you can't have a story without transformation, dude.

It happens.

People can disagree on the story. Part of the journey, right?

At least I have a clearly defined character. Although he might seem to be an asshole, he still is *my* asshole. Is he me? Hardly. Come on, I'm an artist, not a narcissist.

Billy Zane announces my departure with, He's an inspiration, people. We're doing this all for you. Never forget that! We'll fix your script. Humanity, right? That's the secret. Bon voyage, dude.

Everyone on set clapped.

The grip whistled.

The best boy did a follow spot as I crossed the set and got into my car and drove off. I could see him turn off the light in my rearview mirror.

So, they continue on the island of Cortes while I continue outside, circling the island. In a kayak built for two. Yup. We bought three kayaks. Two singles and a double. And only 4500 bucks.

I'm in the back.

Dressed in red in the red kayak, Anna forges ahead. Her paddle cuts through the water soundlessly.

That's an exaggeration. You can't cut water without some splash. But it feels quiet. No gulls, no hawks, no eagles. That, too, is an exaggeration.

They're here, but they're hidden from us, and I believe some of them crouch in dark pines and watch us stroke the water.

No fish, no whales, no seals.

They're hiding too, but deep under us, probably. Maybe they're circling. Shapes we can only imagine.

In the distance, I can see the ominous clouds curling into themselves with pent-up rage. They're coming, they're coming. The question is: how bad will it get and how soon?

Actually, two questions.

And, what will we do about it?

Three questions.

In the meantime.

Just us and our tiny, insignificant wake and the dark darkening.

Punch the air and pull back on the paddle, push the water away … one, two, one, two … etc.

There's a rhythm to our strokes, and I'm surprised to see how much we're in sync. I don't even think about my timing. We're switching to glide. Big time. And I have no idea where we're actually going. But I'm in the back where I belong. We both pause in mid-stroke to get our bearings.

We need to get out of the water, Anna says over her shoulder.

Good idea.

Our voices hit the water and end up kilometres away just like that.

We follow the shore looking for a place to beach our craft.

This side of Cortes Island juts out of the water stiffly and at the knees, sheer rocks hold up trees sharply. You'd need a rope to scale them. They push us away because of the waves. We try getting around the next bend to find a flat beach.

The waves slap at us.

It's a bit miserable out now. An inconsistent drizzle. Air occasionally colder than expected.

I shouldn't complain. We're out here. We're doing it.

It's an adventure.

It's taking my mind off things.

I'm getting exercise.

Actually, this trip was Anna's idea, but I started her thinking about it because she wanted to come back to Cortes after I told her I was fired.

We're making lemonade, right?

Although to be fair to Mister Zane, I probably punched my own ticket when I said the feature was really about a man who may not be redeemable.

I think that's when he said, Then why make it? What's the point to the journey? Are you just going for the easy laughs? Because that's not fair for any audience. People need change.

He said that while we were smoking pot with Norman.

Show me the love, Billy said.

Sometimes the story needs to find you, he said.

Yeah. You capricious bastard.

There you have it.

I'm better off circling this island as the dark creeps in. Who cares?

I slap at the water with my paddle more than once.

Shit.

Stop thinking about your stupid project, Anna says. Look for a landing.

Okay, I say, dipping my paddle in the water, pretending to push hard.

It all looks the same to me, though. Desolate.

We paddle. The cold grows. My arms hurt more. Darkness settles.

Spotting a slight incline of a beach between slabs of tall, grey rock, Anna turns us toward shore. A couple dozen more strokes and I feel the earth scrape underneath, and before I can bail out, my wife grabs the front of the boat and hauls us to shore.

She holds out her hand and I grab it.

I get out stiffly. My legs are numb from the ride. So are my fingers.

But I'm dry.

I help yank the red kayak away from the water. It's really getting dark. Grab the camping equipment from storage — in big, waterproof, yellow bags — and throw it down like dead salmon. I notice Anna has the Coleman out already, a small flame lighting her face. A grimace. She puts on water for hot tea. She sits on an air doughnut — the kind you buy at the airport to put around your neck during sleepy flights to Toronto — and hunkers down on her tender pudendal nerve waiting for me to hunker with her.

It's the time of night between dusk and dark. I'm not sure there's a word for that ... Nautical Twilight? Let's call it barely-there time because I can barely make anything out including the water. But I can sense it. It writhes nearby. These are my thoughts as I shiver a bit.

Anna clears some hair from her face. Some of it sticks to her high cheekbones from the dampness. Her eyes are narrow and without her glasses it looks like she has a slight squint.

She ceremonially hands me my tea in a metal cup — tin, I think. And when I sip it, I immediately burn the tip of my tongue.

Crap.

Put it down on a flat rock. Adjust my squeaky seat — my special air doughnut — and try to see some fucking stars, but it's still misty out, and there's only a faint twinkle behind that thin veil of whatever hangs over our sorry-ass heads. It's calmer now. The menacing clouds look more innocent now.

Anna clicks on her headlamp.

Becomes a cyclops.

Turns to illuminate the surroundings: pile of rocks there, a bunch of pines here, rocks and a little sand, and then me.

I bite my lip, too.

Anna maintains the light on my face.

It blinds me.

I know this is a weak metaphor, but at one time in my life I would have loved being in the spotlight, especially during shoots with beautiful people.

And openings at theatres.

Dinners with fewer than eight people.

Walking my dog at the outdoor market.

And wine bars. Always wine bars. With oysters.

Yes, with women who are really into me. And tell me I'm just their type. Whatever that means.

Then Anna reaches into the waterproof pocket of her waterproof jacket and pulls out the note from Sarah. Yeah, that note. Still in the envelope, and no, I never did read it. I was tempted, but I wanted to do at least one good thing with the affair — although to be fair, that sounds very stupid.

Anna's headlamp lights the paper like it's irradiated, the orange paper turning bright as a miniature sun — a red dwarf maybe, to put it in scientific terms.

Anna sighs.

I think you know what's going on here, she says quietly.

I actually don't. I try to get comfortable. But I'm on the rocks.

Okay, I say. But first, can I say something?

What are you going to say? That you're sorry for having a bunch of affairs on me?

I put my face in my hands and realize how cold my cheeks are, like I've been in a snowball fight in Stanley Park in January. My fingers aren't much warmer. Although my eyes sting.

Yes, I say. I am.

And that's going to make things better?

Well, there's more than one indiscretion between the two of us, right? I say.

Just stop, she says. Stop right there.

Anna waves the note at me. I'm not sure whether it signals a surrender or an attack.

Well, I say. I'd like to explain some things.

She holds the note up now almost above her head. It flutters a bit.

I'm going to read this, she announces to the forest.

Okay, I say. You've had that note for a while and you haven't said anything to me. And now is the time? Now you want to discuss it?

She sighs and the air going out of her matches the air moving around me. I can't explain it any other way.

A moment as things hang.

I rub my forehead hoping for insight tonight.

Anna puts on her glasses. The ones with the expensive blue frames that give her an owlish look. Here goes.

Reads.

I guess you're wondering why I did what I did. I know it was an awful thing to do, particularly to your best friend.

Is this in the note? I ask.

I get a look and not the kind of look you like to get from your wife. So, I shut my pie-hole and play with my fingers. I try steepling, but the church collapses. My fingers are losing their grip.

Anna continues slowly.

It's a betrayal of the worst kind, I know that. When you commit to a relationship and then throw everything away.

Anna's headlamp slowly pans up, a laser beam at the end of a sniper's rifle. It hits me just above my Gore-Tex heart. Impermeable.

Swallow hard, I do. Look around for help, but really it's completely black now. I can feel the trees bristle.

Anna holds the lit note up to her eyes now for a closer look.

Then.

I only know I love you and whatever happened isn't as important as us. We will always understand what being together means and where we get our strength. A laugh here and there. A glass of wine even though we know it's only lunchtime. A snowstorm where we get to make snow angels even though we're too old for that kind of shit. And kayaking when you know the water might kill us.

I haven't had a deep breath of air for a bit, so I try to get one in.

Anna folds up the note like it's origami purchased from Crate & Barrel.

Looks at me and the headlamp light hits my headlamp light so that we have one stream of bright, eye to eye.

I blink because I'm blind.

And I can't stop shivering for some reason.

I try to clear my eyes, wipe at them, look up to the heavens for help or inspiration, but then the mist hits my eyes, and what the hell, it's useless. It's all useless. Fuck. Me.

I love you, Anna says.

I do too, I say.

No, she says, that's how the note ends.

Oh.

I take a moment to try to figure things out. During this moment, my doughnut decides to lose all of its air and with a hiss, sinks me into the cold gravel of the beach until my ass cheeks turn cold.

It's a bit of a slow-motion sink.

A lowering of sorts until my beam from my headlamp hits the dirt.

Anna giggles.

What's happening to you? You've sunk to new levels.

Shit, I say. Shit. I've sprung a leak.

I get to my feet and try to brush off my expensive kayaking pants that feel like lizard skin, which is entirely appropriate for what I'm feeling right now.

But I notice I'm also really leaking from the eyes. I mean, it's a stream.

Try to compose myself by looking around the night sky, and it's then most of the clouds part enough to show the moon, big and still somewhat low on the water.

A couple of deep, deep breaths.

Look at that, I say, wiping away tears. Look.

Anna sees me see the moon and also stands, but her air doughnut sticks to her ass before falling back to the beach gravel.

It bounces.

Did you hear something? she asks.

No, I say. I mean, I don't think so.

I stare down our surroundings. I'm stalling for time.

With the moon out I can make out the stand of trees hanging around our campsite. They crowd to the end of big, black rocks, some of their roots meandering down the beach toward the water.

Yes, they look like snakes, but almost everything does at this time of the night.

Super-quiet in the supernatural tonight.

We just stand on the beach and feel small.

On the blue planet third from the sun.

Did you want to go out a little? I say. Maybe just a bit? The water is so incredible right now. Calm. Look at the way the light is? Look at it. It's amazing.

I mean it honestly.

The world is around us. We are as insignificant as you can get.

I think I actually say that aloud.

We have a moment here, and it's important to stress it because it appears we are the only humans to exist in this time and place.

Anna grabs my hand, takes a few steps down the incline, and we move to push the red kayak out, ankle-deep in the cold water.

It's easy.

And then stabilizing the craft, briefly waiting for me to settle, Anna does the same thing, plopping her ass in. With our paddles scraping the bottom, we push ourselves out into the water away from the flame of the Coleman on the beach.

Just like that, we slide out together.

Soundless, mainly.

Watch for the rocks, one of us says.

We brace our paddles against the hull and drift into the unknown.

ACKNOWLEDGEMENTS

This is a work of fiction. Names, characters, business, events and incidents are the products of the author's imagination.

There are some people within the world of film, theatre, and literature that need thanking. First and foremost, Marc Côté and Cormorant Books for continuing to support me. Marc's edits are always fantastic, and Cormorant is always an exceptional publisher.

I also recognize and thank the contribution of Melanie Little, who gave it the first read through and edits. Susie Moloney, who read an early manuscript and "blurbed" me. Vern Thiessen, who always inspires my characters. Johnna Wright also helped with editing, notes, and shaping. Thank you, Johnna. And thanks to Jane Male, who I often stole from and sent random chapters for feedback. Jane is very, very funny, thankfully.

Inspiration thanks also to: Bill Dow, Sarah Rodgers, Gili Roskies, Emma Slipp, David Hudgins, Holly MacKay, Christine

Reinfort, Deborah Williams, Norman Armour, Colleen Dockstader, Dawn Brennan, Rodger Cove, Colin Murdock, Stephen Miller, Dennis and Eunice Liesch, Ash Lee, Arlene Etchen, Wendy Gorling, Yvan Morissette, Kat Graham, Sean Oliver, Joel Voss, Malcolm Dow, Tom Locke, Mike Kopsa, Simon Johnston, Bruce Sweeney, Colin Rivers and Marquis Entertainment, Kathryn Shaw, Ami Gladstone, Studio 58, Langara College, Vancouver Film School, Kwantlen University, Solo Collective Theatre, and my trusty dog Vibe.

A major contributor and inspiration was also Diana Lyon ("Anna"), my wife. She pushed me to finish this book, but never got to see it completed after passing away at 57 from appendix cancer during the writing process in 2019. Diana was an inspiration to me and to many others that I know. She was a force of nature who loved to kayak and introduced me to Cortes Island, kayaking, and the Salish Sea. She is greatly missed. The empty kayak belongs to her.

We acknowledge the sacred land on which Cormorant Books operates. It has been a site of human activity for 15,000 years. This land is the territory of the Huron-Wendat and Petun First Nations, the Seneca, and most recently, the Mississaugas of the Credit River. The territory was the subject of the Dish With One Spoon Wampum Belt Covenant, an agreement between the Iroquois Confederacy and Confederacy of the Anishinaabe and allied nations to peaceably share and steward the resources around the Great Lakes. Today, the meeting place of Toronto is still home to many Indigenous people from across Turtle Island. We are grateful to have the opportunity to work in the community, on this territory.

We are also mindful of broken covenants and the need to strive to make right with all our relations.